THE JUSTIFICATION FOR INJUSTICE

THE JUSTIFICATION FOR INJUSTICE

David Francis Cook

Clovercroft Publishing

The Justification for Injustice

©2019 by David Francis Cook

Published by Clovercroft Publishing, Franklin, Tennessee

Edited by Lee Titus Elliott

Cover Design by Debbie Manning Sheppard

Interior Design by Suzanne Lawing

Printed in the United States of America

978-1-948484-86-2

Contents

Contents

PROLOGUE

It's time to bring all our readers up to date. We are now beginning the third and final book in this trilogy. But, first, I want to recap what has taken place in the previous two books. The reader can also read about more details in "The Forward," Book 2. The first book *The Rise to Power*, starts at the beginning of James Bannerman's education at his new school in Scotland, at the age of thirteen. The year is 1958, and he is ready to undergo all the challenges that this will bring. With the death of his father after his fourteenth birthday, he becomes the Tenth Earl of Penbroke. The first book continues through his education, until the young age of twenty-one, when he finds his place at the head of the Bannerman empire. The year is 1965.

The second book, *The Temptation to Greed*, takes the reader on a journey to discover how this young man copes with the world of business; having inherited a vast empire, which needs capital investment, can he rise to the challenge or not? In so many cases, people of fortunate birthright are blessed, but they don't always fulfill the mission of taking what they have inherited to a higher place. It is often said, "It's one thing to build a business and another to inherit one." Simply put, the tradition set by the initiator is only of value if the work ethic, discipline, and principles are handed on to the next generation. The book continues from 1965 until 1980. In between the world of business, the story of family life brings about change through marriages, love affairs, and, as always, the challenges of human nature, from its worst to its best qualities.

This brings us to the third and final book, *The Justification for Injustice*. James has now to confront the greatest trial of his life. We are all tested in many ways, and as the saying goes, "To whom much is given, much is expected." James will have to dig deep in order to rise to his destiny. Even with the best laid plans, life can teach us in so many ways.

The purpose of my work is to bring about a higher understanding of life's purpose in between the daily drama of our journey on this planet. I attempt to prompt the reader to read between the lines and decipher a message that lies through the pages of this saga, to untap the true mystery of this special place called "Earth," our galaxy, and the universe beyond.

CHAPTER 1

CONFRONTATION

James barged his way through a dense crowd of reporters and television cameras, all asking for answers to the tabloid accusations that had been made against him by the *Statesman*.

James worked his way up the steps to his bank, with the help of his security guards from inside the bank.

"Ladies and Gentlemen, please be patient; I will have all the answers you require," he said, in a loud and commanding voice, showing his confidence and authority, for which he was known. I never avoid the press or the media, so give me a moment to find out the source of these egregious and slanderous attacks on my personal credibility."

"Do you deny these accusations, my Lord?" shouted out one reporter, as others quickly followed with comments of disbelief.

"How could you do this?" asked another reporter. "You have a bank; people need answers."

"Answers you will have, I assure you." With that, he made

his way into the bank, leaving a stunned audience outside.

"James, my God, how are you doing?" said a concerned Claudia.

"Call a meeting for all the department heads immediately to the conference room, and I will attempt to explain the whole saga," he said, knowing that he was going to have to explain himself first, before he took action against the persons he knew to be his aggressors.

They all filed, in one by one: Roger Bell, head of his merchant banking empire; Stephen Gates, head of his properties; John Higgins, who had already been called up to the London office from Trans Global at Felixstowe to be a part of the meeting; and Claudia.

"First," James said, "I will explain exactly the situation, and then I will attempt to appease the media and all those that have doubts about my actions and integrity. Some years back, I decided to separate the buildings out from the businesses we now own. I knew we would be buying more buildings and building them, too, in order to enhance our expansion, all of which has taken place. Since the bank's beginning in 1838, my forefathers have always put back money from our businesses into a trust fund, annually. This trust was there primarily to protect the bank and our other investments, in the event of difficult economic times—for example, in the 1890s and during the time of the Great Depression that began in 1929.

James caught his breath; then he continued, after taking a sip of his morning coffee: "The fund was transferred to Switzerland in the late 1930s in fear of the Nazi occupation of Germany and World War II. No one at that time knew what the potential outcome would be. The trust has been in existence for over 140 years. It contains, at present, a considerable amount of money. The trust was passed down to me by my father, as it was to him before me, so it has now become my responsibility, as the sole trustee, to see that we guard and protect this valuable asset, for the goodwill and faith we have in our businesses today. I looked at this fund, and, as a chartered accountant, I made the decision to make a better return on this investment, which was only making 5 percent per annum. You all know the incredible inflation we have experienced in the last few years—not to speak of bank interest rates, which have climbed above 20 percent, as of right now. We are not out of the woods, yet. I decided to use a portion of these funds in order to invest in the properties and pay much-needed capital back to the bank and to our other businesses, for their growth and development. It has proved to be a very wise decision, as each area of our business interest has grown exponentially, as you are all well aware."

James continued: "The property income is paid back to the trust for the interest of insuring our financial strength for the future. It has grown considerably, much to the benefit and strength of all our futures." James had finally got out on the table what he had been burning to say all of last Sunday. After a sleepless night of outrage and anger, he had brilliantly masked his thoughts in front of his eagerly listening audience.

"James, this sounds perfectly logical," said Roger, thinking that James did have more financial risk-taking abilities than he had at first thought, in the area of finance and investment. "In fact, I think what you have exercised here is of extremely sound judgment, and I would have done exactly the same thing." To Roger, James's decision was a "no-brainer"; he would have done exactly the same thing.

The little gathering all started to murmur, and then started to clap at his intense and well-thought-out plan. James had demonstrated good faith. They knew he was wealthy enough already. Any thoughts of him trying to line his own pockets would not even be a consideration. His dedication to his staff and employees was unequalled, and to the importance of his forefathers, even more so.

"Well, there you have it," James said. "I now require you to all stand behind me. Spread the word, as I will in due course, with the newspapers and the media." With that, the meeting adjourned, and everyone proudly shook James's hand.

"John," James went on, "you can leave now; I know you have much on your agenda, and I thank you for coming at such short notice."

"Sir, I am 100 percent behind you," said John, politely. "What we have achieved in shipping is short of miraculous, and we haven't stopped growing. I am as proud to be working for your organization as I was the very first day I met you." Then, he left the room.

"Okay now, the rest of you, stay present, "James said. "We have to have a plan of action to deal with this newspaper."

"First, though, Stephen, I want you to now look for a person to head up the security in all our buildings and to develop a private investigation force beyond just security. Our business model has grown to such an extent that we need to increase accountability. We want to know that all those we employ are respecting all our business practices. For example, we know, through our audit and accounting procedures, that people are following our system, because we can track our business daily. However, what we don't know, with our worldwide organization, is our management team following aboveboard business practices."

"James, what are you referring to?" Claudia asked. "I don't understand. I think we have the best auditing procedures and team possible, especially since Sally joined us." Claudia felt slightly offended at James's line of thinking.

"Listen; I'll give you an example," James said. "How do we know that a shipping agent in Hong Kong can be giving a backhander to ship cargo to one of our staff and all the paper work is there for the shipment but that after the merchandise has been shipped, it becomes erased from the accounting system? Okay, here is another example: what is there to stop a Charles Kin or a general manager from doing a side deal with the growth of our fast-expanding textile business? The possibilities are endless. I'm not saying this is happening, but the potential is there. So we must have a safeguard system, through the head of security, to infiltrate various parts of our business in order to eradicate any potential for misdealing. We are in a new age, and it's getting more sophisticated by the moment." James had taken them all by surprise, but they knew he had a point.

"When would you like me to start, sir?" asked Stephen.

"Right now," James replied. "We need to choose someone who has a military background and who has experience with espionage, marine training, and business practices. A person who is a heavyweight and who has a good number of years of 'hands-on' knowledge in the field. Okay, Stephen, you can leave us now; I need to finish up with Roger and Claudia. Thank you for coming."

"Let's take a short break, and then I'd like to have a plan about what has just happened to me, and I want feedback from both of you," said James, now looking relieved at what he had just accomplished so far.

*****

After a short break, James started in: "Roger, the *Statesman*, I believe, is a publicly held company. Can you quickly check that out—who the shareholders are, and so on?"

"I'm on it, boss; I will be back shortly." "James, you've been through so much," said Claudia. "What on earth has happened to make someone do this to you?" Claudia felt pain for James and for what he must now be facing.

"It's simple," James said. "Gordon Peterson is the editor of the *Statesman*; through Flick, he has maliciously sought to get back at me after what took place when we were together at school." James went into all the details of their altercation, including the information he had received from Lisa, from whom he had withheld Flick's nam, and including the night when Flick walked out on him at the Brass Bell Restaurant. It all made complete sense; it now remained for James to have a plan to put Gordon and his brother down the pike for good.

"This is outrageous James; don't men ever grow up?" asked Claudia. "To use his father's newspaper to do this—just to get cheap circulation—is unthinkable, and to think your sister is in the middle of all this. Your mother would be furious, if she knew."

"I have a plan," said James. "Don't worry; my concern is that I don't want Flick to get hurt. She is my sister, and as naïve as she is, she's got a great lesson to learn."

"I think so," said Claudia. "To do this to her own brother is beyond comprehension. It has to be jealousy; there can be no other motive." So spoke an angry Claudia about his sister's behavior.

At that moment, Roger Bell returned with some news: "You're right; it is a public company listed on the London stock exchange. The father, Henry Peterson, who is now managing director of British Television, has 25 percent of the stock; his two sons have 12.5 percent each. It appears they've been selling off their shares, and it's hard to understand why."

"So now they can't block a takeover, right?"

"Not unless they find what we call a 'white knight' that could invest to save their company."

"So, Roger, how do we get control?"

"James, you want to buy a newspaper; what next?" asked an astonished Claudia.

"Yes, we are going to teach these Petersons a lesson, once and for all," said James. "It's my hunch they have gambling debts. They are desperate to make their losses back, and I happen to be the perfect reason for them to take a shot at. This would increase their circulation and share value and get them out of hock."

"Brilliant, James!" said Roger. "I bet you are right on the money. I know the perfect PI who could do a background check. If we smell a rat, I'll have a strategic plan to start buying up the shares from offshore companies slowly. When the shares reach an all-time high, we'll dump the shares and run for the hills."

"Yes, Roger," said James, "but we'll go back in and buy that newspaper with their own money!"

"Even better!" said Roger, laughing his head off.

Claudia looked back in amazement; this was a side of the business she knew nothing about, but she was receiving a quick lesson.

It took a few days for Roger's private investigator to do a background check, but, sure enough, he found out all he wanted to know.

"James, I now have the lowdown on the Petersens," said Roger. "Apparently, Gunter Kirk has been given shares by the brothers, to hold temporarily in exchange for debt, as well as for cash."

"Let's move fast," said James. "Get that Gunter Kirk to come and visit; we will find out firsthand from him. Assure the PI that we will pay Gunter off for any of their gambling debts and will buy his shares. Start buying up shares, as we agreed; then after we settle that deal, I can visit with Henry Petersen and try to make a deal."

It wasn't easy trying to get Gunter Kirk to visit, so James relented and agreed to meet with him on neutral ground, at a pub in the east end of London. The pub was in a rough neighborhood, but James wasn't scared. He took a taxi and met with Gunter. Gunter was a tall, heavy man with slick, black hair combed straight back from his forehead. He had on an expensive, black suit that was typical of a man you would expect to meet from the Italian Mafia. He looked the very part of a crime boss and thug. His henchmen were close at hand. James was escorted to a booth, where the two men could talk privately.

"So what makes me so important to talk with an English lord such as yourself?" said Gunter, with a cunning smirk that implied he knew he was about to make some money.

"Well, Gunter (my name's James, by the way), I understand these Petersen boys have been running up their tab at your nightclub."

"You could say that they have been good clients for our business, which I'm sure you are aware of."

"So, to cut to the chase, how much do they owe you?"

"Close to half a million; I'm also holding shares until they pay off the debt. They have won money over the years, but recently they've been on a bad losing streak. They are good customers, but no one likes their arrogant ways. I hear you were at school with those pompous brats?"

"Yes, I was, and I'm having to deal with their slanderous accusations in their newspaper. They were notorious bullies when I was in school with them. I shut them up when I was there, but now they're trying to get their own back through my sister, Flick."

"Yes, we've seen her with Gordon; she's a pretty girl, but this is not a place for a lady of her background to be hanging out."

"I agree, but she wants to be a journalist, and I think this is a case where people are using people to get what they want. So if I pay off the gambling debts, will you give me the shares?"

Gunter thought for a moment, and then replied, "They are good customers; if I give you these shares, I risk losing business."

"You will, anyway, because once their father knows of their activities, he will go ballistic. I'm sure you know who he is."

"Indeed, I do, and I've had it in mind to see him, if the boys don't pay up soon. They've been warned, and a terrible scandal could arise. I've no wish to impose that, but I know he would pay me in a heartbeat, not to risk his sons' reputations. So, what's my best alternative?"

"I will pay you over the top for the shares so you come out the winner. As for further business from them, that's going to be gone by the time I've dealt with them."

"You're tough; I like that. I can see why you've been so successful. When I came to this country, I had nothing, and, because of my broken English, no one would hire me or my brothers. We had to make a living and get tough so our sons can go to schools like you. I want them to have a fine education and be someone like yourself one day. Our life is not easy, but it pays the bills. One day, I want to retire and to forget I was ever in this line of business. I'm not proud of what we do, but if it builds a future for our children, then it's served its purpose."

"Gunter, I'm not here to criticize what you do. I have a score to settle, and settle it I will. I'll pay you 10 percent above the debt; do we have a deal?"

"Make it twenty, and the shares are yours," he said slyly, grinning again, knowing this was his opportunity to score.

"Come on; fifteen; that's more than fair."

Gunter knew that 15 percent interest on a few months of half-million pounds of debt was more than he could get from anyone.

"Done," he said, and grinned again, liking the challenge and glad to get his money without any hassle.

I'll write you a cheque here and now; do you have the shares?"

Gunter motioned to one of his men, and he quickly served up the share certificates, as James wrote his cheque. He had come to do business, and he liked James and his direct and to-the-point way of doing business.

"I will now bar them from ever returning to our club. You have sealed their fate with me."

Gunter was harsh and not a man to mess with, but men like the Petersen brothers he had no time of day for.

"If you ever need a change of environment, you will always be welcome at our nightclubs, and I assure you that no one will know who you are!"

"It may not be me, but, from time to time, I do have to take care of a business client, so you can be of help in that respect," said a curious James, wishing he could have a night on the town, but he knew it would be more than his reputation would permit.

"A pleasure to be of service, my Lord James."

The two shook hands, and James yelled to himself inside, *Mission accomplished.*

James hailed the next taxi and was back at the bank, making his way to Roger's office.

"So here are the shares," said James. "How are we proceeding with the buyout?"

"With the shares you've got and what I've bought over the last few days, I would say we have about 21 percent of the company," said a smiling Roger, pleased with his meticulous method of buying without making the market price for the shares show too much activity. The Petersens expected the share price to jump in view of the breaking story. They would not be alarmed at the share value increasing and would be unaware of what James was up to.

"Now, I'm going to have a meeting with Henry Petersen and buy his shares; then we shall have control of the company," said a happy, smiling James.

"James, be careful; they are his sons," said Claudia. "I know you can be direct at times, but you are about to disappoint a proud father." Claudia knew how intense James could be when he was on the warpath.

It took Rose a good hour to reach a busy executive like Petersen, Senior, at BTV, but finally she was able to track him down.

"My Lord, I was wondering when I would hear from you," said a jovial Henry Petersen. "I'm sure you are not pleased with what my sons have printed in our newspaper, but they're just doing their job. I'm sorry that you've been exposed to this scandal, but there's always two sides to every story. I'll be happy to hook you up with one of our broadcasters, if you want to make a television appearance." He was pleased with his boys breaking the news ahead of everyone else in the media.

"I'd like that opportunity, sir, but first I would like to visit with you," said James. "There may be some facts that you're not aware of, and I'd like for you to know this in private before I go public." James spoke cautiously, not wanting to burst his bubble yet.

"How about tomorrow at nine at my place?"

"I'll be there; thank you for taking the time, sir."

"Not at all; this is a hot story. I want to learn your side of things, before we proceed further."

"Absolutely; tomorrow at nine it is."

James arrived at BTV headquarters early; he liked to be punctual and to show respect. A smart-looking, young secretary ushered James into the elevator to the top floor. He passed the broadcasting center on his way up to the executive suites. The offices were impressive, and then she opened the door to Mr. Petersen's office, which had a panoramic view of the city. He had a long conference table and a large partner's desk at one end, with two high-back, leather chairs in front.

"Thank you, Jenny, if you could close the door on your way out," said a commanding, confident managing director of Britain's largest television station.

After the two shook hands, James was seated.

"Always loved watching you play cricket at Sterling. What a sight to see those wickets tumble under the furious pace of your deliveries."

"Thank you, sir; I miss those days . . ."

"Well, James, let's hear your side of these allegations."

James went into explicit detail to explain what the trust fund was, its purpose, and that he was, by tradition, the sole trustee.

"So, you see, sir, I was only acting in the finest interest of a business I've inherited from my forefathers."

"Fascinating; so why does your sister have a different perspective, according to Gordon?"

"With all respect, sir, my sister is studying journalism, has very little business acumen, and has naively shared her view with your son in order to get a job at your newspaper."

"She's obviously not very loyal to you; why would that be?"

"She and I have always been at odds since childhood. It happens in families, but we've always settled our differences in the past. It appears she's become very jealous of the success our business has achieved. She feels that, with the wealth I have acquired, she should have received more from my father's will. However, it's been a tradition in the family that the next surviving heir would inherit what I have, and it's not for me to change what my father's will was."

"So, what you're saying is that these allegations are totally unfounded?"

"Totally, sir."

"Well, I'll be damned, if that's the truth, James."

"There's more to the story than that, and please don't be offended by any of the remarks I now make about Gordon."

"Gordon! What in the world has he to do with this, other than that he's printed what a jealous sister has told him?" asked Mr. Petersen, looking curiously at James for what he was about to hear.

"Sir, I don't know whether you were aware of this or not. I'm trying to find the words as diplomatically as I can."

"Well, spit it out; say what you believe."

"Both your sons were known for being notorious bullies at Sterling Heights."

"For God's sake, they were young school boys that got up to some mischief, like we all have done. They're grown men now, running a newspaper. You're not telling me anything a father doesn't already know." Mr. Petersen was fiercely defending his sons, making James's task even more unpleasant than he'd expected.

"Well, here goes nothing. I put an end to their ways when we had a punch up in the Coffee Pot Restaurant in St. Andrews. I embarrassed them in front of everyone and made them swear in public that they cease and desist from their bullying ways as long as we were in school."

"Really? I had no idea that they were to that level of being such a menacing threat to the other students. Go on . . ."

"When I left to take the train back to London, at the end of our time at Sterling, Gordon told me, in no uncertain words, that now that schooldays were over, the gloves were off and that he would get even in any way he could. After he dated Flick and promised her a job, she has confided in him all about my life. He's used this opportunity to tarnish my reputation. I can tell you there will be lawsuits flying in every direction."

"My God! I had no idea; what must they be thinking to behave like that? I admit they were a handful growing up, but I thought all that was in the past."

"There's more; I have just paid off your sons' gambling debts in the East End of London to the Kirk brothers, in return for the shares your sons had given them from your company. They had over half a million pounds in debts. So, this scandal they've brought against me was to increase circulation and share value and to pay off their gambling debts. They've lost more than that, but that was what was outstanding."

"James, this is terrible; they must be mad to hang out with such vicious criminals. The whole lot should have been locked up ages ago, but they have cleverly got the police covered with kickbacks to leave them alone in that region. This is a shock. I own 25 percent of that company, and I've given the other 25 percent to my sons; the rest is public. So now, by their actions, we could be taken over. I started the business many years ago. I took it public when I came to run BTV, knowing we would always keep 50 percent of the company and block any take-over bid. By their actions, they have put the company into a minority stakeholder position."

"Precisely; and if someone wants to acquire that position, they could issue more shares and diminish your interest considerably."

"James, if all this is true, and I have no reason to doubt you, my boys will be kicked out on their rear ends; you can count on that."

"Sir, I don't want vengeance, and I don't want a damaging lawsuit that could wreck the reputation of your newspaper. This is what I now request that you print on the front page: that the information that was given to you was erroneous and that you humbly apologize to the world at large, and to me, personally. Anything short of that, and we will be in the courtroom, and you, your television station, the media, and the press, will have a field day. I'm sorry, but your fine reputation, that of your newspaper, your job, and your sons will be finished by your sons' stupidity."

"What do you propose? I'm sure you have an angle, James. You're not the successful businesman you are for nothing."

"We have bought up close to 25 percent of the shares on the open market. Your company is worth around fifty million. I will pay you for your shares and for those of your sons. I ask that I pay only the sum of one million apiece for the shares of your sons. In view of what they have done to me, to you, and to the other shareholders, I will pay the going price. That way, we all walk away with something and avoid a costly lawsuit and considerable embarrassment to you and your family. You still have your job here; your sons can run away and hide, for all I care. I will have a restraining order on them for what they've done. I'd better not see either of them for the rest of my life. After meeting with Gunter Kirk, I can tell you they have no friends left in that part of London."

"James, you have grown into a powerful young man. I should

have known better, watching you bowl that cricket ball, the very force that's inside you. My sons are a disgrace. What you have explained makes perfect sense. I'm glad you have chosen the high road. I wanted to sell the newspaper some time ago, but I kept it for my sons. Somehow, it's a relief it ends this way."

Petersen knew he had gotten off lightly. He saw James in a whole new light and realized the powerful person he could be, when he demonstrated his power. Sir Thomas and his law firm and James's accountants would carry out all that was asked.

James was ecstatic with his new enterprise, and he couldn't wait to get into the business and see what needed to be upgraded and improved and whom he would now choose to head up the business.

He would wait to make his move after the newspaper would print the words to clear his name and to admit the erroneous facts it had given to the public. He also knew that the share value would drop, as public confidence would hold the newspaper in question.

James would reestablish confidence, after his name was cleared in the press, and the transaction would be complete with the Petersen family. The *Statesman* would now be a privately owned corporation. With time and new management, he would increase circulation and slowly make his way into the world of media. He knew that this was a fast-emerging arena for marketing, advertising, and promotion and that it would give him an opportunity to quietly influence public opinion in the political world. Once again, James had masterfully shown his skills in transforming what could have been a disastrous and scandalous affair into opportunity and the hope of good fortune.

CHAPTER 2

THE STATESMAN

With Roger's help and the drop-in share values, they were able to buy out the newspaper for around thirty-five million, saving a good fifteen million. Henry Petersen got a decent return from his original investment, as he had already made his money when he took the newspaper public.

James headed to the factory in St. Albans on the northwest side of London. He was interested in seeing the layout and in choosing his new editor in chief for the management of the newspaper. He realized that Henry Petersen had been the owner of the business for over twenty-five years and that a lot of the staff had been handpicked by him. After hours of interviewing all the top editors from the various parts of the newspaper, he was particularly struck by one woman. Her credentials and CV were outstanding: a scholarship to Durham University and a master's degree in journalism. She had also been an English teacher at a high school in Durham, an ace tennis player, and a musician. There seemed to be no end to this woman's talents. He took time to read up on her political views. She was left wing and had a socialist viewpoint, a kind of politics not uncommon for women editors. She had attended Benenden, one of England's finest girl schools, and was nominated "head girl." James thought she was perfect for the task. She'd been with the newspaper for about five years and lacked in seniority to many others, who had been with the company more than double that time, but she had all the skills at twenty-seven to do the job.

One of the secretaries ushered her into what used to be Henry Petersen's old office, where James had decided to carry out his interviews. The company needed swift change after the embarrassing departure of the Petersen brothers.

James was immediately struck by her. She had a large amount of blonde hair, with darker highlights. She was around five feet eight in height, and she was dressed immaculately, wearing a tight-knit, pink blouse over a very stylish, dark grey skirt and jacket. Her long legs and matching high heels gave her dignity and class. She was every bit a woman of standing and culture. Her strong face, her large, bold, electric blue eyes, and her brushed-back long hair that fell to her shoulders gave her a sophisticated, but natural, look.

"James Bannerman; I'm glad to make your acquaintance, Ms. Watson," said James, fascinated by this confident, yet stylish, young woman, who had an attractive, intellectual air about her.

This was a lady, he thought. *Definitely top-drawer, but with an outdoor flair; her response and accent more than concluded that.*

"My Lord, it's an honor to meet you," she said. "I would have thought a man in your position wouldn't take the time to interview a candidate for such an important position by himself." As she spoke, she sat down and crossed her legs in a way that was slightly flirtatious, but in a way only a woman of class could do: naturally, with such confident body movements.

"Well, at the beginning of a new enterprise for us, I like to know and understand all the facts for myself," James said. "No doubt, that will change later on. Most of the management of our other businesses report directly to me, but my coordinator, Claudia Ringstone, who is our group managing director, is my right arm. It's not easy for me to be everywhere at once. Our company employs tens of thousands of people around the world." James found himself attracted to this woman and was trying to impress her. There was something about her that made him feel off guard.

"Well, it's an honor, sir, and I respect that you take the time personally," she said, looking him straight in the eye, trying to weigh him up. It wasn't every day that she met people of his stature, and she wanted to make an impression.

"Your scholastic achievements are exceptional, the finest schools and university, yet the columns edited and written by you lean very strongly towards the left," James said. "Is there a particular reason for that?"

"Well, sir, our newspapers are not all read by the upper classes," she replied. "We have to appeal to the majority of people, and most of those people believe that the world is not fair and equal. They work hard in factories and with very little pay. That being said, there are writers and journalists here that write for those of us that do have a higher level of income."

"I understand, and I have thoroughly looked over yesterday's paper," James went on. "My concern is that the editor in chief should have a more right-wing view of matters, even though we must have writers who understand the world we live in."

"I report and edit the news, and it's not always pretty, but it's the truth," Ms. Watson said. "I may appear to support those who are less fortunate in life. The real fact is so many people of privilege do things that certainly don't improve their image."

"Like the story that was printed about me," James said. "I notice you had a hand in that. I'm anxious to know how well you did your homework on such an ill-founded nonfactual report. How is it a newspaper of such high standing could risk stating facts about a person like myself on hot air? My point is how well do you check the facts before writing articles of this nature?"

"Sir, I had no choice in this matter," she replied. "Gordon Petersen was certain of the facts presented by your sister, and, to him, it was a guaranteed fact that you were abusing a trust fund for your own personal use. I was in no way able to discount firsthand information from a member of your family. As treacherous as I thought your sister to be, it was news, and Gordon was overjoyed at the opportunity of being the first to report it."

"Really?" James asked. "Are you aware that we attended the same school, and are you aware of the personal details of our relationship there?"

"No, sir," she replied. "I know nothing of his personal life other than what rumors have been recently circulated. I was hired by his father, Henry Petersen, a man I have enormous respect for."

"So, what do you think now?" James asked.

"I think he and his brother have done a terrible thing and have rightfully been dismissed, although it's hard not to hold your sister accountable, too, sir," she replied.

"How well do you know Henry Petersen?"

"Well."

"Do you see him out of working hours?"

"Sir, that's a very personal question, no? He's a wonderful adviser, and I respect him greatly."

"Not if you end up running this newspaper," James said. "I need someone who is loyal and trustworthy, and although I have no axe to grind with Henry, it is important that your relationship with him be kept separate from this newspaper now."

"Sir," she said, "I had it in mind to leave the *Statesman* and go work for BTV, until meeting you. But if I'm going to be put under house arrest, it's best I go." Her confident style intrigued James; Henry had to be over twenty years older than her, yet she was seeing him.

"Well, if you are seeing Henry, how would that look in a professional television station like BTV?" James asked. "His sons must know about you two. He must have shared more private information about this whole matter with you, if you are having a personal relationship with him."

"He is a free man," she said. "His wife died some time ago; yes, his sons have been a handful; he knows that. Trust me: our relationship and what we share are professional."

"You've been honest with me," James said. "I like that. It's obvious you don't know the whole story, but I'm sure Henry will bring you up to date. I like you; there's something about you that has class and potential. I believe you could run this newspaper, and your knowing Henry isn't a conflict for me. He's a very good man, and I respect him, too. He could actually be a helpful contact and advisor to you, as he started this place. You strike me as a woman who has a mind of her own; I don't think any man is going to tell you what to do, from what I've seen of you today."

"Sir . . ."

James butted in, "Look, call me James when we are alone;

I like informal; if we are going to be a team, we must work together."

"James, this won't be a popular decision," she said. "There are many editors from various departments that have been here much longer than I have. I'm not sure it would be the best choice for the newspaper." She knew deep down she wanted the job, but she wanted to appear considerate.

"It's not always easy making these choices, but I like your style, intellect, and educated disposition," James said. "You are exactly the right person for the job. I would like you to come to London tomorrow to meet Claudia. She's my closest and most trusted confidant; she's like you, and she has a mind of her own. I think you two will hit it off."

"Sir, I'm overjoyed," she said. "I will have to pinch myself tonight; it's like a dream come true!"

"So, you'll be sitting where I am," James said. "Let's wait to make the announcement for a day or two, and tomorrow we can discuss a plan to move this newspaper forward and increase circulation."

"James, it was a pleasure to meet you," she said. "My name is Kimberli, with an 'i'; you can call me Kim, if you so choose. I'm sure, in time, your capitalist views will slowly rub off on me." She departed slowly from the office, staring once more at him; feeling a strange connection, she somehow felt that she would be with him for a long time, but she didn't know why. Their minds connected, but she knew how independent she was, and she wondered if he was a controlling type of man. *Claudia would give her the lowdown tomorrow,* she thought.

James decided to return home to Penbroke; he hadn't seen Sabrina since reading the newspaper last Sunday. He wanted to tell her all the news before heading back to London the next day.

The helicopter landed just over half an hour later at his estate. He walked over to the house to see her.

"James, I read the news today," Sabrina said. "It looks like you took care of matters: hopefully an end to those ghastly Petersen brothers and your sister's disloyal behavior." She gave him a big hug and a kiss.

"I know I didn't have them print the details of the deal, but I will have the newspaper print out a story," James said. "I know tomorrow I'm going to have to meet all those reporters at the bank. It's all hush-hush at the moment. The allegations have been dropped, but they'll still want an explanation from me personally, which means I'm going to have to deal with Flick for her disgraceful behavior. Mother would be furious if she knew. Best kept a secret for now, but she'll learn about it sooner or later."

"James you look distant somehow; is something bothering you?" Sabrina asked.

"No; it's just been one hell of a week," James replied. "Thank God tomorrow's Friday. All this uproar has upset me, knowing about our funds in Switzerland. I don't like the public knowing about private matters like that; people are not always trusting. Flick has certainly cast a shadow for now. In time, I'm sure attention will become drawn to other, more engaging news. Even though it's all been put straight, I could throttle Flick for giving people a chance to know about something that's private. It's really nobody's business but mine. She can be such a pill." Deep down, he was still thinking about his meeting with Kimberli Watson. It was rare he'd ever met a woman that affected him so deeply. She had something; he could tell it by her aura. The moment they shook hands, the whole room lit up. It was an attraction—not sexual but heartfelt. He knew he had found a special person of immense force and intellect, yet he couldn't put his finger on it.

"We'll take it easy this weekend," James said. "Relax and play cricket in the nets with Samuel, and just do stuff around the estate, and ride the horses. You and I can go out for a nice meal, just the two of us."

"Let's get back to some sense of normalcy, after all this hoopla!" said a happy Sabrina, loving to have James home and being with the kids on their summer holidays.

Samuel was now ten years old. James loved throwing the composition ball to him in order to show him how to bat. They spent hours together, James showing him how to bat and bowl. Sam was starting to learn cricket from the best; his own father could see he had an eye for the game. It was early days for his bowling, but he could teach him as his body developed.

"Dad, do you think I'm any good? said Samuel, looking into his father's eyes. Sam knew what he would have to live up to if he was going to be anywhere close to his father's achievements.

"You have what it takes," said James, "but, like everything, it takes practice, a will, and a desire to be the best. I have no doubt you will be great at the sport, but somehow I think you are going to be a better batsman than I was."

"Really? As long as I'm good, that's what matters," said Samuel, knowing he had a long way to go, but, with James's experience, he had the best coach a son could want.

Sitting on the front lawn was Sabrina, with their daughter, Annabelle. At seven, she was also developing, very conscious of being feminine. She liked to capture her father's eye. She looked forward to the day when she would receive as much attention as Sam was getting.

"Do you think I'll be good at sport, Mom?" asked Annabelle, playing with her Barbie doll.

"I don't know," Sabrina said. "I loved tennis, but I can't say it was what I did best. You're still young; time will tell, amore, but I think you are very pretty, so don't worry about that yet. Focus on your schoolwork first, and enjoy playing with your friends and your dolls. You have the rest of your life to discover those things."

James and Sabrina then left the children with the nanny, and they changed clothes to spend an evening out and discuss the experience of the last week over dinner. It was now their alone time.

They went to their favorite restaurant, in Horncastle.

"James, how are you going to deal with Flick after the treacherous act she took against you?" Sabrina asked.

"I don't know," replied James. "I've been racking my brains over this whole debacle. She's so rebellious and won't take advice. She attempted to hurt not only me but also our business reputation. I know I haven't heard the last of this. She just doesn't think. It's all about Flick and Flick's world, and the rest be damned. She nearly ruined Henry Petersen's career and reputation, not to speak of her gullible assumption that I would ever do such a thing by taking money incorrectly from our family trust fund for my own personal use. She's naïve, and too pretty for her own good. She thinks she can manipulate anyone for her own purposes. If she's not feeling guilt and shame for what she's done, I am at my end with her."

He knew she had something up her sleeve after she left so abruptly when she and Becky had dinner at the Brass Bell that night. However, in his wildest dreams, he could never believe something of this measure.

"Well, someone has to put a stop to anyone that would be that disloyal, especially to her own brother," said Sabrina, angry at the very thought she would do such a thing. James had all a person could want; what personal gain would he have by doing that? She had to know of her brother's integrity . . . Flick's disloyalty was enough to dumbfound anyone.

"I don't have the words or answer to that," said James, shaking his head. "If she doesn't attempt to make an apology, she will become an outcast of the family by her own choosing. I can only pray that she has the courage to come forward and straighten this whole affair out. I'll be damned if I'm going to talk to her. She's made her bed, and now she can learn to lie on it."

Sabrina put her arm across his shoulder to give him a kiss. She knew the pain he was suffering. What had he done in his life to deserve such behavior from his own sister? In spite of all her escapades and shenanigans, this one was over the top.

The couple enjoyed a quiet evening together and then retired to bed, after drinking a glass of port on the terrace outside their bedroom.

James awoke to an early morning breakfast with the family. After reading some factless comment in the newspaper, about which he would go on television and talk to the press during the next week, he went to his study. Here he could smoke a cigarette, which he never did in front of his children, and drink his morning coffee, while scanning the business agenda for his upcoming week. All of a sudden, he heard shouts . . .

"James, James, come quickly," Sabrina shouted out to him anxiously. "Becky's on the phone; it's urgent."

James picked up the phone in his study.

"James, it's urgent," Becky cried out. "I was out last night, got back to find Flick out cold on the floor this morning, ten minutes ago. The ambulance has now taken her to emergency. She was barely conscious. She'd drunk a whole bottle of scotch, and then downed God only knows how many sleeping pills."

"Calm down, Becky," James said. "At least, she's alive. I'm

going to take the helicopter to Battersea Heliport; meet me there in an hour; then we can both take a taxi to the hospital." James sounded composed, in order to calm Becky down.

"Oh, James, in spite of all she's done, I do hope she's all right," said Sabrina. "She knew that what she had done must have finally hit home."

James entered the emergency room, only to see his sister semiconscious. She was alive, and that was a relief.

"We've pumped out everything she had in her stomach," said the attending physician. "Now we've got her on a saline solution that should at least knock out the alcohol she's drunk. As for the sleeping pills, we've injected her with some stimulants and suppressants to negate their effects. She's just going through withdrawal; it's going to take a good twenty-four hours before she can talk intelligently. My suggestion is we will now take her to her room and let her sleep this off; she will, of course, be under constant observation, my Lord. It's lucky her sister is in the medical profession and knew what to do. With that amount of alcohol and drugs in her system, she's lucky to be alive."

"Thank you, doctor and your staff, for the swift action you have taken."

"Yes, my Lord."

James knew he could use some of his healing powers to help her, but a voice was telling him to wait so he could see how she would progress. They stayed for a while and then let her rest. They decided to return the next day in the morning to visit with her and to try to understand her actions. James chose to stay in town and went out to dinner with Becky.

"James," said Becky, "hopefully, this crazy, treacherous, and disloyal behavior she's taken against you will be at an end."

"Who knows?" asked James. "Maybe; but as terrible as she's

been, it's not worth her life."

"Hopefully, we can get matters worked out," James went on. "I just wonder how long it's going to take before the press gets hold of this."

*****

James and Becky made their way to the hospital from his office in the city. They were hurriedly escorted to Flick's room; she was now out of recovery.

Flick was lying propped up in her bed, and she had a look of dread, as the couple entered the room.

"Oh, James, there are not words enough I can say for the remorse I feel, and for all the trouble I have caused you," she said, with tears starting to stream down her face.

"Flick," said James, "the most important thing is you are here, and recovering from something that had us all worried beyond belief. All you had to do was come and see me. Your life is worth more than that, for God's sake!"

"I know," said Flick, "but when I saw and understood the truth of what happened, I didn't know how to forgive myself. Through my blindness, jealousy, and desire to get ahead through Gordon, I delivered a most disloyal and unthinkable deed to my brother. I was naïve and selfish. I didn't take into account the pain I must have caused you. How can you ever forgive me? How can anyone? I just want to go away and hide. Leave England and start over in Canada or America. The embarrassment I feel is too great." She shook, as she delivered her words with a quivering expression.

"Look, what's happened has happened," said James. "We can't change the past, but we can do something about now, and about the future. What you must say is that, at the night we all met at the Brass Bell, you came away with a complete misunderstanding of the facts. You deeply regret the misinterpretation, and you had not realized that this was a trust fund that had been handed down through many generations, by tradition. This family trust was now the sole responsibility of my brother, the Tenth Earl. It's not something I asked for; it's a tradition that was put in place in order to protect the interests of the bank and its shareholders. That's all; you can write a column in our newspaper, and that will put an end to this entire hullabaloo!"

"James, how can you forgive me? Can you ever trust me again?"

"We are family, and if we don't stick by one another, then what is family for?" asked James. "Flick, I was a little confrontational that night, because I sensed where you were going. Frankly, I was upset that you didn't realize that, as your brother, I would protect you with my life. It's not a question you even had to ask. I am responsible to all the family. Surely, you know me better than that?"

"I do," said Flick. "I've been such a fool by listening to the evil, jealous, plotting words of Gordon after your schooldays. Just because I wanted to get ahead."

"Anyway, we own the newspaper now," said James, "and I'm going to put you under the wing of Kimberli Watson, whom I have chosen to run the newspaper. She's smart; learn from her, and she'll get you where you want to go. As an anchorwoman on BTV, she has all the right connections. This could be a huge opportunity for you, so let's all stick together, okay? Becky is now in charge of all the medical staff for Trans Global Shipping, and you now have the opportunity you've always wanted. Just a little patience! Flick, I know you have the personality for this; I know it."

"James," said Flick, "I will work hard to show you my loyalty, and I will repay you for all the heartache I have given you. Your love and your forgiveness are more than I could possibly ask for."

James got up to hold his sister, as she sobbingly embraced him with thoughts of total disbelief at his magnanimous dealing with the whole affair.

"Let's take care of business," said James. "It's all in the past; there will be some more questions from the media, no doubt, but it will all pass, and then we can focus on the future."

Flick could feel the tremendous energy that her brother was passing to her in their embrace, and she immediately started to feel better.

Over the next few weeks, James talked with the media, as did Flick. Slowly, more impending news started to take the spotlight.

CHAPTER 3

A CHANGING
OF THE GUARD

Kimberli had delayed her visit with Claudia, but she arose early the next day to prepare herself for her meeting with Claudia. After taking her daughter to school near her cottage not far from the printing works, she made her way to St. Albans to catch the train to the city of London.

She was nervous, and she had thoroughly gone over what she was going to say. She had inquired about Claudia from Henry Petersen, who didn't know her well but who did know of her excellent reputation. He had spoken to her on many social engagements and had spoken to her husband, Sir Thomas Ringstone. She knew that she was the eyes and ears to James's empire and that impressing her was paramount to her future relationship with James and his other staff. She also knew that she would be the youngest and that she would have to earn their respect. James had elevated her to a position that could create great jealousy, which she was starting to feel amongst the other members of the editing staff. News was traveling fast. She now needed all the support she could get to enhance her dream of becoming an outstanding leader and to be known as one of the best editors in the business.

She was slightly intimidated as she walked up the steps to the newly renovated bank; the paintings of James's ancestors in the lobby, along with the lavish furniture, now gave a presence of power and stature.

The hall porter ushered her to the top floor, which was now the corporate headquarters to the most senior executives and staff in the Bannerman hierarchy.

Rose took her raincoat and brolly as she exited the lift. She then ushered her to Claudia's newly wood-paneled office. Since the renovations, there was only one small conference room, as all the offices had been increased in size to appropriately administer the activities of the day. This gave an appearance of confidence and financial "well-being," as was necessary in the world of finance. The new conference rooms had been set up on the floor below.

"Kimberli, it's a pleasure to meet you," Claudia said. She instantly loved her appearance. Kimberli had chosen her favorite purple skirt, with a white blouse and a light beige leather topcoat with matching high heels. She wanted to appear bright and warm and not to appear stuffy and stereotyped, as so many people in the city looked.

"I love your choice of clothes—warm, yet so appropriate," Claudia said. "Please come over here and have a seat."

Claudia led with an open hand to offer Kimberli a choice of seat.

"Rose, please fetch Ms. Watson some coffee and another for me," she went on.

"Thank you, Claudia," said Kimberli. "This is certainly a

very beautiful building, and I love your office."

"Oh, you should have seen this place a few years ago," said Claudia. "Since the expansion of our business worldwide, it was so outdated and so old-world that it was laughable. It looked like we belonged to a place associated with pre–World War II. James finally agreed to renovate the entire building. At one time, we rented space out to other companies, but now we utilize every square inch ourselves, for all our worldwide operations."

"Impressive," said Kim. "The operations at our printing plant look exactly like what you're describing as pre–World War II." She was hoping for improvements toward her well-thought-out business plan.

Changing the subject, Claudia said, "Let's take a tour of the bank; then we'll go to lunch."

"Great; lead the way," said an anxious Kim, ready to learn all she could about her new business owners.

Claudia wanted to treat Kimberli to a really nice luncheon, so she hailed a taxi and headed for the Connaught Hotel, where Sir Nicolas had taken her many years ago.

After ordering the traditional roast beef, she ordered a bottle of Volnay wine, and then the conversation started.

"Kim, tell me all about yourself—how you are so confident and appear much more mature than your years."

Kim blushed at the inference, but she found talking with Claudia easy; she felt she could tell her anything. She knew Claudia had to be discreet and would not be a gossiper and would hold in privacy any personal matters she might share. Kim also knew she had to have James's confidence, as he would never have a woman in such a place of authority, if she was anything less.

"Well," Kimberli said, "after leaving school, I met the man

of my dreams at Durham University. I was studying journalism and political science, and then I went on to take finance, amongst others—"

Claudia butted in, "Finance! I didn't see any mention of that on your CV."

"I know I try to stay focused on the profession I'm in," Kimberli said. "I don't like to appear as a jack-of-all-trades. It was actually one of my best subjects, as I had almost a scholarship level in math at school. After leaving university, I took classes in accounting as a backup in the event my journalist career might not take off. The world of journalism is a tough one, and it's not for everyone. Chasing down the story and getting the facts makes you have to push and be on the spot first. Getting interviews firsthand, with the right parties, and becoming a person that people want to go to before others, takes twice. Once you are trusted with what you print, you start to climb the ladder. There are not only jealousies amongst other reporters, but there are also jealousies within the newspaper you work for; it's not a profession that many are cut out for. So it's wise to have a backup plan."

"Impressive; so to what level of accounting are you capable of?" asked a curious Claudia, becoming more and more intrigued.

"Not to sound full of myself, the degree I hold would stand me in good stead for any company small, medium, or large," Kimberli said. "I would be capable of a career in banking, if I so choose. I'm competent to tax-level accounting, and I would, of course, learn more about that if the necessity arose. However, I believe I'm on the edge of my dream career as editor in chief. It won't be easy, but I hope to present a full and complete plan of implementation to you very shortly. A plan to double circulation and streamline our operation with fewer people, by having better and later equipment."

"You are certainly a go-getter," Claudia said. "I can see why James picked you. You exude energy and enthusiasm, and your CV certainly backs that up. The finance knowledge you have is fantastic for running a business like yours. I would be nervous if I was the bookkeeper in your organization."

"You would be right," Kimberli said. "The woman we have is close to useless, and that's a change that will take place soon!"

Kim laughed, and so did Claudia. Kim would implement change slowly and wisely, but Claudia could already see the fire in her eyes and the passion she expressed for her work.

"So back to your first boyfriend: are you still together?" Claudia asked.

"Alas, no," Kimberli replied. "We married when I was only nineteen, and, after finishing university, we had a baby girl. She's nearly five, and she lives with me at my cottage, not far from the business. I drop her off at a small private school each day. We have a nanny because of my hectic work schedule; she takes care of the home and makes sure my daughter is properly attended to."

"So, it didn't work out with . . .?"

"Jeremy? No. He teaches at a very good school in Durham, teaches chemistry. I loved him. He couldn't put up with my being gone and my ambitious work schedule. It was sad we were too young. He's found someone else, but he takes Jennifer every other weekend. He's a good father. Not ambitious enough for me; I like a man with drive; I prefer older men, who don't require a mother."

They both burst out laughing, as those were Claudia's sentiments completely.

Kimberli continued, "I take her to our family estate each

weekend; there she can see her father, and I can give her my complete attention, as well."

"I respect your work ethic, but it sounds like you are a very caring mother."

"Of course, the phone never stops in our business, but I try to leave it to the evenings when Jennifer goes to bed."

"You have a family estate in Durham County?" Claudia asked. She was having a blast listening to this enterprising young lady.

"Yes. I was an only child to a second marriage. My mother and father were Texans; I was born in Texas and raised there until I was twelve. My birth father died when I was eight. My mother then met my stepfather-to-be on holiday, and that's how I came to be raised in England. It was hard at first, but I've grown to love the way of life and the people here. I have a half brother who is older and now lives in Surrey, so I see very little of him these days. My stepfather owned many collieries for the production of coal, which he inherited from his father. I hated the business: the toll on peoples' lives, black lung, so little pay, while we lived in a mansion. To think of all those tenement houses, street after street, where the miners lived. Some of them working all day and yet barely seeing the light of day. Their only refuge was the local pubs. So many people huddled into tiny, little places with barely enough to live on."

"A Texan, indeed," said Claudia. "I thought you had a different accent but had passed it off as upper-class North Country English, but now it makes more sense. It's actually very pleasant to the ear. Sorry, please continue."

Kimberli paused to take a deep breath and then continued to tell her story. "That's why the columns that I write lean towards the man in the street, the rank and file, the people who don't live in the world I do. I worked with the Salvation

Army at holiday times to help with the underprivileged when I was younger, and I still help out now at Christmas and other times of the year."

Kimberli was certainly different, a rare find, Claudia thought. James had chosen well. His instincts for understanding people's talents and qualities were unparalleled.

"I'm given to understand that you inherited what you have from your father?" asked Claudia.

"Yes; he had sold the mines and left everything to me in a trust. I miss him greatly, but I was never so glad when he sold the mines off. Today, of course, there are unions, which I hate, but were necessary in those days. Technology has provided better equipment, and men are paid more, with superior standards for health-related issues."

"So, do you have anyone special in your life now? Such a pretty woman surely doesn't go unnoticed?"

"I did, but it's my work, Jennifer, and my trips to Durham most weekends that make it almost impossible to have a relationship with anyone. Men just become frustrated and move on."

"You must come and spend a weekend with us and meet my better half. We women must stick together. I spend my life surrounded by men. Some feminine company is always appreciated, and certainly a young lady like you, who has such a fine mind. I'm old enough to be your mother. I can teach you more about the amazing Bannerman Empire and the pivotal person that's turned a fortunate inheritance into an enterprise that spans the globe."

"I was fascinated to meet him. I was surprised he conducted the interviews himself. Surely that's something he would delegate?"

"Not James; he likes to know all the heads of each sector

of the business. He does, however, like a second opinion, and that's why I'm with you today!"

"I can see why," said Kimberli. "You seem like a perfect fit; would you please tell me a little about yourself, if you don't mind me asking?"

"Not at all," Claudia said. Then she told the story of how she knew James from the age of thirteen, when she was about the same age as Kimberli now, and the story of her love life and losses. The two had an intense conversation, and Kimberli was fascinated to hear about Claudia's modeling career. The couple then parted. Kimberli went to the train station, feeling exhilarated with her new position in life. Claudia felt encouraged by the encounter.

The next morning, an anxious James couldn't wait to hear Claudia's opinion of Kimberli.

She brought him some coffee to his office, and then proceeded to take a chair.

"Well, you have been a busy boy!" Claudia said. She was being mischievous, and she knew that James, in spite of his better judgment, had to have noticed her looks.

"What are you referring to?" James asked, with a puzzled look.

"She's quite a woman, not only good looking but brains out of this world," Claudia said. "I absolutely adore her. She's tough enough to handle pressure all right. To be that confident at twenty-seven blows my mind away. She reminds me of the female version of you. There will be no stopping that ambitious lass."

"Does she have a personal life?" James asked.

"Ah ha! I thought you might have an easy eye for her!"

"Well she's a looker all right, but it takes more than that." James was acting a little coy, feeling threatened that Claudia knew his taste inside and out."

"No, she doesn't have a personal life, so you must behave yourself. I know how men get that second itch; I could also see she's quite enamored with you."

"I know she's power-packed and can definitely do the job."

"She's preparing to submit a plan to you to double the circulation."

"That does sound like me."

"James, she also has a degree in finance; the woman is smart; she's my replacement one day. I'd put money on it."

"She's got a lot to learn. Claudia, you are still a very competent and knowledgeable woman. I know you'll be here for at least another ten years."

"James, I'll always be here on the board and to help; even though I'm a small shareholder, thanks to you, it's worth a fortune. I'm fifty-one, and Thomas is now sixty-five. It would be nice to take some time away, even though I know Thomas will relax only when Alex is old enough to go into the business."

"You can take time off whenever you want. It's time you had a competent backup."

"I know; it's hard to let go. We all suffer from the same disease; we're all workaholics!"

"Well, Ms. Kimberli certainly fits that mould, too. A degree in finance to what level? And why wasn't it on her CV?"

"She didn't want to look scattered. She wanted to present a more focused image towards reporting and journalism. She's good to tax level."

"Fascinating! So you could be right about her being a future potential. Let you off the hook after say twenty years or more. Anyway, not now; we have far too much to accomplish; we're not there yet, but almost."

"Almost, and what does that mean? As in never . . ."

They both laughed, knowing the chemistry they shared was unequalled. They also knew it would take more than a moment to fill Claudia's shoes, but the future potential was there.

CHAPTER 4

A TERRIBLE SHOCK

Since 1981, and over the last ten years, the business grew exponentially to even greater heights. The business had to be run from London, New York, and Hong Kong. Many more chief executives were hired, and the ever-growing chain in James's empire seemed boundless. Flick had realized her dream of becoming an anchorwoman, and Becky had remained happy growing in her authority within the medical field at the shipping line. Both James's sisters were now married. Kimberli Watson had done wonders with the newspaper by more than doubling circulation, with increased efficiency and more modern equipment. The closing of the old factory and the building of a new facility towards Bedford had smashed the old union movement and had resulted in the rehiring of the best printers of the day. Kimberli had completely transformed Henry Petersen's dream, having added so much more for the reader to enjoy.

James had stayed true to his masters and guides, taking

more time for family and traveling less. The month before Christmas 1991, James received some soul-destroying news.

A weary Sabrina returned from a regular checkup with her doctor, after feeling more tired than usual.

"James, hold your breath, my love," she said. "After my last checkup, the doctor delivered some very disturbing news; please sit down, I have cancer. It's fast growing and very advanced."

"My God, we can stop this!" James cried out. "There's chemo; things have changed since my father's day, and we can fight this."

The couple hugged each other with intense heartache. The very thought of James losing his Sabrina would be earthshaking. He had all the money in the world, and he would go to the ends of the Earth to save her.

"They will start chemo next week, so be prepared for my new look," she said. Then she flopped down in the armchair in the living room and started to sob. She had held her composure up until she told James; now she had to let it all out. James rushed to her side to console her.

"We can beat this; I know we can!" shouted a determined James.

"I wish we could, James, but they only give me three months," sobbed a dejected Sabrina. "It's pancreatic cancer, and it moves fast. I wonder whether it's even worth going through chemo."

"Of course, we must try," said James. He was thinking about using his healing powers, but a very strong voice from Serena told him that it was her time.

Why? Help me! Why are you not allowing me to change this outcome? he thought, and the answer came back: "It's meant to be. She knows it, because she will now return to us. It's the body she chose to be with you, and she knew before birth the genetic weaknesses." James knew that when his guides spoke, there would be no change. He ran out of the room and into the backyard, where Sabrina couldn't see him, to a private spot in the garden.

He then shouted, "God, how can you do this to Sabrina, my family, and me? Czaur, all of you, my guides. What have anyone of us done to deserve this terrible tragedy?"

He then fell on his knees and sobbed in a pathetically humble state, his head buried in his hands and rocking himself backwards and forwards. To have to watch his beautiful Sabrina wither away to this ghastly state that he witnessed with his father was too much.

"Not again, not again; this is too much!" he cried out.

A voice then came to him from Czaur: "There is a very important reason she will be coming to us. You will find another, but not now; rest assured: it's all part of a greater plan." James just wouldn't listen to what he was hearing, and he blamed himself for concentrating on his empire too much. He felt that God was punishing him for not appreciating her more throughout their marriage, although he had greatly improved over the last several years. It was devastating, to say the least, and James didn't know how to cope with a tragedy of this magnitude.

*****

Sabrina's funeral in Lincoln was a major event. She died in February of 1992. She managed to stay alive long enough to see Christmas through and the children off to school. It was a sad event, as James rose to the pulpit to give his eulogy.

"My Lords, Ladies, and Gentlemen, today we witness the departure of a woman I have loved since the day I met her, on one summer day on the lawn outside our drawing room. When our eyes met, I knew she was the one for me. She also felt the same way. It was a magnetic moment, one that I can never forget. Not only was she a beautiful woman to look at, but also her inner beauty went far beyond that. She was an exemplary mother, never ever missing any of Samuel's or Annabelle's events. She was a wife that stood behind me in all that I've worked so hard to do and that never ever complained for a moment. No man could have had or known a better wife."

His voice was now starting to quiver, as the tears were starting to roll down his cheeks.

"She was my everything, and now that she's gone, I pray that I can find a way to carry on."

He paused for a moment to regain his composure; he then continued, "I will take time away in order to understand this terrible loss, in order to understand why a woman is struck down in her prime. I thank God she was able to see her children become adults . . ."

James continued to sing her praises in front of a sobbing audience, from his mother, Antonio, and all the immediate family, to a huge entourage of admirers and friends. It took all James's strength to descend from the pulpit. It was at that moment Sabrina chose to show herself to him. He ran out to hold her in front of an audience who thought he'd become delusional and could see nothing.

"Sabrina, Sabrina, my beautiful Sabrina, you look just like the day we met on the lawn!" he cried out. Then he fell on the floor, in front of the altar. People helped him stagger out to his car, where his chauffeur drove him away. The whole affair was too emotional, and people were concerned; they had never seen this side of James before. The cool, hardheaded, pragmatic tycoon was now reduced to a fragment of his normal being.

*****

James had Claudia book him a place to get away. He took a small island in the Caribbean. The island's mansion was the only building. It had all the staff and medical support from neighboring islands around. He could now live in complete isolation in order to recover from an experience he could never believe possible two months ago, before Christmas. His staff, under the excellent stewardship of Claudia, knew exactly what to do. Claudia would not bother—James knew she would manage somehow—and she would put on hold any major decisions for the moment. She knew his pain, and she was grief-stricken that she could not do more. She knew how to instruct Keith Pruett at the estate so that everything would be in the best hands until his return. She had arranged for medical staff to be on alert, after seeing the despair he had shown at the church during the funeral. It would take time—she knew that. A man like James was so committed and passionate in all that he did. His strength could be his weakness, and his heart was broken, and now he would have to find a way to recover.

The days passed, and then the weeks. All James could do was walk along the beach, falling down, then sleeping, from his drunken stupor. The staff would drag him back to his room and put him to bed. He could be heard screaming aloud night after night, "Why God? Oh why?" He couldn't eat. Alcohol was his only friend. It was indeed a pathetic sight to see a man of such great means brought so low.

After nearly three months, the medical staff was brought in. James was so thin; his unwashed, matted hair had fallen almost to his shoulders; and his beard was now down below his neck. They injected him to put him to sleep, and then they put him on a saline solution to clean out the alcohol from his emaciated body. The ingredients of the solution would slowly cleanse him and restore some strength. The staff would regularly take him to the bathroom, where he would wrench his aching stomach and pass the water in his body.

After several days, he awoke and started to feel alert. It was as though the love of his masters and guides had healed him from the destruction he was doing to his body. The memory of Sabrina was still firmly in his mind, and it was as though she was with him. He could be heard talking to her, but the staff could only guess to whom it was.

"James, I'm still here with you; I will not go until you are well," said Sabrina, as he started to sit up in bed.

"Oh, Sabrina, how do I carry on without you?"

"You must; it's all planned, and you will see when the time is ready. Someone is coming to visit you, so get ready!"

"Who?"

"It's a surprise. You must get back on your feet; you have too much to do, and, right now, your children need you more than ever."

"Yes, that's true; my Sam and Annie. How could I forget? I just miss you so much, Sabrina; I know I must start to recover; life goes on." So, did he speak, shaking his head, finally processing all that had taken place. He felt selfish in forgetting his children and started to get a grip on himself.

"Sabrina, I have been replaying all the beautiful moments of the life we shared together. Even walking along the beach, I remember the first moments when we met. The time when you would come over before the modeling started, our long-awaited wedding day, and honeymoon. I hope I was a good husband to you."

"James, you were, and you are still my everything. I watch over you; we are twin souls. You are my other half, and just know I'm still with you, until you cross over. My journey of life on earth is complete, and I shall wait for you until we meet again. In the meantime, our masters have experiences that they want you to live and learn from."

"What experiences? Being with you is all I want."

"James, you will see, and, in time, you will understand that there are others to meet and that you must integrate our children, for the future of the Bannermans. You have much left to do, and you will find the right woman: I will help you achieve that. I must leave you now, but know I'm watching over you, but be free to find another for your life. We will be together when the time comes; you will see."

With that, she was gone. James kept asking, but he had been answered, and now he would have to make his own way.

*****

At that moment, who should burst through the door but, lo and behold, Lisa!

"By God, James, look at you! I've come to straighten you out."

"Lisa, what a pleasant surprise. I couldn't think of anyone more I would like to see. I've barely had a conversation with anyone on this planet; I've been truly lost."

Lisa got rid of the staff after asking for a bowl so she could shave and bathe him, and then she cut his hair. She was the perfect person for the task, and James knew it.

"We'll have you back in shape in no time," said Lisa. "My God, you look a bloody wreck! Not the James I'm used to." She had him smiling in no time, and the color started to come back into his face. After all those days of dropping on the beach, stone drunk, he had developed a serious tan.

"Look at you!" she said. "You look like a native, not the tycoon and empire builder I know. If I could love you looking like this, I suppose I'll always be infatuated with you. James, you give it all. As intense as you are in your work, so you are in your love life. What woman in the world couldn't admire that?"

"Oh, Lisa, I've always had an easy eye for you, and I so love it when you talk in your best sexy Cockney accent."

James was noticing that, even in her mid-forties, she was still a beautiful woman, with more maturity and force than ever. Sir Nicholas had known she was just the right tonic to get him back on his feet. Lisa's mother, Sally, had worried about James, and she knew how much her daughter adored him. She told her to go and ask Nicholas if she could take time off to travel and see James. Nicholas didn't hesitate for a moment, as he remembered the night they had all met at the Fantasy Bar in London. She was not a family member, and that was best.

Over the next week, James started to regain his former self. The positive energy he was receiving from Lisa had opened his eyes. He had moments of reflection for Sabrina, but the emotion was starting to leave. His memories of Sabrina would, however, never fade. He somehow knew she was there, and that comforted him. He felt she approved. He also felt the warmth and joy of her love, and he started to realize that Sabrina was in a happy place, too. In time, he thought he would revisit the stars and maybe rekindle his Sabrina in a different light. He knew it wasn't now. He felt a great force for him to move on with the journey that lay in front of him.

After going for long walks on the beach and discussing old times, Lisa and James had decided to have a dinner prepared on the veranda. He could now have a cocktail, as they sat down to a beautifully prepared meal under the stars, and, over a good bottle of wine, they could finally enjoy discussing the present.

"James, I know you've been through a lot, but how do you see your life moving forward?" said Lisa, in a thought-provoking way.

"I must get home and see my children; that's number one. It's enough that they have lost their mother; it's time to pick up my responsibilities as a father and attend to their needs. The business, I'm sure, is in good stead, under the competent hands of Claudia, whom I will call tomorrow. I will be lonely, at first; then when I feel all is in a good place, I will slowly work at meeting someone else; I'm not in a hurry, but I need company, and you, Lisa, are a godsend."

"James, you know how I feel about you; for me, you are the love of my life. I am, however, a practical woman that knows I will always be your friend. You need someone with intellect and style. I have, thanks to you, risen way above my station in life. I know I could never match that mind of yours, but always know we have an attraction for one another. In your pursuit for Miss, or maybe Ms., someone, I will always try to make myself available if you feel lonely and are in need of comfort and love."

Lisa was so humble in her presentation that James's eyes watered at her unconditional love and acceptance of who he was. He would always see Lisa right, and she knew she would never have to worry about a job or financial well-being, as long as James was alive. He also knew she would never take advantage of their relationship. She was, in all essence, the greatest female friend a man could have.

In the remaining nights they shared together, she would

cuddle up next to him, affectionately. He was not yet ready for any physical pleasure, but he felt the love and warmth that Lisa provided. She, too, was in a state of bliss to be able to feel his love and give hers, thinking that there was much more to life than sex.

CHAPTER 5

STARTING OVER

James arrived back at Penbroke and took time to think his life through. He felt so lonely wandering through the house; the children, now adults, were in university. How was he going to deal with this emptiness he was now feeling? The very thought of not having Sabrina was starting to hit home.

Who could replace her? She was my everything, he thought. *I must change my life; the memories of her presence here are too great. But where? Who? I must get back to work; I need company, I'm not ready for living here right now. I must go to London and stay there, work, and, with time, I will slowly return. Claudia will help me. She's my closest friend. Maybe I'll fly out and see my mother and Antonio. I'll get back into work; that'll take my mind off everything.*

All these thoughts were buzzing through his brain, as he had his pilot take him back to London. He just wasn't ready to face the inevitable—yet.

"James, it's wonderful to see you again," said Claudia, giving him a big hug.

"Claudia, let's go into my office, and let's have a chat."

Claudia had coffee brought in so the two of them could have a good discussion about himself, the future, and the business.

"You look like you're on the mend, but I know what you must be going through," Claudia said. "We must get some weight back on you. You're still a fine-looking man, so you must start taking care of yourself. I know it's hard to eat when one feels grief."

"I just can't stay at Penbroke right now; the whole house has Sabrina's stuff everywhere, and the memories are too painful for me to face right now."

"That's normal, but all of us have to face those painful experiences life deals us. You don't remember how I felt. You were too young when I came to Penbroke. Your father lifted my soul after my loss of Paul So, I know exactly how you feel."

"When Father died, I felt pain, but nothing like this. You were there and comforted us all. I just knew he was in a good place."

"As much as you loved your father, and I know you two were very connected, this is a different kind of love. Sabrina and you shared a family between you and adored one another for nearly twenty years. If you didn't feel like you do, I would have questions."

"She was my everything, and as much as I know my guides have told me that it was meant to be, I just have a hard time accepting this."

"It was a shock, not only to you but the whole family. You must focus on your two young adults and realize the pain they must be feeling."

"It's true; life goes on, but I have to say this is, without a doubt, the lowest point in my life. How do I ever meet another Sabrina?"

"James, you will, and I know Sabrina would want that. I found that out from being on your throne; I felt total release from Paul, and that's what changed my life!"

"When I'm ready, I will make the journey and do that; I've just been so angry that this could happen to the one I love. My guides have told me there is a reason and I will meet someone else, but it takes a moment. I'm just not ready yet to release my love for Sabrina, if ever."

"James, the spiritual person I know you to be, as crazy as it seems now, it will all make sense eventually."

"I know; as much as I try to make sense of it all, my heart has not yet dealt with what I'm going through. I'm so structured, and I'm learning that life can definitely deal you a left fielder. I am sure that, with time, it will just make me stronger; it's the missing part that's so hard."

"James, over the years, I've got to know Kimberli well. She's stayed with us on a number of occasions, and I have been to her home in Durham. She may not be the person you may want right now, but she seems very enamored with you, and I think she has always been a favorite person for you. She's single, highly educated, and attractive; I think she might be a good tonic for you and what you're going through."

"Yes, I've always had a close working relationship with her. She's a woman I admire greatly. Yes, she's had the financial backing to completely overhaul the newspaper, and I can't take away the fact that she's made great progress with the company. Claudia, you could be right. I think I'll pay her a visit; it's been a while since we last spoke. I've always left it to the both of you."

"James, you need change, and she might be just the person; even if you just strike up a friendship, she's every bit your equal intellectually; and who knows? You might have fun. I do know she's a workaholic like you. She's too strong and independent for most men. She's shared her feelings with me that she would so like to meet someone, but she just hasn't found the right fit. She's tired of just having the casual relations she now shares. It's her lifestyle that most men find hard to live with, and the fact she is so strong-willed. I do, however, think you two could hit it off. You two are certainly match enough for each other!"

"I think you could be right. I know I was struck by her when we first met; she has presence. I'm sure that could be intimidating for a lot of men. A strong and single-minded woman . . . Who knows?"

James's eyes started to light up at the thought.

"Give it a shot; go see her; have lunch and see where it goes!" said Claudia, glad to see James starting to light up at the idea.

*****

"Now for business—where are we—any emergencies?" James asked.

"Everything is going well, but, James, I'm concerned for the future," Claudia said.

"Why?"

"James, I'm in my sixties; Thomas is in his seventies. As shareholders, we will always be there for you and this empire you've built. It's time we worked less, say part-time. Alex is now with his father in the law firm. We want to travel and share a life together while we have the health."

"That's understandable, so you want to train a replacement?"

"James, it's time, and you know who the perfect person would be?"

"Now I see why you want to hook me up with Kimberli;

you have an ulterior motive, aha!" he said, laughing.

Claudia was slowly bringing James back to the man he truly was. She knew him too well. Their connection would probably never be repeated in the same way again. Claudia had been an essential ingredient in helping James on his ambitious journey. She was in good health, still a fine-looking woman, but she would always be in the background. She loved the business, and James knew she would always be there, to advise him at crucial points.

"I think she would be perfect," James said. "She has more than earned her stripes at the newspaper. Who knows? She might leave me for dead. I know she has all the force and brilliance to be an even greater version than I have been."

"I doubt that," Claudia said. "Outside Sabrina, but more particularly in the world of business, it would be hard to find a person of your caliber. Smarts are important, but it's chemistry that counts. It's that inner intuitive understanding of each other and how we think that has made our relationship such a success."

Claudia went on, "I thank you, James, for your vote of confidence; we do, without doubt, share a great admiration for one another, and that is an essential component in our long journey of knowing each other. Changing the subject, I also have another question to put to you."

"Shoot," said James, looking at her with curious anticipation.

"Who's going to run this empire you've built when your time comes? Have you thought about that?"

"I'm not dead yet!" shouted James, though he felt close to it. "However, I do have a will, but I'm not completely sure. You bring up a good point. Samuel, I believe, would be a competent administrator, but I don't think he's entrepreneurial enough to reshape and reform businesses as we move forward in this new age of technology. He's like my father was. He's extremely literate and more even-keeled than I am. He has all the speech-making skills, authority, and confidence to run this business. He's doing well at Oxford. He would be an excellent figurehead, but he doesn't have the same drive I have. Scholastically, he's great, in history, sciences, politics, and people skills come naturally to him. His acumen for math and numbers is not so good, but he could hold his own. Money, I think, isn't important to him. He's going to be a leader and a man of the people.

"Now, that being said, Annabelle is sharp with numbers and does have that drive. She's doing exceptionally well at Cambridge and will pass out with honors. She's fascinated with what I do, and she is totally up on all the latest technology. Her IT skills are up there with the best. So, ironically, she seems to have more of me in her than Samuel. She's so beautiful, just like her mother. A little taller, I had always thought she would want to be a model, like her mother. She could have boyfriends all over the map, but she has one goal, and that's to be the best at what she does."

"Now, that's food for thought," James went on. "She may be my next replacement if Kimberli still wants to run her own company."

"I plan on taking them on a long summer cruise," James continued. "It's necessary now that we spend time together and have this type of conversation."

"James, think about this, too," Claudia said. "Maybe it's the right moment to do some public offerings. Trans Global's shares would rocket, and your textile business would also do extremely well. Take public all the companies that are not associated to the bank. That is, keep the bank, the credit card process for now, the properties worldwide, the newspaper, and let all the others out to the marketplace. You have the perfect man in Roger for that. In that way, you could harness a huge return that would benefit the next generation. They may or may not have your skills to run an operation of the magnitude we have now."

"Sound thinking, Claudia; the money could be held in trust, and, in that way, they would be insulated from any world depression or financial catastrophe in the future."

"I'm sure they could both play a role in this company, with Samuel as chairman eventually and with Annabelle, who could, in fact, be the managing director and be more involved in the day-to-day. How do they get on?"

"Extremely well; they have very different natures, so it works. Samuel is more outgoing, is a great sportsman, one of the lads. Annabelle is more studious, which is ironic; given her beauty and looks, she could even surpass her mother. Life is funny that way."

*****

James took Claudia's advice and drove his way up to the new newspaper business to see how Kimberli was doing. It had been a while since they last met. Kimberli was nervously taking care of all her daily obligations. She was anxious to see James. She was excited to show him all the hard work she had done. She had put her heart and soul into transforming the newspaper. She was proud that he had chosen her above all the others. Now was the moment to show him that she had more than returned the faith he had in her abilities. She also had other plans she wanted to expand on.

James entered the main lobby and proudly looked at the work the architects had done to update the image of the business he had bought out. The new buildings and offices were appropriately styled to reflect the newspaper's history. He enjoyed seeing the original photographs of the place where Henry Petersen had started the company, from its modest beginnings.

Kimberli made her way to the reception area to meet James. She was immaculately dressed in a black skirt and topcoat and was wearing a purple blouse (her favorite color), with matching shoes. Her tall presence, in higher heels than she normally wore to work, gave her entrance to the reception area definite attention from James.

"Kim, I like your attire," said James. "You have a formidable presence, something I've always liked about you, since the first time we met."

"Well, thank you, my Lord; coming from you, who I know are always surrounded by those who dress with elegance and style, I take that as a great compliment."

Their eyes met, and James could feel she liked his words, and she liked that he'd taken a moment to notice that she had made an effort to look pleasing for him.

He followed her through the main office, where many of the phones were in action. People were frantically talking, trying to get the latest scoop from their various contacts. He followed her down a hallway, which was carpeted, as the drone of the voices lessened. They then entered an area where the administrative offices were located. They climbed a stairway to the upper level, where her senior staff operated, in offices adjacent to the large conference room, which was directly connected to Kimberli's office. There were two conference rooms, one for larger groups and the other for smaller ones. Kimberli had her own secretary, who had a smaller office in front of her much-larger office at the rear, and which was also connected to the two conference rooms. Her office spoke well of her interests and her life. She had large photographs of her daughter and home behind her desk of paintings that showed landscapes and sunny places that looked inviting. The office had a feminine touch, but it was extremely tidy and exuded a warm and inviting energy. Above her credenza, she had a window that looked out over the shop. She struck James with the thought that this woman keeps her eye on everything. No detail passes by her without her knowledge.

"So, Mr. James, what do you think?"

"First class, I'd say. A slight difference to the other factory we had outside St. Albans."

"James, you don't know how much I love it here; I can work as many hours as I want. On second shift, I like to walk the factory floor and keep in touch with the people there; it's good for morale. I usually make a round first thing when I arrive in the morning and then on second shift before I leave. This equipment we have is great! It can spit out twice the number of newspapers in half the time and with half the staff. We are barely up to the number we had at the old factory, and yet we are doing over twice the circulation."

"That's remarkable. I feel you command a great deal of respect, as I see people look up at you when we walked through. You have a lot of force about you. A woman in this day and age who can command the respect of all the work-force without a union has to have something going for her!"

"I have regular meetings with everyone. So there are no misunderstandings about what our vision and direction is. Staff and shop managers alike—we all work as one, united in our effort to be the best. That means we can pay higher wages to fewer people and have more productivity."

"So how well do you know how to operate those printing presses out there?"

"There's not a job that I can't do or a machine that I can't operate or a story that I can't write or edit," she responded. "I can do it all from the ground up. I've spent many weekends and long hours to learn how to operate all that exists under our roof. That being said, we have a great team. I'm just a jack-of-all-trades!" She laughed.

"I think you're one of a kind; I don't think I ever met a woman like you before."

"Well, I used to work with my father growing up; although we don't have a big farm, I can be a farm girl, too! We have to multitask, and that, together with the fine education I was afforded, has put me in a good place to do what I'm doing today."

"Why don't we go to lunch and talk further," suggested James.

"I've made a reservation," said Kimberli. "It's a little drive, but it's the best pub around here." She hoped he would be pleasantly surprised.

James was impressed with Kimberli; she could do it all. They climbed into her Jaguar, and, like everything else, she drove out of the gates with same determination she had in her walk.

It was a lovely Tudor pub close to Bedford, just off the A1 motorway. They had a legendry old-world dining room there. The couple found a table that was private, where they could talk about business and about life.

"James, how are you coping after the loss of Sabrina?"

"It's not easy; when you love a person like Sabrina, the difficult part is the emptiness you feel after someone who has been that close to you for over twenty years has died. I have dealt with the pain and the heartache; now it's adjusting to the fact that person will never be on this planet again, at least during my lifetime."

"So you believe in reincarnation?"

"I do; do you?"

"I'm not sure; being brought up Roman Catholic, we are not believers in that."

"It's not part of Christianity, I know. But when you look around the world and see such a disparity of wealth, the difference in spiritual evolvement, it makes it hard to understand the inequality of the human race."

"What do you mean by spiritual evolvement?"

"We are getting into a deep subject," said James, starting to laugh with Kimberli. "It's like this." James was choosing his words wisely, as he knew Kimberli was first and foremost a reporter and a very intelligent one, at that. He wasn't going to go too far on their first encounter outside the business, but he wanted to make a point that would be thought-provoking. He didn't know Kimberli's personal beliefs, but he could tell by her aura that she was very inquisitive so that she did not necessarily believe it herself, but he knew it would help her understand him better.

"When you meet someone like me, for instance, or anyone, don't you feel a level of spiritual essence within that person? I just believe we are all at different levels of understanding about the universe we live in."

"I agree, although I've never given it much thought. I just take each person I meet at face value, and then I proceed from there. Some I feel a chemistry or connection with; with others, I don't. In business, of course, we can't always discriminate, but, thank God, we can personally."

Kimberli was a down-to-earth type of person; however, James did feel a level of curiosity, as they both laughed. This was not a normal conversation to kick off their meeting, but it signified a comfort level the two of them had with one another. This was unusual on a first encounter.

James felt Sabrina's presence and knew she was happy that they were enjoying each other's company.

"So, do you write much about those kinds of things in the newspaper?"

"Yes; we have horoscopes and interviews with psychics. There's quite an interest in the paranormal, but we tend to keep that towards the back. We have to be careful not to lean in any particular direction and to remain neutral and impartial, always reporting the facts."

"I had a reason for seeing you today, one of which was to get to know you better, but I also wanted to offer you a job that I believe you would be tailor-made for."

"Really? And what would that be?"

"To step into Claudia's shoes; she would train you, of course. She's now in her sixties and has been invaluable at what she does, but she wants to work fewer hours. She would, of course, remain on the board of directors. Outside me, it's probably the most senior position in the company."

"Wow, I am flattered; so, what would that entail?"

"Coordinating all the businesses we own worldwide, financially overseeing them, and reporting directly to me. That's a gross oversimplification, of course; you would have to spend time with Claudia in order to understand the role completely."

"That's quite a role; would I make more than I do now?"

"Absolutely; the only factor is that you are so good at what you do here. You have a certain autonomy in your role as head of this newspaper; you might feel that you don't have the same independence that you have as being the boss here."

"That's true; I do like my position, but I have an idea I want to present you with."

"Shoot."

"James, I would like to branch out our business here. There's a small television station that I know we can buy very reasonably. Then we can invest and go into cable news and have our own satellite station; this could be twice what this newspaper could be."

"That's a big step, so you are an entrepreneur as well!" James shook his head, laughing; it was about the last thing he had on his mind. Kimberli was now thirty-seven years old; she had more than proven her worth with the newspaper.

But why not? James thought. I have another Roger Bell on my hands. There will be no holding back this gal! She has a mind of her own and all the force in the world to go with it. As great as she could be in filling Claudia's shoes, she has the mind of an entrepreneur, and she would be wasted in a role like Claudia's.

"James, I've done my homework," said Kimberli. "I know all the right people and before you leave, I'll let you have my presentation, if you wish to make this acquisition."

"Okay; so, tell me all about Kimberli."

"James, you know all about me; you have my CV."

"If I'm going to start investing in television stations and cable news, I need a deeper understanding of the woman I'm about to invest in; don't you think?"

"There's not much to tell; I just work all week, all the hours God can send me; then I go to my home in Durham, to my daughter, who's now fifteen. She is a weekly border at a school there, and she comes home for the weekend. Have to keep an eye on those teenagers, you know! Then I like to paint in my studio; when I get time, I ride my horse or work in the garden and tend to the plants I have in my greenhouses."

"It seems all you do is work," said James, trying to understand this very independent woman. "Don't you have a man in your life?"

"I have been married once, as you know; yes, I do have boyfriends I see, but who wants a relationship with an independent-minded workaholic like me?"

"Kim, you are a beautiful woman; don't you want someone in your life?"

"I do, but it always ends in misunderstandings or arguments. Men like you to feel owing to them; they don't like it if you're too independent. It's okay for them to do what they want and sometimes drag you along, but I have never met a man that sometimes wants to do what I want."

"You are certainly different; do you prefer the company of women?"

"Yes, but don't go down that road; I've heard it before. I just find women easier and more heartfelt in understanding another woman. So, yes, I have to say I do prefer the company of my own sex."

"What do you mean by 'don't go down that road'?"

"You know what men think; just because they see an unattached lady who is attractive, they naturally assume she's . . . Well, I'm not. I would love to meet the right man, but where in God's name is he?"

"Kim, you have to understand that living with you and not seeing you, unless they work with you, would almost never work. Then you would probably want to get away from each other, because you see one another all week." James shook his head, laughing.

"What?"

"Ms. Kimberli, never mind, but if I can't whisk you away for a fun evening in London once in a while, I will feel very disappointed."

"Lord James, are you propositioning me?"

"Absolutely; you want that television station? You better play ball!"

"You are a bad man; you just have to have your way!"

Kimberli, deep down, was flattered at the inference; she knew a man of his stature and looks could get almost any woman, but he found something he liked in her, and that was hard for her to resist.

"Need to get you out of your rut and away from all those women that talk bad about us. Dance, have a great meal and a good bottle of wine, and be a little crazy now and then!"

"So I don't have a choice?"

"No."

Kimberli knew he was teasing; he was a man of too much class to force himself on her, and she liked the way he went about it.

She thought, *If I'm going to get my way, I might at least return the favor; after all, he didn't have to help me if he didn't want to. Besides, it would be fun. And who knows? What the hell? Here goes nothing!*

James took the presentation back with him to London.

She's a first, he thought. *More drive than a thousand horses. She's like Queen Boadicea and her chariot, blasting her way to the top. I guess I have met the female version of myself?* He chuckled.

CHAPTER 6

THE REPLACEMENT
OF CLAUDIA

James was puzzled; he had thought long and hard about Kimberli, and he handed over her presentation to Claudia, to see what her thoughts were.

"James, this is a very ambitious project that Kim has in mind," said Claudia. "Are you serious? After all you have, are you at it again? You can't resist a challenge? On the other hand, it might be good therapy for you after all you've been through. My advice is if she wants to do this, you have a clear message."

"What do you mean?"

"Don't get too attached to her; I'll talk with her. But, weighing her up, I know she's not going to be anybody's woman. She may want that, in the romantic sense, but the world is as it is. James, I know her hardworking drive ethic; you could get frustrated. If you back this project, she will be up to her ears in this. That means if she's not interested in settling down with a man by now at her age, she has one thing that is paramount in her journey of life."

"I don't understand; a project like this could bring us closer together. I'm not asking for marriage, just an opportunity to get to know her better."

"At what price? I can see why she enchants you, as you are total in all you do. I'm just warning you; don't get too close to the flame."

"Look, let's evaluate her presentation and see the merits of her plan, or not?"

"Just as long as you go forward with that in mind."

"Of course; I don't expect anything else."

"James, I know you too well; most women would jump at a chance to be working with you on a day-to-day basis, a huge increase in salary, responsibility, and prestige. What you are offering 99 percent of women would jump at. She has all the competence to do that and still push for the TV station, as well."

"So what are you trying to say? Speak plainly."

"I will talk with her and evaluate the process, and if you choose to do this, be prepared to see her now and then, keep good relations, but see it for what it is. You've been through too much with the loss of Sabrina. All you need is another disappointment in your personal expectations. I'm sure she would be successful, I have no doubt about that, but don't be doing it for the wrong reasons; do it because it makes good business sense. Your sentiments I feel already are not like you have towards any of our other staff. I just want you to realize that from the get-go, because it may not be the same for her."

"Point taken; let the chips fall where they may!" said James, laughing at Claudia's protective concern, but underevaluating the fine instincts of a woman like Claudia.

*****

Claudia and James now delved deeply into all the businesses they owned worldwide. He needed to know exactly where he stood in order to integrate his business holdings for the future—whether to go public with certain businesses or to continue to hold his private status, which he cherished for the heritage of his family in the future. It would be necessary before his cruise and intended summer holidays with his family. He would make his decision after spending time at his new corporate headquarters in New York. The three head-quarters—London, Hong Kong, and now New York—were at the epicenter of his world empire. The final decision would come from London. In the new world, it would be easy for the soul of what he had now created to cash in and to take the wealth. It depended on the people he had now and the next generation of Bannermans. It would be profound, and it was a decision he could make only from his cruise and from a final visit to Hong Kong.

Rose knocked on the conference room door and said, "Sir, you have a call from your mother; do you want me to put the call through here or in your office?"

"I believe we're finished; my office, please."

The meeting broke up. James was anxious to talk with his mother, whom he had seen only briefly at the funeral.

"Mother, how are you? It's been a while."

"James, darling; more importantly, how are you doing?"

"As well as can be expected. I'm so sorry not to have called before now; it has taken me a moment to get back on my feet, as you can imagine."

"Look, we are in town for a few days, so why don't we meet up for dinner this evening?"

"I'd love that; let's meet at, say, the Brass Bell at seven o'clock?"

"Seven, it is; see you then."

James finished his calls, as was his normal practice; then he went to his townhome to change for the evening. He was looking forward to having a long conversation with his mother and Antonio about all he had been through.

The three met on time, and, after all the hugs and kisses, the maître d' sat them at James's favorite table.

"James, you've lost a lot of weight," said his mother, concerned about how he looked.

"I know; it has been a trying time. I find it hard to go back to Penbroke with all Sabrina's stuff there. Do you think you could work with the staff to clear away all her things? Obviously keeping her jewelry and valuables for Annabelle?"

"Of course, darling, I will go first thing tomorrow and organize everything. We can meet up this weekend, as you must make the effort to move past what's happened. It's hard, I know, but I went through the same thing with your father. So you must man up and face life."

"I know you all loved her, and it must be sad for you, too, Antonio."

"James, to lose my first wife and then my daughter in my life, as I have, is more than painful. We must pray and find the strength to move on. Look, I found my first love again, your mother! We can never know what God has in store for us. We must maintain faith and trust that as hard as it is to understand, there is always a reason."

"I feel her; I know she's with us and she only wants the best for me and our family and she has, as crazy as it sounds, no regrets."

"James, you have always had that extra sense and intuition

about you; if anyone can rise above this, I know you can."

"Thanks, Antonio. You help me to believe in myself again. I have never ever loved someone like our Sabrina, ever. She will be hard to replace. However, as you say, who knows what the future holds?"

They finished the evening with lighter conversation and then parted. James was glad that he'd finally spoken to his mother and Antonio. They promised to meet up on the weekend and sort through Sabrina's belongings.

It was Thursday afternoon, and James knew Kimberli would be headed to Durham for the weekend. He had it in mind to take her out and to dig more deeply in order to understand the future she truly wanted. The satellite business was a huge undertaking, and he saw that her future would be best served under Claudia for now. She could then keep a watchful eye on the newspaper.

"Kim, how are you?"

"Fine, my Lord, to what do I owe the honor of your call?"

"Well, I was thinking if you would like a change, come down to London tonight and let's go out, discuss some business, and have a fun evening; are you up for the challenge?"

"Let me see; I have some things that could wait; yes, an evening out would do me good; where do we meet?"

"Let's meet at the bank; then we can go from here."

"But I need to change; I can't go in these clothes!"

"Go by your house; bring a change of clothes; and you can stay here."

"Where is here?"

"My place."

"Now you intend to be a kind, polite gentleman, I hope, sir?"

"Look; I have plenty of space here, and you can choose

whatever room you want to sleep in, and you can change clothes in absolute privacy; I promise."

"Well, if that's the case, I'm on my way; say, six o'clock at the bank?"

"Sounds good to me!"

James was elated, and excited. It was his first encounter with a new opportunity, since Lisa, and he couldn't wait. It was just the tonic he needed to get his mind off matters.

*****

Kimberli arrived on time and was escorted to his office; her suitcase, she left in the lobby. The staff had gone for the day, and it was an appropriate time to impress her.

"So here is my Texas lady, on time!"

"I see—. Claudia has informed you of my roots."

"Every detail."

He had a plan: he wanted to show her around so that she would have an idea of where she would be working if she didn't decide to stay at the newspaper and not pursue her dream of running a satellite television network.

"I think I could be very comfortable in these surroundings, plush offices and a magnificent boardroom, with a map that pinpoints all the entities owned within the Bannerman Empire."

"So, you are having second thoughts?"

"Absolutely; who wouldn't want to be located here at the epicenter of your world?"

"Not everyone; it's a demanding job," said James, putting on his jacket and coat and making motions to leave the bank. After hailing a taxi, they soon arrived at his townhome.

He showed Kimberli to her room. She was delighted to have time to prepare herself for the evening.

Kimberli was excited as they entered the Fantasy Bar; taking it all in, she said, "James, I can't tell you how long or even if I've ever been to a place like this before! I'm such a country girl in my personal life; this is a whole new experience."

They made their way to James's favorite booth, whereupon he ordered a bottle of Crystal to kick the evening off.

"So it's time we took the country out of you, don't you think? Clear away some of that structured routine you've become so used to and have you let your hair down for a change."

"I guess this is welcome to London and all the bright lights," she remarked, grinning from ear to ear, feeling a sense of abandonment and freedom.

"So, this is where you take all those fine ladies when you want to have an intimate evening?" she said, looking at him, realizing he could be a lot of fun when he got out of his normal routine.

"Now, Kim, not to talk business all night, but we've read your proposal about the TV station you want to buy out. We think that we would be venturing a little outside our zone of expertise. The money it would take to be a major player to get this venture off the ground would be massive, so as much as I would like to back you, I have my doubts."

"James, I agree. I would like to take you up on your offer to work at your corporate office in London. This would open new horizons for me. As much as I have loved running the newspaper, I have someone who is more than competent to take my place."

"Who?" asked James curiously.

"Why, your sister, of course."

"Flick? You're joking? She's a competent anchorwoman and definitely has all the confidence, the 'gift of the gab,' so to speak, but to run a business? I think not."

"You would be wrong; we get on famously; she knows the business in her sleep, and she has all the energy to make people get out there and collect the latest topical news. Look how successful she is in what she's doing now. Henry Petersen thinks the world of her. She may not have all the factory skills that I possess, but, in all sincerity, we have very capable staff who can well take care of that. It's about the news and getting along with people. Flick is a leader and has energy for sale. Her husband is also in the media business, and, believe me, they have all the right contacts. You might be surprised!"

"Well, I'll be damned; I must admit I haven't been following her too closely lately, but I am proud of what she's become."

"James, she would be so overjoyed if you offered her that opportunity. She's her own person, and where she works now, they pretty much leave her alone, because she knows exactly what she wants and knows how to get it done."

"You think she would give up being on TV? I know she likes the spotlight."

"I'm sure she would; she's often hinted to me that if I ever changed, would I put in a good word for her. You may not know it, but she's been a useful connection and has helped me a lot."

"I'm happily surprised."

"Since those days with Gordon Petersen, she's always wanted to show you what she can do. This would be an opportunity for her to shine. In my case, I get along with Claudia; I value her as a friend and dream of working with her to one day be your right-hand person, as she has been to you."

"Well, let's make a toast to that and go dance."

James noticed that Kimberli was very reserved. You can tell a lot about a woman when you dance with her. She was slightly stiff and didn't want to get too close. He thought, *Was she over-*

come with the surroundings, or shy dancing with a man that everyone in the room knew who he was? Or was it because she wanted to keep the evening formal and more businesslike, until she felt more comfortable in the hands of a celebrity? Perhaps she wanted to be sure she had the job before showing a more intimate side of herself.

Kimberli knew well the dangers of mixing business with pleasure. She was going to keep her distance in that way until she felt well assured that she was firmly established as James's right-hand person at the center of his empire. Kimberli was ambitious, and nothing would get in the way of achieving her goal. The thought of a higher salary, prestige, and power was uppermost in her motivation.

They returned to the table, where James ordered some light snacks.

"So, what do you think of this place?" he asked.

"James, it's out of this world; forgive me if I'm a little nervous being with you in a setting like this. I'm not used to being in the company of such people or a person like you."

James was flattered and said, "Nonsense; we are all people at the end of the day, and a little fun and libation never hurt anyone, so lighten up. If you're going to take over from Claudia, give me a chance to know you a little better. Is there anything you'd like to know about me?"

"James, naturally I'm a little overwhelmed just being with you here tonight, but please don't take offense to my next question. You have to know I was once a reporter?"

"Indeed, I do, so shoot."

"What about your personal life? Are you seeing anyone in particular right now?"

"Ah ha, checking me out, Ms. Kim? The answer is no; it would be hard to find anyone to replace what Sabrina and I shared. My mother is taking care of all her personal belongings as we speak. Naturally, a lot of her possessions will go to Annabelle, my daughter, who has to finish her studies at Cambridge University. I plan to take Samuel, my son, and Annabelle on a cruise this summer and have some together time after the shock of their mother's passing. I just take it one day at a time; I'm sure the right person will come into my life one day. It's not easy, but we must all have faith."

"A handsome and eligible man like yourself must have a host of admirers, but I do know it takes time to get over someone you loved so dearly. I know what that feels like; I had a boyfriend I loved very much, but, as always, my work got in the way, and then came the arguments. I'm hoping, although I know I will work my tail off when I'm with you, to meet a fine man like Claudia has done. It's time for me to have some personal life, and I've been thinking about that a lot recently."

"Everyone deserves a personal life; don't get too used to being alone. It takes work, give and take, but if the love is there, you will find a way."

Kimberli looked deeply into his eyes, with emotion, as tears started to well up. James stretched out his hand to comfort her; he could see she had been hurt, and he wanted to console her.

"Come on; let's dance; enough of all this serious stuff; we are here to have fun."

Kimberli started to relax; as she could see, there was a gentle and kind side to James. She moved closer, starting to feel a warmth and connection for the first time.

The couple shared a lovely evening, having started to connect with an emotional bond. Kimberli really felt good about her decision to move to London. As Claudia had done, she needed a life, and London was the place to get her out of her rut.

They slept in separate rooms. As was appropriate, Kimberli thought a lot about James before finally falling asleep. The next morning, she got up early to make some tea and toast. James was appreciative of her efforts, as the two sat, chitchatting and enjoying an early-morning cigarette before Kimberli left on her return.

CHAPTER 7

A NEW REVELATION

It was Saturday morning, and James went into the bank to update Claudia, knowing she would be there.

"So where did you guys go for the evening?" asked Claudia, with a sly grin.

"Oh, I thought a night out at the Fantasy Bar would do her some good. Shake off the cobwebs from a regimented routine and create a slightly more intimate environment for discussion."

"So much for a restaurant and business as usual!"

"Claudia, I'm just trying to get to know her; if she's going to be working here, I have to know whether we can all get along. Besides, I wanted to show her a more friendly, fun time, a different James—you know what I mean?"

"So, what is the prognosis?"

"She likes working with you, and, yes, she wants the job. She agrees the television is ambitious and, as I believe, outside our scope of activities. I don't want us to get too diverse and spread out of our business model."

"Who's going to run the newspaper?"

"Kim recommends Flick, which surprised the hell out of me, but she's sold on her abilities."

"Really; well, she has come a long way and improved immensely. She's great and confident in what she does on TV. She was definitely born for media."

"She's good with people apparently, and the best at getting the latest scoop."

"Kim said she would keep a close watch and work with her, even if she wasn't there."

"Sounds like a plan. Yes, I enjoy working with Kim. She's smart, works hard, is dedicated and a quick study."

Rose broke into the office at that moment and said, "Sir, Sarah is on line three; do you want to take it? It sounds urgent."

"Yes, of course."

"Sarah, my dear, how are you?"

"James, I've just made an unbelievable discovery!"

"Really, what?"

"Are you coming this weekend? I know your mother's here at the main house."

"Yes, I had planned on it."

"Well, see you tomorrow; it's too much to discuss now over the phone; believe me, you will be taken aback!"

"I can't wait; I'll be up there in the copter first thing."

"Sarah has made a discovery," said James to Claudia. "She sounds very excited; I can't wait to find out."

"I wonder what that can be," said an intrigued Claudia.

"Let you know early next week; my mother is helping to clear up all Sabrina's personal effects into storage, not a pleasant job. I'm glad she's doing that; it helps me a lot."

*****

James arrived at ten o'clock and hastily made his way over to Sarah's office.

"James, so pleased to see you; how are you doing since the funeral?"

"I've been better, but slowly getting over the event. It's coming here I find difficult, so my apologies for keeping my distance."

"I know; I felt the same way after Victor passed. That's why I wanted to change my life and live here. Since the children took over, I made a clean break. This was the best therapy for me. When I returned, they had made so many changes. It seemed like living there was a distant memory. Sometimes we have to make a change, not forget the past, but focus on the future."

"That's not going to be an easy task here, but I'm making an effort. It's just things that remind me of Sabrina. Except for some very personal items, I shall gradually change. It's just too painful. Anyway, as you say, I should remember the beautiful memories and start over."

"James, I have found a way to transport the body, as well as the mind, onto the Throne!"

"Wow! How?"

"Let's go over there now, before it becomes too busy," said an exuberant Sarah. Soon after, they were at the Throne.

"Now look carefully; you see these gold pullouts at the rear of each gemstone, which we all thought had been attached to the gemstone of the Throne."

"Yes."

Sarah pulled the top one, and, to James's astonishment, he saw the amethyst chakra light up."

"What just happened?"

Sarah continued to pull out all the gemstones from behind, as James looked on in disbelief.

"How do they do that? There's no wiring or capacitor attached to the Throne."

"It's simple; the light from the dome above shines through the crystal crown chakra," said Sarah. "It is then, in turn, transmitted to the other gemstone chakras." Sarah was proud of her new discovery.

"They look magnificent; I can almost feel the extra energy from standing in front."

"Be careful; don't get too close; this is why I have put extra barriers to keep people further back, so no meddling hands can reach the Throne. I have a person to keep a constant eye on the Throne."

"This is truly a revelation," said James, barely believing his eyes."

"When I pull the plug from behind the gemstone, it opens a portal to receive the light, so the gemstone glows with energy."

"Now, I will turn them off, and we can go back to my office and discuss the implications."

Sarah brought some coffee for James and for herself. She knew that as much as this could be, it was a blessing; this could also be a curse in the wrong hands.

"James, here's my concern, which I have not told you yet. I have transported myself in my entirety to my guides, and it was the most incredible experience I could have ever dreamed. When I returned, I had enough energy to work without sleep for a week. When the atomic structure of our body is transformed to light energy, every single part of us is positively charged. I have never felt so positive and well in my life. I had more energy than a young kid. It leads me to believe that possibly this energizing of the body could heal people of all kinds of disease. In addition, it could possibly be an antiaging formula; the possibilities are endless."

James sat in silence for a moment, taking it all in.

"If this got out, half the planet would be lining up at our doorstep. I see the dilemma, as positive as this is: whom could we trust after experiencing such a sensation. In addition, it could become addictive for all the wrong reasons. Once the cat is out of the bag, there's no telling where this could lead. There's one man I need to talk to about this."

"Who's that?"

"Jeremy Soames; you don't know him; he's the head of what is known as the Law Lords in the House of Lords. He knows all about that Throne, because he was my manservant on Atlantis, who took the Throne to Egypt. I wonder what he knows about this?"

"Really; so he knows you from that time? Fascinating."

"He told me that even if the boardroom at the bank would have rejected my proposal, he would have stepped in to help finance the project. He must know all this and is waiting for us to discover this for ourselves. He will have good advice as to how to implement this; as of right now, other than keeping this whole matter undercover, I don't have a worthwhile suggestion."

"James, of all my experiences of life in this dimension, there is a balance in all matters. I have to believe that as positive as it sounds for what this Throne can do, there has to be a counterbalance."

"What are you saying? I don't understand?"

"I believe that if this new-found discovery is abused for any reason, there has to be an equal and an opposite reaction."

"Newton's, third law of motion! I'm sure Lord Soames will know that, all the more reason to show caution. However, a soul has to be aligned to travel the vortex, and, for most, that requires a lot of work. If a person was using this for the wrong reasons, it's my gut feeling the vortex wouldn't receive that person."

"Good point, James. Anyway, we will slowly unravel these new found mysteries, will we not?"

"Absolutely," James said, then gave Sarah a hug, and then made his way over to the main house to see his mother.

****

"Mother, I can't thank you enough for doing this task. I know you have had to do this for Father, and it couldn't have been easy."

"Darling, I'm happy to help, all her clothes I've had packed away in the cellar with mothballs. Annabelle, in time, can choose what she likes, and the rest is hers or yours to do with as you wish. Her jewelry I have carefully put in the side drawer of her dressing table. That is a serious collection. I doubt that Annabelle has a clue of the value. If I were you, I would be very selective as to what you show her and as to what you allow her to have now. Some of those pieces are worth a fortune. You may want to hold some of that back. My advice is to put this in a safety deposit box at the bank. Do not spoil her yet! You may want to keep some pieces for someone you might meet. Someone else should appreciate these pieces. Jewelry should be worn, not locked away. Only give Annabelle those items that were close and true to Sabrina over time. Knowing Sabrina as I do, she would want that for you, or just sell them, but you won't get your money back. Sabrina would want your happiness, so don't feel guilt by letting someone else have the special gifts you made available to her. I know you will be wise in your decision."

"Mother, you are right. I'll also keep some of the pictures, but I will change some of the decorations to create a new beginning."

"That's the spirit. I can see my boy is on the mend."

Phillipa and Antonio spent the weekend visiting over the past, and they invited James to spend some time in Italy after his cruise with the children.

CHAPTER EIGHT

THE SUMMER CRUISE

James arrived early at his bank, ready to talk with Claudia about his plans.

"So you always beat me into work!"

"'It's the early bird that catches the worm,'" said Claudia, laughing. "So what's got you so motivated, my Lord?"

"Let's get some coffee; I want to talk about Kim with you."

"Kim on the brain; she's got you intrigued: I can see that, I know that twinkle in your eye."

"Yes and no; as you know, I'm about to take my young ones on holiday, so I thought this would be an excellent opportunity for you to plan the transition of Kim here, and Flick to the newspaper."

"Yes, it will give us a chance to get her acquainted with all we have to contend with. The sooner the better, as far as I'm concerned, although she won't learn this job quickly."

"That's what I wanted to discuss with you. I feel absolutely certain she will have no trouble learning what we do; my only concern is that she's an extremely self-willed person."

"How could that be a problem?"

"Learning the job is one thing; learning people and working to integrate is another. Claudia, outside your administrative skills, you possess tact, diplomacy, and etiquette. Our staff has been with us for some time; they are senior executives in all that they do. With changing and enhancing their efficiency, I don't see a problem, as I'm sure Kim can bring that quality to us. It's in the implementation that concerns me."

"Why?"

"When I spent the evening with her, she was extremely respectful and polite. There is a side to her that is locked away. She's not a person to open herself up to just anyone. From a professional standpoint, that's good. To work with people who are on an equal footing and who, at first, will be more knowledgeable than she will be has me concerned. Look at her track record; she's competitive and knows how to get to the top. A large part of what you do is to improve but implemented in a way that is supportive. Our staff value you highly, as you show equal respect and measure; you don't seek to dominate; you seek to help people, whether it's to your gain or not."

"I haven't found that quality in her," said Claudia thoughtfully. "But, yes, I don't work with her on a day-to-day basis. She tells me she's team oriented."

"Yes, I understand that, but that is only if she's the boss. I could be wrong, but she's younger and must tread carefully; people don't like change, and you were here before all of them."

"I understand; I will work with her to make sure she fully grasps that. I'm not as aggressive as you, and you and she are alike. The only difference is that you are revered and looked up to. As a younger man, you have more than earned your stripes; she must understand that and must realize that new

ideas, which are needed, must be implemented in a constructive way, not to diminish another but for the good of the team."

"If you go with that in mind, running a newspaper certainly
takes talent. What we have here are people who are well able
to think for themselves and to come running when they need
help. That's how we work, and the business model has been
successful. In a position like yours that has a lot of authority
and power, it's easy for one person to disrupt relations, so she
must realize how important this position is."

Then he continued. "Anyway, being away will give you
time to analyze all that. I've put forward the thought, and,
who knows? She may be the best choice ever, outside you
of course!" James laughed. But knowing the importance of
change sometimes is not always easy.

"Next matter is the Throne!"

"The Throne?"

"Yes; Sarah has made a startling new discovery. Behind
each one of the gemstones lies a gold, pull-out plug, which
we have always thought kept the gemstones in place. She has
pulled these plugs and has noticed that the gemstones light
up."

"Really? So what does that mean?"

"It means there is enough energy in the Throne to transport
an entire person through the vortex to another dimension."

"Wow; I would love to experience that!"

"Sarah has already experienced that. She was so excited by
her experience from the energy she received that she could
hardly sleep for a week."

"That's outstanding. So, the energy she received from the
vortex had that effect?"

"Yes!"

"That's just what I need."

"I'm not going to go into detail; you can discuss that with Sarah. I would like you to call Jeremy Soames and, if possible, to arrange a meeting here at his earliest convenience."

"I'll get on it immediately."

James felt relieved to talk with Claudia. It was just an insurance policy in case matters didn't work out. In every business decision, James always looked at the worst- and the best-case scenario. He wasn't afraid of risk, but he knew how easy one person could upset the apple cart, especially in a situation as important as this one.

*****

Jeremy Soames wasted no time in coming by to see James; he was curious, as he knew James wasn't one to call for no reason.

"Jeremy, thanks for coming by; I have something that deeply concerns me with the Throne."

"What can that be?"

James continued to relate the story he witnessed with Sarah.

"Have no worries," said Jeremy. "I was wondering how long it would take you both to figure out the full potential of what that Throne could do."

"So you know all about that?" asked James.

"Yes; as I've told you when I was on Atlantis, I remember all of its capabilities; that's why I was closely watching to see if your board at the bank would support you in the endeavor to restore it to its former glory. First, there is absolutely no danger of abusing the Throne. The vortex, which has been created between this world and the fifth dimension, will not carry anyone unless they are aligned. Yes, it can heal, but only if that person is at a certain level of spiritual understanding. However sick people may be, they have to have the authority of the divine to be received. The Throne cannot be used for any purpose that is not good. The vortex is created by a spiritual force that is way beyond our level of understanding here on Earth. Even if a person abuses its force to seek energy or to create a nonaging process. The vortex knows the mind of its entrant. We are not allowed the right to outwit the laws of this three-dimensional world unless the entrant's purpose is for good."

"Is there no fear of having people line up in a frantic craze to use the Throne for that purpose?" asked James.

"None."

"However, if word gets out, you will be barraged by would-be people, who will want to use it for the wrong purpose," Jeremy continued. "This is a world that has a barrier between the spiritual dimension and this one of materiality. It is for us through the divine essence to seek that road and arise to what we call the 'The Law of Grace'. When you are ready, you and I will take time to expound on this. The universe is a place of learning and understanding, and the creative light force protects itself in its entirety. I am not saying another Throne cannot be created to project people throughout the Galaxy and the Universe, no. The entrant will end up only on another three-dimensional planet like ours. It can be more primitive or maybe more advanced. No one can break the boundary between this dimension and the fifth, without an inner awareness of where their souls are intent on going within their spiritual journey, not their material journey."

"Then an aligned person could travel the vortex through the mind without the body, by leaving the gem stones unplugged?"

"Yes, indeed; that's its true purpose. To transport the whole body is given only to a soul that's much more advanced, and that soul will know the reason why."

"I will pass this information onto Sarah, which I'm sure she's aware of already. Anyway, that's reassuring to know. What of the fourth dimension, though?"

"The fourth dimension, or the astral plain as it is referred to, is the dimension that lies between the fifth and the third. It's where a mishmash of souls go who are lost and who will probably return to a three-dimensional world again until they learn the spiritual laws. It is where you have satellite communication and technology abound. It is the transitional dimension between the two dimensions. It is where Jesus stated to Mary Magdalene, 'Do not touch me, for I have not yet ascended to the Father.' It is a transitional dimension that concludes where we go after this life, return, or move on, or stay in a place of Purgatory."

"Jeremy, you have much wisdom and a lot to teach me."

"That's what I told you; I am once again here to lead you to that rightful place and help you to take over from me in our inner sanctum. Your time will come soon, but you will be well prepared."

"I have much to ponder on; your meetings with me are so inspirational," said James. "I can't thank you enough." James was always surprised about what more he had to learn.

"I know you are about to embark on your holidays with your young adults; I still feel for your loss over Sabrina, but please know I am always there to comfort you."

"Jeremy, you are a lord over the judges in the house; why don't you take up your title?"

"James, I am happy with 'sir'; it attracts less attention. You, on the other hand, have a long line of inheritance and must live up to a proud institution that has served this country with great example."

Jeremy got up to depart, and the two shook hands. For the

first time, Jeremy smiled at him with an inner reverence that he was beginning to understand about a man who had hitherto remained an enigma to him.

*****

James, his son, and his daughter met up at London's Heathrow; they had a long flight ahead of them, and the happy threesome were so excited to share time with each other after Sabrina's departure. James flew first class, while Sam and Anna flew business class. Periodically, James would walk back to check on them both.

"Anna, so far so good?"

"Yes, Daddy, catching up on all the movies I've missed."

"I can see your brother, Mr. Social, chatting up some fine lady further back."

"You know Sam; he doesn't sit still for long; he has to get up and walk around. I'm content enjoying the trip, catching a nap here and there. I can't wait until we reach Los Angeles. I'm so looking forward to the cruise and working on my tan. It would appear a number of people here are going to L.A. for the same reason. That's why Sam is trying to get a head start."

"Who knows? He may find some dark, handsome stranger for you."

"Knowing Sam, anything is possible, but I'm in no hurry!"

"That's my girl."

The plane landed at 4:00 p.m., California time. After clearing customs, the weary trio made their way to the ship. James had booked the master suite on the ship. Unlike many, who would be boarding the ship the following day, they were allowed to board early, escaping the normal formalities and lines that took place for others. James was a celebrity, and, therefore, he could avoid the usual hustle and bustle that most people didn't enjoy on embarkation.

"Dad, this is fantastic; we have a front view overlooking the bow of the ship," said a surprised Anna.

James had a master bedroom suite and a bathroom for himself. Sam and Anna had their own rooms, with an adjoining bathroom that they could both share. James's bedroom was on one side, and the two other bedrooms were separated by a huge panoramic lounge, with comfortable armchairs and a formal dining table that could seat six for in-room dining. The lounge was surrounded by a large, wide deck that opened out from two, glass sliding doors on each side of the ship. The deck had outside sun-lounge chairs so they could all stretch out with ease, catch some sunrays, read, eat, drink, and spend their days as they pleased. The room was stocked with sodas, alcoholic beverages, and all kinds of snacks.

"Dad, this has to be the tops," remarked an excited Sam. "Wow, this is going to be a trip to remember. All I can say is thanks. It doesn't get better than this! Beats the hell out of my dorm room at Oxford!"

"As soon as the bags arrive, we shall have an in-room dinner, as I don't think the main dining room will be open tonight; then we can have an early night and try to get on this time." James was happy to be close to his little family, and he was feeling a great sense of freedom of being away from all the cares of the world.

After dinner and a light discussion about the both of them finishing up their university days, Sam and Anna went to prepare for bed. James poured himself a large scotch and took one of his favorite cigars to sit outside on the veranda.

He felt the warm breeze from the ocean wafting across the deck, as the stars started to alight the heavens. He thought about Sabrina and about how much he wished she were with him. Annabelle so reminded him of her that it helped him feel closer to Sabrina. Then a voice popped into his head.

"James, I'm with you; do you feel my presence?"

"Yes; it's your perfume; I can smell the fragrance."

"I have news for you; this trip will change your life. It's no accident you are here!"

"Really? How's that?"

"You will see; just trust your instincts and know it's all meant to be."

"You are always surprising me, as you did in life. I can't think what that could be; I'm learning to be content knowing that you are here and that I'm surrounded by my kids."

"Just keep an open mind and look to the future."

With that, Sabrina was gone. She didn't want him to live in the past but to open his eyes to what lay ahead.

James awoke late, after having had trouble sleeping in the middle of the night. He noticed the kids had gone and must be discovering the ship. After taking a shower, he made himself a coffee and started to read the events of the day posted outside his cabin. He perused the guest list, but nothing jumped out at him, except that he was looking for any potential, single women.

Anna came blasting through the cabin door and said, "Dad this ship is the greatest. It has dance floors, rock bars for the younger ones, and others for the older guys like you!"

"So you are out scouting about for any potentials?"

"Nothing serious yet, but there's a lot more passengers to come aboard."

"I notice we have a request to sit at the captain's table; we are all invited," said James. "That will be on the next formal night, which will be Wednesday." James was wondering what the captain's guest list would be like.

"I hope it won't be too stuffy; I will put on my best airs and graces. I'm sure it's an honor to sit there!"

"Indeed; so we must let that gallivanting brother of yours know so that he is prepared and not off on some wild goose chase somewhere else."

"Come on, Dad; you can't sit around here all day; let's go discover."

"All right, all right; give me a moment."

As they left the cabin, he passed by a very noticeable woman in the hallway with her son. Their eyes met for a moment; then they moved on.

"That looks like a lady for you, Dad."

"Steady on; she may have a husband; don't jump to conclusions."

Anna took him to a coffee bar two decks below. There, they sat on stools, drinking hot chocolate, while enjoying a shipboard snack. They noticed all the couples being escorted to their rooms. James was happy they had the evening before to get settled when he saw the crowds.

At that moment, Sam showed up and said, "Dad, we are going to have a blast; definitely some talent walking through these hallways."

"Steady on; I don't want to give you the old-parent lecture, but do realize to not make any mistakes. When they get to know who you are, be weary and smart; there are plenty of young people who want to sow their wild oats. Speech over; message received?"

"Yes, Papa; we know!" said Sam.

"Dad, we are both in university without you being there, so do trust us; we are not little children any longer!" said a teasing Anna, giggling at his old-fashioned ways. Besides, who knows what's in store for you?"

Little did they know that their dad was no saint, either, but that he'd always been true to the woman he loved.

The formal night arrived; James had not attended the "greet-the-captain ceremony" on Tuesday night; he let the kids go and chose to take a snack in his room alone. He wanted to catch up on his business affairs he had brought.

The formal night was a black-tie affair, and the family busily prepared themselves for the gala evening at the captain's table. They took the invitation with them. The affair was taking place on the main-floor dining room three decks below.

The headwaiter ushered Annabelle to the captain's table, while other waiters were available to usher other ladies that would be sitting there.

After greeting the captain individually, they each took up their seat at the respective card that held their name. The captain had been careful not to sit James next to any woman in order to respect his privacy, so he had him sit at the opposite end and had his children seated on either side of him. The captain asked people to introduce themselves individually and state their home and country of origin. The Bannermans introduced themselves without titles. Many people in the main dining room glared over at the captain's table and knew exactly who James was. The woman sitting next to the captain and the one who appeared to be her son sitting next to her particularly intrigued James. He thought it was the woman had passed in the hallway, where their eyes met for a brief moment. Their eyes met again, and he felt his heart beat quickly. He couldn't explain it, but she had something apart from her graceful appearance. Sam was sitting next to a very eligible young lady, as Anna was sitting beside a nice, young gentleman.

The captain knew his passengers and had done his homework. In a sense, James felt slightly isolated, as, in order to have any conversation, he would have to talk across his children. He enjoyed his conversation with a property tycoon in the States, who was fascinated by his holdings in the United States, and with an older lady who was a widower from Santa Barbara, California. The entire table had consisted of seasoned travelers, knew England well, and exchanged conversation as best they could. It was a first introduction. James wished he'd sat next to the woman by the captain, but he thought this was the first night and there would be plenty of time for that. He hadn't come on the cruise to talk business or to be recognized; he was there to have fun and be with his children first and foremost.

James retired to the small bar off the theatre to have a nightcap with Sam and Anna.

"So how did it go for you guys?" asked James.

"It was fine, but he was not really my type," said Anna thoughtfully. "Who knows when we are all dressed up? And I'm sure they knew who we were; it must have been awkward."

"I don't know about you, but I really liked the girl I was seated beside," said Sam. "She is from Florida, and her dad is in the construction business and builds giant hotels for Hilton, Marriot, and others. Definitely going to follow up on her; she is hot!"

"I could tell you guys were getting on," said a slightly jealous Anna. "She definitely had an eye for you, Sam; if she told you one more time how she could listen to your accent, I was going to start laughing my head off."

"Now you two behave," said James. "We are not here to have an argument. You had fun, and I'm happy for you, Sam." He was hoping at least one of them enjoyed the evening.

****

The ship was now well out to sea and on its way to Tahiti. The ship days at sea were fun. They danced into the wee hours and then tanned the next day on the sundeck. They were having the time of their lives, meeting young people of all ages. James didn't mind them coming and going late into the night. He then decided it was time for them to have a night together and talk about the future. He let them relax first, but now it was necessary to talk. He reserved a table at the Italian restaurant, where the atmosphere would be more casual.

"So, Dad, is this a formal family business meeting?" asked Anna, laughing.

"No; but since the passing of your mother, I think it's important we all discuss the future, don't you?"

"Yes, Dad, I agree; not only was it a sad day for us, but it also had to be devastating for you," said Sam, feeling for his father and what he'd just lived through.

"It was, and I'm sorry that I was a little too distant for a time. I had to get a hold of myself. It was a shock for all of us. Anyway, Anna, you are in your first year at Cambridge, and, Sam, you are about to finish up, unless you want to continue on and get your master's?"

"Dad, you know I'm not an ace at academics. I prefer the classics; I'm okay at numbers, but I will never be the business-man you are."

"Sam, what would you like to do now?"

"I have thought about that, and if it would be fine by you, I want to travel. I want to learn our business and to understand all that we do. Then I can return home and start learning from you about how to run the business from London."

"I don't see a problem with that; get out there and see the

world. You can set sea on one of our merchant vessels, help out in different areas, meet the people, and see what they do for our business. Start with Trans Global, then banking with Roger, and, after that the property business. Some of us learn better by doing. School is not everything."

"Dad, I want to do what Claudia does," said Anna. "I have a head for mathematics and business; it comes naturally to me; I have three years to go. And, during the holidays, I can work with whoever takes over from Claudia and be a backup to help Sam. Sam has all the social skills and is very confident. In a sense, we make a good pair, as we have different abilities, and that's why we get on."

"You don't know how pleased it makes me feel to hear that. I have been battling whether or not to take certain parts of the business public. It's not everyone that's an entrepreneur, so I could, in a sense, divest from the business and leave you both in a strong financial position."

"Dad, I don't think either of us are blessed to do what you've done with the business," said Sam. "Maintain it, yes; grow it slowly, yes. I do know timing is everything, and you may be right. Economics could change at the turn of the century. We have been through a fast and furious pace of growth, thanks to you and the world market."

"Wise words, my boy. You think well upon such matters; I am pleasantly surprised. I will think this through. Now off with you; I know you want to get with the young ones and have fun."

"Papa, before we leave, I don't entirely believe that, between us, we couldn't continue to match the empire you've built," said a deep-thinking and thoughtful Anna. "Once I'm on board at the business and understand the way things work, I believe we are moving into a different age, and with my IT skills and my interest in bio-tech businesses, I might be able to take the business in a new direction. I'm not as social as Sam, but I do feel I have an entrepreneurial instinct. Who knows? But, with time and experience, I hope I can learn from you the art of business and to build on businesses that I find that may have potential in this domain."

"I'll think that through," said James. "Maybe, Anna, I've underestimated the possibility that you may have the talent to be not only a financier but also a future entrepreneur, as well! It's certainly a world where women are starting to come to the front. I somehow believe you do have those gifts. I'm proud of you both, and even prouder if you can do a better job than I have. That means I can back away in time and watch my new generation of Bannermans flourish! Nothing warms my heart more than what you are both telling me." James was thoroughly excited at the very thought of his two children dedicated and wanting to be a part of his world.

As James started to leave, he could see the young lady he had been enamored with sitting at a table close by, without her son. This was his chance. He took a big breath and walked over to her.

"May I introduce myself? I have passed you many times in the hallway and know you must have a suite close to us."

"Please do, sir, my Lord."

"No formalities, please," said James.

"Camilla."

"I have noticed you from the first day you set foot on the ship, but I didn't want to appear inappropriate."

"Not at all; I would have liked to speak with you, but, somehow, I didn't know how without seeming too forward. I am so glad you have come over to talk to me."

"How are you finding the cruise so far?"

"I'm loving it; since my husband died in February, it's been hard, so I thought this cruise would be good for both my son and me."

"What a coincidence? My wife died at the same time, so we can share our grief in common."

"Would you like to go to the pool deck and have a cocktail there?" she asked politely. "I find it so relaxing to hear the sound of the sea and feel the warm breeze."

"Lead the way, and I will follow."

James took the time to notice her form, as he walked behind her to catch the elevator.

She was tall, at least five feet nine, and lean, with a classy deportment. Her hair was black and long, falling well below her shoulders. She wore a bright green summer dress, with a lot of gold and expensive accessories. He noticed her green eyes when they entered the elevator, which went well with the color of her dress. She had a natural tan, and he judged, by her accent, that she was probably Portuguese or Spanish. She spoke good English, but with a hint of an American accent. She smiled at him, as though she was happy he'd introduced himself. In that moment, James could see the beauty she possessed. She was nothing like any woman he'd ever met. She had inner warmth, and he felt she was completely comfortable to be in his presence.

They silently made their way over to the pool bar and found a table away from the others, where they could talk privately.

"So, my lady, Camilla, what would you like to drink?

"A glass of Chardonnay will do just fine."

James brought the drinks from the bar; then he noticed her pulling out a packet of cigarettes from her handbag.

"Ah ha; now I know why you like to come up here!"

remarked James, laughing.

"Would you like one, my Lord?"

"Yes, I would. I sneak a smoke now and then; I'm a bad boy, too!"

"That makes you all the more exciting!"

The two clicked their glasses; then she lit his cigarette.

"I couldn't find a more perfect setting for a night like this, meeting such a beautiful woman. I must pinch myself after all the sad days I lived through, without my Sabrina."

"I'll drink to that; welcome to happiness and laughter, as of right now."

He hadn't thought or realized what she, too, had suffered at the loss of her husband. Now he could see that inner glow more brightly, as her aura started to increase.

They both started to talk at the same time, excited and nervous at their encounter.

"No; you go first. Tell me all about Sabrina; she must have been a lovely woman for you to miss her so much."

"She was; we met when we were only eighteen, and we dated on and off for a number of years. Then we were married for twenty years after that. She was a model; you may have seen her in magazines?"

"What was her name?"

"She went by her maiden name, Sabrina Rossi."

"Of course, she was famous and so beautiful that she exuded happiness. I loved her styles. So she was Italian?"

"Yes, half-Italian and half-Scandinavian."

"That makes sense, because she was tall and fair, but she had that flair about her, very photogenic and natural."

"What about you?"

"My family were well to do. I was raised in Roman Catholic private schools. Then finished my university years at Princeton, in America. After receiving my B.A. in business administration, I applied for many jobs and ended up working for a company that was in the mining business. Three years later, I married the boss!"

"You were twenty-five, I guess? About the same age when Sabrina and I got married."

"Yes; he was much older than me, though, nearly fifty years old at that time. I have always preferred older men; I'll tell you the reason later. We had a good marriage, and I looked up to him for all he had achieved. He mined for silver in Argentina, copper in Peru, and gemstones in Brazil. We had one son, Nicolas, who is now nearly ten. We don't pronounce the 's,' like you do in English. He's a little on the heavy side, like his father, but I'm working hard to encourage him to do more sports. Our marriage lasted ten years, until his death last February."

"So, you are nearly thirty-six?"

"Yes, and you?"

"Forty-eight; so older, but a little closer!" joked James.

"I like to see a man that has a little gray in his hair; I think it's so attractive."

"So why do you prefer older men?"

"Now I hope I don't scare you with this, but I was born with a gift. I'm a psychic!"

"Doesn't scare me; I'm always intrigued when people have paranormal gifts!"

"My husband took my advice, but not all the time. When I was in school, I had no problem being asked out, but, after a few dates, guys thought I was weird."

"It's not for everyone, and there are a lot of charlatans who profess to have the gift, but not all are true, and they are in it just to make money."

"I know; I do readings for people, and I like to think that, most of the time, I'm correct, but no one is perfect."

"So, who runs the business now?"

"I do; I've been there since I was twenty-two. I know the business very well. It has expanded greatly since I started there."

"Let me test your psychic skills: so what haven't I told you yet that you sense about me?"

"I'm going to have another glass of wine," James continued, "and I think you need one, too. Then you can ponder about my question, before I return."

James gave ample time for her to think; he was enjoying her immensely. He loved that she might have abilities and thought that Sarah and she would get on like a house on fire.

James retuned, anxiously awaiting her conversation.

"James, I see you as a man with determination and force. You are good to your staff and all those that work with you. You control an immense business, which spans the world. You have grown this business beyond anyone's expectations. I see ships and buildings. Also, you have something to do with finance. You are into a variety of businesses, but those are the main ones. I see a woman who is by your side; she's older, but she's known you for a long time. She's loyal, loves you, and admires you very much. Is that enough?"

"Wow! Pretty good start. I'm impressed."

"There's lots more, but those are the basics."

"You have had this gift from childhood?"

"Yes; it was a curse at first, because I used to see things I didn't like, and it scared me. My mother worked with me, as she, too, had the gift. It makes you more mature, and I was lucky to have someone to guide me. A lot of children have the gift. But after nightmares and after parents thinking it's just a child's imagination, the skill can be lost. To develop one's intuition takes work, discipline, and effort."

"I, too, have some gifts, but they only work when they come from above to help. I can heal."

"Funny; I can feel that energy from you. Let me hold your hands."

James stretched out his hands, and immediately his hands went red-hot; he could feel her pain, and slowly she started to glow again.

"You do have the gift; I feel the best I've felt in months, and you were meant to give me that energy. My guides told me how you channel. It comes through you from above. You have a very high master, and he's happy you and I have met."

In just one evening, the couple was totally on the same page. They could have talked all night.

James escorted her back to her suite.

"We are going into town in Tahiti tomorrow; want to come with us?"

"James, I'd love to!"

He gave her a hug and good night kiss, feeling that this could be the start of a relationship that was truly special.

*****

The two families met up and wandered into the town of Papeete, the capital of all the islands of the archipelago; then they took a plane ride to see Bora Bora. This was the honeymoon paradise of the world. James wanted to visit the huts that lay out in the calm, turquoise waters and then to enjoy a luncheon at the resort there. He was scouting out the area for good reason. It was a place he had heard many couples rave about. One day, he hoped to return with a prospective bride-to-be for his future life.

"This has to be as close as it gets to heaven," laughed a slightly inebriated Annabelle, after drinking her second tropical-fruit punch. "Who couldn't love this place? A romantic place for a honeymoon?"

"So you are a romantic, my dear Annabelle," laughed James, as he teased her. "I was beginning to wonder, after all your studious pursuits with education."

Later, the two families returned to the main island, observing the many other destinations from their private jet.

"So many islands; we could spend a week or two just exploring this place," said Samuel, observing the islands that strung out in front of them.

"For sure, definitely a place to return to, "said James, turning his eye toward Camilla.

Once back on the main island, the families were enjoying practicing their French as they walked the streets looking for souvenirs. Tahiti, the main island, had the most to offer for activities. It was similar to Hawaii, but with a more continental flair and with a more relaxed environment. An island created from two volcanoes made the vegetation very lush for one of the world's best-known destinations to paradise.

It was a perfect outing for the two families to have a chance to know each other. Camilla and James agreed they would have dinner that night, and Sam and Anna offered to take Nicolas and to keep an eye on him. They wanted their father, who was now showing a keen interest in Camilla, to have some free time to learn more about each other.

James met Camilla in the cocktail lounge by the theatre for an evening cocktail before dinner. She was now dressed to the nines. Her makeup really added to the natural beauty she already possessed. She wanted to look her best after a typical tourist day on the island.

"So, my dear, you arrive in full form to all those turning heads."

"I like to dress up and look my best, especially for you," she said. "After your being with Sabrina, who was a model of fashion, I have to show you what I can do." She spoke with a twinkle in her eye and a smirk across her full lips.

"Your son appears well-behaved and didn't mind being with all us adults today."

"I've brought him up strictly. So many kids today don't have manners, and they are spoilt. In Argentina, we are probably more old school. Manners are important. He can be a little scoundrel, though; I can assure you."

They made their way to dinner, and the head waiter found them a quiet booth to continue their discussions.

"James, tell me about your home in England; I want to know more about what you do and your life."

"Being an English Lord, I have an estate I inherited," said James, continuing to apprise Camilla all about his life in detail, leaving out the Throne room for later discussion.

"A lot rests on your shoulders; it sounds as though you spend your life working."

"Yes; but, in recent years, I travel less and stay closer to home. I am blessed with a great team, but, like all businesses, my staff are getting older, and I have to think about the next generation. I am the youngest of the group, since I started at twenty-one, and most of my team are ten-to-fifteen years older than me."

"You are obviously faced with decisions, especially after the loss of your wife."

"The main reason for taking this trip was to evaluate how dedicated my children would be to the business—whether to take some parts of the company public and to stick to our core business of banking."

"James, I can see what you're faced with, and you need a

companion to enjoy your life and to relax more. You've been through a lot, as I have, too."

"Meeting you is certainly an unexpected revelation. I could never dream that I would find a woman that would rival Sabrina, but in a totally different way."

"Now you tweak my interest; how so?"

"You are cultured and soft-spoken, not to mention all your other attributes. I feel it's early days, but I already feel comfortable being with you."

"James, I will now tell you something, and I know I'm not the first. I was on Atlantis, too. We had our ups and downs; we both were very spirited people; our lives since then have made us wiser. We are also meeting later in life; we were too young then, but I know I loved you, and when we parted, it was a sad moment. Our souls have waited because I believe you and I have a very special purpose. It's no accident that our paths cross now."

James remembered what Sabrina and his master had said: It is meant to be!

"I knew when I first laid eyes on you, it was like a magnet. I never would have believed I would meet someone like you, and yet you are completely different. With Sabrina, it was very special, something I can never forget, physical yes, but spiritual in another way, I was, of course, younger. With you, it's my heart and my soul that somehow feels we were meant to meet. It's an experience I've never felt before, but equally compelling. I'm not, for one moment, implying that your physical appearance is not appealing. I'm amazed to awaken feelings again that I once had."

"James, as much as I loved my husband, the feelings I now sense I have never felt in this lifetime. Come on; let's go and have a cigarette on the balcony of my suite and enjoy some good wine."

"Let's go. I love listening to you speak as the waves rush in against the side of the ship."

For the first time, they held hands as they walked through the corridors to her room, eyeing one another with warm approval, waiting for that appropriate moment in anticipation. No sooner had they opened the door and she had put down her handbag than James pulled her into his arms, starting with a gentle kiss, then a pause, and as their temperatures rose, the passion started. He then stopped.

"James, I do want you; I know it's right, but we still have time."

"I agree I want to savor every moment of what I feel as I learn to love once again!"

She poured the drinks; then, arm in arm, they went to the outside balcony, feeling an intense feeling of oneness and connection.

"James, I have to tell you I will remember this, our first kiss; I could never dream to meet you again, and if it were not for my psychic abilities, you would have been a distant memory of my Prince Charming. How lucky we are to meet again! We must, however, be truly sure that we are ready for one another, even though I feel we are meant to be together."

"I agree; we are not teenagers, although I feel like one."

They both laughed, staring at the stars, knowing they had found that elusive, yet overwhelming, force of love.

*****

The ship journeyed onward to other smaller islands. The children were doing their own thing with their friends, while James and Camilla were becoming closer and closer in their relationship. They were well on their way to Fiji, and James was completely relaxed and rejuvenated from his normally busy work schedule. It was time to go to the next step with Camilla. They had waited, and now it seemed appropriate. He could see the twinkle in her eye and the adoring way she walked through the streets holding onto his arm, constantly looking up to see his expression. They were in love, and it was plain for all to see.

As the pair wandered up to the pool deck after breakfast the next day to stretch out by the pool, James decided to pop the question.

"Camilla, how about Nicolas staying over at my suite tonight, and you and I taking some time to be together?"

"James, I would like that," she said. "We can be a little naughty for a change." She laughed, as she squeezed his hand before jumping into the pool.

James followed, and when no one was looking, he swam up to her, fully embracing her in her scant bathing suit, and he finished off with a long, passionate French kiss.

"Wow; that was unexpected; you should do that more often; I like surprises," giggled Camilla.

That evening after dinner, they went to her suite, as planned. After some champagne on her balcony, she went inside to get changed.

CHAPTER 9

CAMILLA

Shortly after she returned in her bathrobe, she sat down on the lounge chair next to him, poured herself another glass of champagne, and started to talk to an anticipating and eagerly waiting James. It was a magnificent evening—warm and with a breeze, as the moon started to lift from the horizon and ran a track of light across the calm seas in front of the ship, as the couple looked down.

After his shower, he, too, put on his bathrobe and made his way out to the balcony. He held out his hand to Camilla. She arose to the beckoning encounter that now awaited them. The two of them stood in front of the bed, as Camilla wantonly looked deeply into James's eyes. He couldn't resist her tempting gaze any longer and stepped forward to take her in his arms. He kissed her gently and slowly, and then he pulled open her robe that fell to the floor. He was now standing in front of what words could not describe. Her lightly tanned body with her long legs and short back awaited his beck and call. He noticed how thin her ankles and wrists were in comparison to her height. He pushed back her long, dark hair over her shoulders, continuing to kiss those soft lips, slowly moving towards her neck. It was then that she reached out to loosen his robe.

He couldn't help thinking that as beautiful as Sabrina had been, the whole touch of her body was so feminine and alluring. This was a new experience. Camilla's elegance and statuesque form by daylight gave her a china-doll appearance, yet she was taller than that. She was like a Latina form of the statue *La Timide*. His arousal was becoming clearly obvious for her to see. The couple fell onto the bed, and the lovemaking began.

James started kissing her irresistible lips again, with more intensity, slowly moving down her body. He was now ready to give her the full essence of himself.

"My God, James, you are unbelievable; you satisfy my everything; please come; don't hold back anymore. I want to feel you inside me."

James drove her into oblivion—then came in a manner he hadn't for some time.

The two lay in each other's arms; he kissed her again and again; and then they fell fast asleep. Thirty minutes later, they were awakened by somebody in the hallway, talking too loudly, probably drunk. They decided to go out on the deck, to have a cigarette, and to finish up the champagne.

"James, that was phenomenal. You certainly know how to make a woman happy and satisfied."

"I can tell you I was nervous, so it can only get better, my love. It was a wonderful experience for me to make love to a goddess like you!"

"I'm pleased that I make you happy. I felt a tremendous

connection between our two souls.

"We will play hooky tomorrow and have room service all day. I will check on the young ones in the morning; then we can join them at night."

"That sounds marvelous!"

The couple continued their passionate rampage during the night and slept late, and after James checked his suite, he left a note, saying they would meet up for dinner that evening. James then continued his endeavors with Camilla until late afternoon.

*****

After the passengers' visit to New Zealand, the ship was now entering the port of Sydney, Australia. It was an emotional evening, as the ship pulled in alongside the dock. It would be a last evening for all the passengers to share their memories of the trip before going through customs the next day. Sam and his girlfriend from Florida had become close. Annabelle had met a young man studying law at Yale, and she was very enamored with him. It was the first encounter for both of them; spending that amount of time with one person and really getting to know that person is exactly what life on board a ship provided.

James, too, would miss Camilla. After dinner, all the friends and family said their good-byes, while James and Camilla went to the upper pool deck to discuss future plans. Everyone else retired to pack. James and his family were allowed to leave the ship after everyone else had disembarked. Camilla had already packed, as she would want to spend the last evening with James.

"So, my dear, are you ready for the long trip home?"

"No, I am going home in reverse. I want to see a little of

Sydney before flying home, but my heart is really not in it without you."

""I will miss you, too; what we shared I could never have dreamed of such fulfillment. The feelings we have for each another are far too powerful to forget. I will remember this trip forever. We are off to Hong Kong tomorrow evening; since we are in this part of the world, I must check on our businesses there and show my young ones the ropes. When you get settled and have Nicolas back in school, please come over to see us—or, more explicitly, me. I don't want us to lose touch; what we have discovered between us is far too powerful to let go, and I know I am going to miss you terribly."

"James," Camilla continued. "I won't rest until I'm in your arms again. I shall make plans the moment I arrive back, and I shall e-mail you my itinerary. I think we are going about it the right way. I've read about on-board-ship romances, but I feel this one is true, don't you?"

"Yes, without a doubt; one doesn't meet another person and have the intensity and attraction we have, easily, if ever. No, it's real. We must not let go of that magical thought. I know we are in the perfect environment for romance, but I feel it's deeper than that."

"I know I will be very busy with the business at first," James continued. "I have a very able second in command, and I plan to make a few changes. I want us to have a more personal life, if it is meant for us to be together."

"We can discuss that when I come to England. I love England and would have no problem living there. In fact, it would be excellent for Nicolas's education and future."

The two got up to hug and kiss each other before retiring, walking together, hand in hand, to their cabins.

"I'll see you tomorrow; we can have a coffee before you

leave," said James.

"Okay, James, I love you; good night."

"Love you, too."

The next morning, amongst all the hustle and bustle, they didn't meet up. Camilla must have had an earlier disembarkation than expected. They had said what was needed to be said. Their hearts were total; it now remained to be seen if their futures would be aligned as promised. Or was it a fleeting on-board romance?

CHAPTER 10

HONG KONG AND HOME

The plane touched down at Kai Tak airport, the new airport, which was under construction and was not yet open. James took a limousine to accommodate their luggage after their memorable journey across the Pacific. It was a long day, and they were all tired and a little sad, after leaving their friends they had become so attached to. Sam and Anna soon woke up when they entered the bank building.

"Wow, Dad, this certainly beats the hell out of the bank we have in London," said a surprised Samuel, looking at his grandfather's portrait and observing the palatial, spacious surroundings.

Annabelle was not a big shopper, but she couldn't help noticing all the ladies' shops on the first and second floor.

"Dad, this is like another world; our bank in London looks like the Dark Ages, compared to this."

"You will have plenty of time to wander around tomorrow; all I want is to have a stiff drink, relax on the balcony, and get a good night's sleep."

Sam and Anna loved the elevator that took them to James's penthouse on the fiftieth floor, and they were even more astounded at the penthouse itself, with its outdoor patio. They all met outside for a nightcap in their robes, sitting in front of the pool to reminisce about the fabulous trip they had experienced. It was a perfect night, warm with calm winds, as they all embraced the magnificent view across the harbor to Kowloon, where many of Trans Global's ships docked.

"I know we just had a cruise of a lifetime, but, Dad, this is a pretty high-end pad; I think I could settle in here quite nicely." Sam was wondering what the Asian women looked like, after the rainy climate of England; he thought that a few years in a place like this would be hard to turn down. Anyway, tomorrow would tell the story. *The women had to be hot*, he thought.

*****

James was up early and left the apartment before anyone had awakened.

"Harold, good to see you."

"You, too, sir; I wasn't quite sure when you were arriving, but I made sure everything was ready for your visit."

"How are we doing?"

"The textile factory is growing in leaps and bounds. We are totally out of space in the building downtown. It's time we erected a purpose-built factory on the mainland we purchased on the Pearl River Delta. We can then renovate the building here, and I would suggest we turn them into low-income apartments. Clean modern, but appropriate for that part of town. We can then give that over to Gerald to manage."

"Good thinking; I bet that building could do with a make-over. It seems that a lot of industry is moving that way off the island."

"With the advantages we have in being able to ship to our many warehouses for distribution, we are seriously able to undercut the competition. There's no end to the worldwide demand for cheap textile products. The population explosion seeks these products."

"The bank; how are our affairs here?"

"Roger continues to be a guiding light, and now I have learned a great deal from him. He's slightly nervous about traditional banking, as he sees a swing towards supporting second mortgages and the financing of debt, as opposed to investment in manufacturing and business that create employ-ment to make consumer goods and to employ more people. It's to our advantage in some ways, but he sees a slippery slope with the American and European shift away from traditional industries. He believes that too much is being manufactured in Third World countries. The result is that the Western world is becoming a giant service industry, making profits on bought-out items that are not being made locally. For example, take Hong Kong, Singapore, and others—who can compete with our manufacturing of textiles and cheaper labor?"

"All good points for evaluation; that's business, an ever-changing scene where we must adapt and see the upside of opportunity in a different way."

"James, the eternal optimist, there's always another way to skin a cat."

The two laughed.

"On another note, I have a son who has finished his tenure at Oxford this year. I thought that working out here might be a good opportunity for him."

"Sir, we would be delighted to have him."

"He's young and has excellent social skills. He's not what you would call a straight-A student, but he is well rounded in his education. I would like you to take him under your wing, so to speak, and teach him the ropes. I believe banking is the first place to start, as it is the very heart of what we do. Like all young people, he likes to get out and about; he can stay here at my place, but I would like you to keep a close eye on him."

"I have kids his age, and so does Gerald; they will show him around. They're in college here. In this way, he can learn and understand the culture."

"Excellent; I'm going to be here for a few days, so we'll get back before I leave."

"Very good, sir."

******

James made his way down to the first floor and wanted to pop in on Nicholas's shop to see who was around and what they were doing.

"Nicolas, what the hell are you doing out here?"

"You know me; I can't stand still; I have to keep an eye on everything."

"Let's grab a coffee and catch up."

"Good idea, old boy; lead the way."

James and Nicolas went to one of the cafés on the ground floor. Nicolas looked older. He had to be in his mid-sixties by now. He looked to be in good health, though.

"I hear you've been gallivanting around the planet on a cruise ship."

"Yes; I took Annabelle and Samuel with me, and I met a lovely woman, to boot."

"That's good; I felt devastated for your loss—after Sabrina."

"I know; I've been antisocial for too long; that was a hard one to overcome. When you love someone like Sabrina and she's snatched out of your life, it takes a moment to understand the why of such a cause. I'm now over it, but I will always miss her."

"No doubt; I can't imagine losing my Davina like that."

"What are you doing tonight?"

"Davina is with me, so let's meet up at the steak bar and catch up on good times."

"Sounds good; see you at seven?"

James went around the first two floors, observing all the activity. It was a bustling place and everything he had dreamed about. He then made his way back to his penthouse to check on the kids.

"Come on you, lazy lot; time to wake up."

"Dad, I woke up this morning, and I had to think twice, not knowing where I was," said Sam. "This traveling for pleasure is one thing, but, for business, I can see it can be rough on the body! Time changes and packing and unpacking—now I can see why you come home exhausted after your trips. Running a world empire takes it out of you, and I haven't even started yet!" Sam was thinking matters through.

"Well, Sam, that's what it takes. If this is the direction you want to go, you'd best get used to it. Grab some coffee and come outside and sit on the patio with me."

James lit up one of his small cigars and sat there, thinking, until his two young ones joined him.

"Come on, you sleepy heads; we'll go downstairs in a minute, and you two can have a late breakfast."

"Dad, this is so different from England; we really didn't take any time to see much of Los Angeles, but this building certainly stands up to any high-rise building I've ever seen," remarked a wide-eyed Annabelle.

"Dad, how do you run all this all over the world?" Sam asked.

"Sam, it takes a team and someone at the top that has a clear understanding of all the businesses we run. You don't have to be an expert in every detail. You must listen to the experienced staff you have, receive all the advice that's available, and make decisions. If you still have doubts, wait. Never make decisions in a panic. Thoroughly evaluate any situation before moving forward. You won't always make the right decision. This way, you will learn, and you will know what not to do the next time. You can, of course, always step in, admit to an error of judgment, and make adjustments. The more hands-on practice you have, the better you become."

James continued, "This part of the world has a lot to teach you, if you take the time. I consider it possibly one of the last bastions of true capitalism. In 1997, of course, Hong Kong will revert back to the Chinese. I believe China will not change the way of business here, even though they are a Communist country. We employ too many of their people, and, with our expansion into the mainland, up the Pearl River Delta, of growing companies for manufacturing in Hong Kong, I believe they will be accepting of our ways. I met with Chairman Mao, and I find him to be strangely receptive. Our country has a deep trading history here, and you would do well to learn all about its roller-coaster ride to becoming the incredible place it is now. I am going to buck the trend when nervous people pull out; because of the change in government, there will be deals all over the place. This could be a fascinating period of change and an opportunity to learn."

"It's going to take me some time to learn all that you have accomplished," said Sam, beginning to realize that the world of business was not all glamour.

"Yes, but two things to remember. I got started at twenty-one, when the business was a lot smaller. So, in a sense, I have grown with the business we have today. I could have sat back and led a more leisurely life. I chose to do something with what I inherited and to make the best of what we had in a furiously expanding marketplace. The world scene may be different in your time. These are the challenges you will be faced with. Come on: let's go have a snack. Tonight, I am going to meet up with Nicholas and Davina; I'll introduce you to Harold Cummings, the managing director of the bank, and he can take you both out; he has young adults your age, so get to know him and make the best of your time here."

They all went down to the ground floor to eat. His two children were fascinated with all their surroundings, watching people come and go. They recognized a whole new world after the sheltered life they had led in school and university.

"So now I've finished with Oxford, could I stay out here to learn the first part of the business?"

"Yes, when you come back, take one of our merchant vessels, as I did. See firsthand how Trans Global Shipping works, after working with Harold to learn the banking side. It will be an opportunity of a lifetime."

Annabelle butted in, "Dad, I wish I could go to."

"Your turn will come, my dear," said James. "You have another three years at Cambridge, so, with your accounting and business skills, I think starting out in London at the bank will be the best place for you." James was testing her, just to see where her heart was.

"You're probably right. Sam, you have to know how to run things; it will be my job to watch the money, right, Dad?"

"I think that's a good way to start. You both learn from each other, and since you both possess different qualities, it should work well."

James took them both up to see Harold in his office, and, after introducing them, he left them both in order for them to have a better chance of getting to know one another. James then retired to his office at the penthouse to catch up on matters with Claudia, after being absent for three weeks.

"Claudia, I wanted to talk with you before you left for the day; how's it all going?"

"James, I hope all of you had a wonderful trip; I can't wait to hear all about it when you return."

"I should be in London by the end of the week; it seems like I've been away for ages, but the rest was wonderful, and I have lots to share."

"I can't wait. Things here are moving along. Flick is excited to be at the newspaper, and Kim has spent time with me and is learning the business. I think she's going to be perfect for the job. Got lots of other matters to fill you in on, but nothing that can't wait."

James felt a little tired, so he chose to take a nap before meeting up with Nicholas and Davina later.

The kids arrived back around six. James had taken a shower and had dressed for the evening. Nicholas and Davina would also be arriving shortly.

"Dad, Harold is great; he is going to take us out to his home to meet his children and his wife; then we are all going to dinner."

"Good; that will be fun for you both; when?"

"He'll meet us in the front lobby around seven."

Then came a knock at the door, and Samuel opened the door to Nicholas and Davina.

"So here we are amidst the Bannerman clan. By God,

Samuel, you've grown, and look at you Annabelle, the spitting image of your mother and a bit taller, I see."

They all sat out on the back patio, drinking Nicholas's favorite champagne.

"Nicholas, what are you up to?" asked James.

"James, I'm expanding our business here, shipping out more and more items, as the staff here become more proficient, and tightening my grip on the factory in the U.K. People aren't happy, but we will always do the final work back in England, especially for the more haute couture dresses we fabricate. Now, Annabelle, why aren't you a model? With looks like yours and with your height, I could have you in my fashion business in a heartbeat."

"Please call me Anna; I know I have been asked that question many times; who knows? One day. But now I just want to get my degree in business administration from Cambridge and to come and join Dad."

"Great pocket money; Claudia can tell you that; she still attended to your father's work and became successful in her career with me."

"Sounds tempting; let me give it some thought; who can't use some extra money, right?"

"That's the girl; come over when you get home, and, in between your work studies at Cambridge, I'll fit you in; that way, you can save your old pop a few bucks. Okay with you, James?"

"It's okay by me; that's what her mother did. Annabelle, just don't drop on those grades and don't let Sir Nicholas get too many fancy ideas in that head of yours."

Davina started in, "Now, Samuel, what is a young, tall man like you up to these days?"

"I finished Oxford, ending this summer, and I'm looking

forward to learning the business from Dad."

"Sensible young man, learn your trade and let the ladies wait; let me tell you they'll always be there for a catch like you."

"Sound advice, Davina," replied James. We intend to keep him busy, but you are only young once, and we are all entitled to a little fun." He knew that he was tougher on himself, yet he knew that Sam was more social by nature. If he boxed him in too greatly, his enthusiasm would diminish. That was something Sam had to learn himself. James would be watching with a careful eye. James's nature was in testing people rather than controlling them, in letting them learn by their mistakes, but not in being too distant.

"Well, kiddos, we are going to dinner; don't be too late for Harold."

James had made his reservation at the steak bar, and they welcomed his arrival with extra attention. He had a private room off the restaurant, where they could eat and talk freely.

"James, how are you doing after Sabrina's departure?" asked an anxious Davina, knowing the sensitivity of the question.

"I take it one day at a time; of course, I miss her terribly, but I'm slowly healing. Thanks for sending Lisa out; she really snapped me out of my malaise. That woman is a riot! Miss Positive."

"I know you two have always had an attraction, and I truly believe that a woman will always love you, James," said Nicolas, being the man of the world he was.

"Life is so funny; we don't choose whom we fall in love with or whom we are attracted to, or both. It just is. I have always believed that love is an involuntary emotion and that although it sometimes takes work and effort if it's truly there, love will find a way. I also think it depends on what stage of your life you are at. When we are younger, we are obviously more into physical attraction, but, with time, we grow in our hearts and minds. That can be more painful when it doesn't work. When you have the whole package like Sabrina and I had, then the loss is even more compounded."

"Very profound. I remember Marilyn Monroe. She really loved Arthur Miller, who was, without doubt, the leading playwright in the late fifties. She adored his brain and conversation, which tells you a lot about Marilyn. His unfortunate jealousy for her photographer, who adored her in a different way but who never did anything inappropriate with her, was Arthur's undoing. She truly married him to be her partner for the rest of her life. So, my point is that I do believe brains and imagination can exceed physical beauty. Arthur wasn't ugly, but Marilyn could have anyone. You can't always find the man who's got it upstairs, as well."

"So, Davina, that's why you married me?"

"You devil, you were a riot and are still one; I couldn't imagine being with another man like you."

"James, any new talent on the horizon, or are you just not ready?"

"We have a new person working with Claudia, who has struck my attention, but I think she may be too dominant for me; we are too alike; it's great for work when we are on the same team, but I have my doubts personally. Time will tell."

"I've seen her; yes, she has appeal and personality and a lot going on upstairs; a good choice to take over from Claudia may be just what you need, now that you are approaching fifty," said Nicholas. "She'll keep you on your toes." Nicolas laughed. He secretly admired her, too, but he was holding back in the presence of Davina.

"I have also met another woman on the cruise; we just finished."

"Will you tell us all about her?" asked an interested Davina.

"I noticed her on the ship in the hallway on the first day; there was something magnetic about her. I shrugged it off, thinking she was probably married or thinking I was just on the rebound, looking for anyone. The more times I saw her, the more enamored I became. Finally, when she was sitting at a table all by herself, I plucked up the courage to talk to her. We immediately hit it off. It turned into a whirlwind romance. I can't stop thinking about her, but I wonder whether it was just an onboard-ship infatuation or whether this could be the real thing."

"Describe her."

"Davina, she has some Latin origin, being from Argentina, and she is very aristocratic and soft-spoken. Chic, feminine, with a body and skin that could melt any man. Tall, with coal-black, straight, long hair and large, brilliant, green eyes."

"Sounds like a woman to die for," declared Nicholas.

"You behave, or I'll give you a good spanking!" said a defiant Davina.

"Will we get to see her, James?" asked an intrigued-looking Davina.

"I believe so; I have to let her know when I'm home, and then she's going to send me her itinerary for her visit to England."

"How old is she?"

"Thirty-six, Nicolas; around that."

"Sounds like another model; I'll check her out; believe me. I'll tell you what I think. Yes, Davina, you, too, my darling!"

"You just saved yourself from a good neck wringing."

"James, on another note, I know you are doing well with that textile business of yours," said Nicolas. "Would you be interested in selling it to me? I would give you a good price."

"I hadn't thought about it. I am taking a serious look at what to do with all my businesses, as I don't know how competent the next generation will be in running the entire diversity of our business interests. I thought about taking part of my companies' public, about freeing up some cash, and about focusing on our core business, which consists of the properties and banking."

"Funny you should mention that; I'm going to be sixty-five soon, and the same thoughts are running through my head. We were brought up differently; I don't know whether this next generation will have the mustard and drive to run these businesses, either, or the interest, for that matter. They'll have more than enough money, and it has to be carefully thought out to avoid stupid choices."

"When I know Camilla's plans, I'll call you, and we can all meet up and talk about business and pleasure."

After Nicolas cracked a few more jokes, they all laughed as they polished off another bottle of wine before departing.

"I've got to come and see how your kids are doing; it's been too long," said James.

"Be sure and bring that woman, and we'll make an evening of it."

*****

James arrived back at the penthouse; he noticed the kids hadn't arrived back and decided to get an early night and catch up on all their news tomorrow.

The next morning, James was up early; he let the kids sleep in again while he made his rounds, read the local news, and had breakfast down at the food court. Tomorrow, they would be returning home, and he was busy thinking through the best plans he would implement when he arrived back in London.

He wondered if he had received an e-mail from Camilla and looked forward to reconnecting with her again. He knew this wasn't just some wild fling he had experienced; he was thinking too much about her. He couldn't wait to show her the Throne room and to meet up with Sarah. He was certain that they would hit it off.

"Dad, here you are," said an excited Anna, as she pulled up a chair to have breakfast.

"At least you are up; what about that sleepy-head brother of yours?"

"Oh, Sam; he will be down shortly. We had a fantastic time last night; I really like the Cummings family, and his son, Charles, was a riot. We danced to the wee hours at a great disco club not far from here. Sam definitely likes these Asian girls; as usual he went all over the place."

"The day after tomorrow, we leave early, so we must pack tomorrow. It will be a long day, as we will be going back in time. So, make the best of it while you're here."

"Apparently they have some fantastic deals, so Sam and I were going to take a taxi and go shopping."

"Yes, there are, but don't jump at the first deal, and do bargain your way down."

"I want to have some souvenirs from the terrific time we've had, not only on the cruise but also during our visit here."

Sam arrived, not looking as chirpy as his sister.

"So, my boy, it looks like you downed a few last night."

"You can say that again," he said, with a big grin. "These girls are hot. This Asian-European mixture creates some very exotic-looking women. Hard to choose, but a pleasant problem, I think I could get used to living out here, although this place gets very crowded at night."

"It's less crowded when you get off the island," said James.

"Remember that, in between your social appetite, we do have a business to run." James smiled widely, knowing Sam wouldn't be any different. However, being left with the responsibility of running the business at such a young age and having met Sabrina, he really had no time to go skirt chasing.

*****

They arrived home, tired and jet-lagged. James left Anna at his London home and was anxious to be in the office to catch up on the latest.

CHAPTER 11

PLANS FOR THE FUTURE

James arrived around ten, still feeling a little off-kilter from his trip, but rested and ready to get back in the saddle. He paid special attention and waved to Kimberli, as he passed her office; she smiled back, in return.

"Claudia, have you a moment to come and visit me and catch me up on the latest?"

"Yes sir, and I'll bring your coffee, because I know you are going to ask me."

"Oh, Claudia, I'm going to miss you."

She arrived with all her notes, as Rose brought in the morning coffee.

"My traveling Lord, so how did your trip go? I want to know everything."

"Everything? That would be really too telling."

"Ah ha, you met someone?"

James always went a little red when faced with direct comments that hit a nerve. Claudia knew him so well after many years of being together.

"You are worse than me; you do like to cut to the chase. The answer is, 'Yes, I did, and she will be coming over to England soon to visit.' But I've yet to catch up on all my e-mails."

"Tell me all about her; I have prayed you would find someone. I know it's hard to top a Sabrina, but you are not a man to live alone; you need companionship, and rightfully so."

"She lives in Argentina, and, yes, I find her striking, but more important, we have a tremendous inner connection. Believe it or not, she's a psychic; Sarah's going to love her, and if things work out, she could be a great asset at the estate. I have not told her about the Throne room yet, and I didn't want to overawe her before getting to know her better. She's definitely different, but classy and refined, and, yes, to say the least, I am enamored."

"So, what does she do?"

"Her husband died at about the same time Sabrina did, which is a strange coincidence. He was a lot older. She works in his business and has now taken over. They are into mining in Peru, Brazil, and Argentina. She is completely self-sufficient, has a ten-year-old son, and, like me, she has been going through a lot since the loss of her husband."

"Sounds smart; how old is she?"

"Around thirty-six."

"Oh, you bad boy, after those young ones, but age doesn't matter: if it's there, it's there. A psychic? Most men would find that a little off-putting, but not you; sounds like a fit, and I haven't even met her yet. Well, I can't wait to meet her."

"You two would get on famously, I know; she's sharp and has a good business head and is well-educated, like you."

"Oh James, you always sing my praises. I have some interesting news to tell you before we get down to business. Kim is doing great, and I see that forceful potential in her, as you do, but she's maturing, and I do believe you couldn't have made a better choice. On another note, she has started to see Peter . . ."

James butted in, "Peter, as in Peter Lloyd?"

He felt a strange tinge of jealousy; he knew he had feelings for Kim, but he did his best to mask his reaction and to remain calm and curious.

"How did they meet?"

"Peter, as you know, has been working with Roger, and he has been down here recently, staying for a few days at a time to work on an expansion plan for their business. He's doing very well with this new venture. In fact, he's here now. I believe she truly has feelings for him. He's perfect for her. Peter is not a businessman, but a very talented artisan working with metal. Kim is more dominant, and Peter is gentle by nature, and she's the perfect woman for his life. Both of them need someone, and, frankly, it's about time he settled down; for God's sake, he's your age, forty-eight; Kim is, I think, thirty-seven and still young enough to have a child, like I did. So, before we get down to brass tacks, why don't you two old pals have a chat?"

"Splendid idea; have him come up, and we'll catch up on the old days."

Peter arrived with haste to see his old friend and to get caught up on the latest.

"James, how are you? Feeling somewhat better after the loss of Sabrina? I knew she meant so much to you."

"Yes, it was a traumatic period, to say the least. I take one day at a time, and, between my family and my friends, I'm slowly making my way back. Work helps keep my mind off things."

"Roger and I have been working on some new plans for the business. We started out using this new process for improving fatigue life on all kinds of components within the aviation, agricultural, automotive industries, and so on. We are now moving toward an area of my own personal expertise, and that is the forming of wing skins. This new process not only increases the life of the wings but also shapes the wing skin to the wing box. This is an ambitious step, and it requires more capital, but we are making good progress, and the industry needs another competitor; we believe there's room for us."

"I always knew you had those unique skills with your hands, so I don't have any doubts that you will be successful in your endeavors. Are you still doing metal forming on other parts?"

"Yes; in between, we do some of the work I did when Dad was around, because there are so few people that do this kind of work anymore, owing to a lack of a skill base; it's kept us busy, and it is very profitable."

"I hear rumors about you and Kim. Is that just talk, or is there something serious there?"

"Yes, as a matter of fact. It's early days; we all went out to lunch one day with Roger and Claudia, and I found that she and I definitely had a connection. I have had many chances to get married over the years, but I have never found the right person."

"Well, it's about time! You're my age, for God's sake! She is at least young enough to give you a child, and you need a lad to carry on the Lloyd enterprise, don't you think?"

"No doubt about it. James, you know me well; you and I have always made a good team. She's like you, dominant and energetic, but she needs someone who's not too aggressive in a man. Our qualities seem to fit. I'm a competitor on the track, but not so much in life, and that's why Kate and I work well together. It's the same with Kim; I think she will be an asset;

I like her drive and ambition; she likes my gentle nature; we balance each other."

"I'm delighted for both of you. She wants to settle down with the right person, and so do you. I'm sure she'll also be a valuable asset in helping you with the direction of your business. You were certainly the best 'wicket keeper' a bowler could have, making me look good when I made some atrocious deliveries. It takes a team, and it looks like you two could be the right equation."

"James, I'm so glad you approve; please rest assured that, as your friend, your personal business will always remain between Kim and you. I'm not an intellect at the higher level of business operations, as you know. I just like doing the work."

"No fears, Peter; you are a trusted friend, and that would never bother me for a moment. More important, it's time you both had a life; I hope it all works out."

With that, they parted, and James was anxious to open up his computer and read some of his private e-mail. Sure enough, Camilla, as promised, had responded, saying how much she missed him and that, in the next two weeks, if it fit with his schedule, she would be flying to England. Her Nicolas would be back in boarding school, and her able staff would keep an eye on him, while she was gone. It took James no time to respond. He couldn't wait to see her again on dry land, to show her the Throne room, and to find out if the feelings he had on the cruise ship were truly real.

James took Claudia to lunch, He had thought out his strategy, and, before meeting with Roger, he first wanted to share his plans with Claudia.

"Busy morning; so, what do you think about Kim and Peter?" asked James.

"No problem; it's good; it's time they both settled down,

especially Peter," said Claudia. "He's a good friend; I trust him. So, I don't see the relationship being a problem from a business point of view. Peter is about the last person that would want to talk numbers all weekend with Kim, and that's healthy."

"You have a point; that was my only concern."

"Getting down to business," James continued, "I am going to discuss with Roger about combining certain enterprises we own, or separately, to take them public. I believe that, within the next two years, we should do this. We would keep the core business, like our properties, the credit card, our merchant banking, and our newspaper, private. This creates a manageable unit for the future. It will increase our cash position, and if we have another entity that wants to take control of those businesses, we will have enough cash to fight them off, if we so choose."

"So you are wanting to take public Trans Global and the textile business?"

"Yes; this will end up with a larger board of directors for those entities, but this will take off some of the weight from running these operations for the next generation, namely my family. These businesses have grown immensely; we would have a large amount of say, but we could step back more from the day-to-day. We have experienced phenomenal growth, but they will need new blood to continue to grow these operations, as the demand is still there. We shall benefit from the ownership of the properties we own, but the operations will have a freer hand to be a part of a bigger destiny."

"James, I like your thinking. Owning these companies privately is very demanding on our corporate staff, so taking a return on your investment now seems smart, and, in a sense, you will still be a big player."

"Exactly."

"So back to Kim," James continued. "How soon will she be able to take the reins, so to speak?"

"James, I'll give her another two months; then I can come in once or twice a week to check on things, but she will have my phone number, if she needs help. She will need backup, though; I think she can manage between the both of us for now."

"Good; I have it in mind to bring Annabelle in behind her; she's very competent, but she has another three years to go at Cambridge. If she needs help, we will fill the gap somehow."

"If you divest from the businesses you are taking public, this will take a load off her. Trans Global demands a lot of oversight."

"So how about you? What's Claudia going to be doing now, with all this free time?"

"While we have the health, we want to travel, to play golf, and to enjoy our time together."

"Makes sense; my God, where have all the years gone?"

"I know, but you're still a young man, and you have some distance left in you. Titans like you don't give up their love of what they do so easily. You live for it, and that's what has created the success you have."

"I must see how things work out with Camilla," said James. "Who knows? A whole new chapter in my life? The only thing about life that's predictable is change." James sat back, finished off his glass of wine, and laughed.

"I could never believe I would ever meet another woman like Camilla, but I am going to be cautious. Oh well, I must speak with Roger when we get back and put this plan into action."

*****

"Roger, come in," said James. "How's life with you and Kate these days?"

"Couldn't be better; she loves her work is doing well, and I am excited at Peter's new proposition. Peter is finally the Peter he should be: creative, happy, and doing what he loves. I am always surprised how a brother and a sister work so well together. Kate is the boss, as you well know, but Peter has the respect of his people for the creative skills he's blessed with."

"Roger, I have been doing a lot of strategizing and thinking on my vacation. I believe we should take Trans Global and the textile business public,"

"I couldn't agree more. I never thought I would ever hear you say the words, but, over the next two years, with the earnings you have and the low-debt position, the shares would go through the roof."

"What about the textiles? Together or separate?"

"Separate; they are two totally different businesses, and the potential for growth into more areas is exponential. First, build the factory on the mainland on the land we bought, then keep the property downtown, convert it into low-income but properly thought-out flats/apartments, and keep that as a part of your property business. That will be a good income generator."

"I like your thinking."

"I would go with Trans Global for an IPO in the next two years and then do the textiles. Keep the properties and the warehouses in Europe and in the States as part of your property business, also."

"Okay, more good thoughts."

"James, I don't like what I'm seeing in the world-banking community. There is a greater tendency to finance debt on properties than investing in technology and manufacturing.

As you know, many businesses have fled to Singapore, China, Taiwan, and Korea, with more to follow, I'm sure. Europe and the States are growing more toward service industries, because they can't compete. Technology is the key and the lifeblood of the future. I know we can't compete with these Third World countries, but more-advanced machinery and less labor and logistics for freight is where our future lies. I see the financial community banking on sure things and taking the risk it should to encourage investment into innovation and creation. This is where our future belongs. Then, those other countries cannot outproduce the modern technology. It's the present trend, and, hopefully, our manufacturing base will return, with time. Property scares me, with the escalation in price; we bought and built at the right time; we have little debt, so going public with our manufacturing is smart, because I believe that, in the next ten years, when the property game is about to go bust, we can pick up buildings and property for a song."

"Roger, you are a minefield of ideas; I love it; you don't see only the now, but you look seriously into the future and position us to be there at the right moment. It's a great gift you have. On another note, Hong Kong will revert back to China in 1997. Contrary to popular opinion, I think a lot of people will want to leave. What are your thoughts?"

"That's what you pay me to do. Business is about seeing the downtimes and taking advantage and cashing out at the top. The financial world has a rhythm; we must see the change before it arrives! That's vision. We will make mistakes, but, overall, the winners must beat the losers! Anyway, to China, yes, I will take a closer look at that. You could have a point. I see you are picking up on some of my ways. It's not bad to be a trend bucker, and you could be right. We can't miss out on that. Potential property deals are all over the place. There also may be some commodity trading deals, too!"

Roger continued, "That's what it's all about, *VISION*, It also made you a very rich man. Instincts like yours are why I guess they pay all those vast sums of money to the people on Wall Street."

Roger went on, "Yes, I know we are going through a boom period, and I'm sure there will be more before the turn of the century, but the share values of some of those companies are so inflated it's scary."

"Well, good to see you Roger. Let's go into action."

"James, it's great to see you looking happy and being back to your old self. I know what you went through must have been devastating. We were all worried about you. You have bounced back, so welcome home."

"Thanks, Roger; keep up the great work!"

Roger left with a smile on his face; he admired James for his decisive, thought-out actions; he loved being a part of a great team.

James sat alone for a minute; then he thought it was about time he had a chat with Kimberli. It had been over a month, and he wanted to have her perspective about how she was doing.

"Kim, please come in and take a seat; I wanted to catch up with you and see how you are doing," She was professionally attired, as usual, and she seemed happy to have a moment with James.

"Sir, can I get you something to drink? A soda maybe? I'm parched."

"Yes, yes, please do,"

She returned in quick order; this somehow made the meeting more relaxed.

"Since that night at the Fantasy Bar, we haven't had a chance to talk, so I was anxious to know how everything was turning out."

"James, I absolutely love my work, Claudia has been so patient and kind, and I feel so welcomed by everyone here. You have a very astute and experienced staff, so I'm treading carefully to understand all their ways and habits and indeed to learn the basics of all your many interests around the world. It's incredible what you have been able to achieve in the last twenty-five years. For a man who could have sat back, you've pushed on, like you were spending your last dollar, to improve and expand on what you have. Having such a small amount of debt does allow you to make serious returns, and, as for Roger, I think he's brilliant.

"Good; I'm so happy to hear your thoughts and that your you are being wise about your integration into the business here."

"I see areas for improvements with regard to IT, which is a favorite part of my training; a lot I can implement myself, but I will patiently wait my time and learn the business first."

"So, when do you feel that we can let Claudia go on one-to-two days a week?"

"I believe that, within the next two months, I can pretty much have this job under control. It's not the work. It's understanding all the businesses, the agendas, the wire transfers, and so on that takes a moment to be thoroughly conversed."

"No doubt; considering the size we are now, I am happily surprised you can achieve this in such a short time. So how is Kim liking London?"

"I love it, but it's always nice to get away to the country, away from the madding crowd, so to speak. I would like to mention that I am seeing a friend of yours, namely Peter Lloyd. He's been down on occasion to see Roger on business.

At first, the three of us went out together, and Roger, knowing I was alone, introduced me to Peter. Because he is a person who is educated like yourself, but from the country, I find we have much in common."

Deep down, James was slightly jealous; he felt this strange attraction to Kimberli from the first time he met her. Her drive, ambition, and go-there attitude were all attributes that caught his attention initially. There was something about her presence, the way she dressed, and the strength of her personality that he felt pulled in by.

"I'm happy for you; Peter is a good man and it's about time you two settled down. He needs a strong woman in his life. Peter was my best friend at school, and still is. He's not a very demonstrative soul, but heartfelt, kind, fun, and a master craftsman—all qualities I admire. Also, Peter can be trusted."

"I'm so glad you approve; working closely with you in the future, I don't want there to be any secrets between us. Having a personal life you approve of is important to me."

"Kim, in all reality, that's entirely your business, provided you take care of business here, but I like that you choose to share yourself, your thoughts, and your trust in me enough to be open about such matters. Yes, you have an extremely important position here, and knowing a little about your personal life is helpful. Claudia and I have always had that relationship, and I look forward to having that with you."

"Thank you, James, for taking the time and interest of wanting to know how matters are working out; that makes me feel important."

Deep down, Kim had feelings for James also, but Peter was great for now, and she would see what the future held.

CHAPTER 12

JAMES RETURNS TO THE STARS

James wanted to be sure about how Penbroke was doing, so he took a break from his normal routine for the week in order to see that everything would be ready for Camilla's arrival on Sunday of that week. He had one thing on his mind, and that was traveling on the Throne as a complete person, in the hopes of seeing Sabrina. He had dreams lately, where he felt her beckoning him to come. She had things to tell him, and he felt more emotionally balanced and ready to see her in her new life. This was his first priority; then he would attend to the affairs of the estate, see Sarah, and be sure that the house was appropriately prepared so as to give Camilla the impression that he had overcome, at least emotionally, all the memories of Sabrina.

Early Sunday morning, he arose and made some tea and toast before making his way to the Throne Room. He hadn't told the household staff and had purposely given them the weekend off so he could have the place for his own privacy. He knew the gates wouldn't open until nine o'clock, so this would give him all the time he needed. The new household butler had seen to it that the door to the Throne Room was unlocked, before he left on Friday evening. All James had to do was turn off the alarm code.

There it was; his heart was beating fast, as he pulled out the plugs from the rear of the Throne. He could see the chakras light up, one by one, to make the gemstones shine their iridescent light. After taking some deep breaths to calm him into a more relaxed state of mind, he was ready to sit on the Throne once again—this time with a whole new experience.

The sensation of feeling his entire body being lifted up through the vortex was indescribable. He felt he had been turned into a ball of light. His mind and thoughts were in no way affected, but he felt weightless. He did not experience that intense pressure he felt on his head the first time he travelled, when he was separated from his human body. He was now travelling as a complete entity, and it was the most peaceful uplifting experience he had ever felt. The joy he was receiving had him wanting to burst out with laughter from within. The level of light energy had transformed all the cells of his body into pure energy. Moments later, he landed in a place he hadn't been before, the garden of a home he had never seen before.

As he became adjusted to his new environment, to his surprise and delight, Sabrina was standing right in front of him in her white, short toga, with golden sandals. Her beauty shone, showing her brilliant aura and her tremendous happiness at seeing James in her dimension.

"Sabrina, my love; it's you; I can't believe it."

The two rushed together to hug. The experience was quite different. It was as though the two of them merged into a oneness, and the feeling of love was nothing like James had ever felt before. It was so powerful, yet it retained all the feelings of sexuality at a completely different level.

"So, James, how do you like this new feeling we have?"

"It's breathtaking, and it's far more intense than the experience we felt in our human form."

"Well, we are just in a higher, more-energized state of being. The beauty is that feeling is ongoing and that we can switch on and off our sexual or heartfelt desires as we want. It's not like human form, where we have to take time to regain our energies. It's abundant in every form."

"Sabrina, you look so beautiful, so this is your choice of habitat and surroundings."

"I suppose my childhood roots made me re-create my little vineyard, smaller than we had in Tuscany. This is like my secret garden I often went to when I was a young girl to escape from my sorrows and to meditate and think. This also has a spectacular view of the Mediterranean and of the steps that lead down to my sandy beach below; it's like being on the edge of an old-world, Italian seashore, close to a small village."

Sabrina continued, "James, come up to my veranda and enjoy the view, where we can drink some of my wine."

James followed.

"I love my life here; of course, I miss you all, but I can be anywhere you are on Earth. I know when you think of me, and I can read all your thoughts."

"That sounds scary."

"Not at all; it's only when you are sad, like you've been; that lowers my energy, because it pulls on me, because we are so connected. Those we love, and especially you, who are my twin soul, are never happy when either one of us is unhappy. In a sense, we are one person; you are my other half. That's the way it is since the beginning of creation. We may lead life with others we love, soul mates, but they are not our other half, our twin. We can make each other however we want to look, because we know what we are attracted to, but that which lives in our heart is the primary essence of our attraction."

"So much to learn; I cannot deny what I feel; we are one, and that's the truth," said James. "Do you see other men in this dimension?" He was starting to feel some of his more earthly emotions.

"Yes, but they can never be our other half. As they say, 'You got me, babe, you got me!' So, don't feel jealous; it just is; what we share is not possible with another, other than an act of God to make change. We usually meet our other half when we are ready to move onto a higher dimension at the end of a cycle of civilization. When we part, it's very traumatic, because the love we share is so powerful."

"You must know that I'm about to see Camilla. I find her very attractive, but there's only one Sabrina."

"We will meet others, James, but, in the end, we will always be together when we have to be. We are each other's strength. Without you, I am half of myself. That doesn't mean that we cannot have love and support those who are helpful for us. But what is, just is!"

"I am working hard to get to grips with all that you are saying, but as I see you here, there's no doubt."

James went on, "It's necessary we meet others who are our soul mates, and, indeed, we make and find new ones. Camilla has a very special talent. In addition to being a psychic, she is a seer. She has gifts. From time to time, she will have visions of the future, sometimes good and sometimes not so positive. This is a special gift that does not have to become reality. When a vision is given, there's a reason, a choice, where a certain outcome can be altered. So why are you here? And why am I still back on Earth?"

"James, you are a very talented soul that has lived many lifetimes. Your very existence on Earth is necessary to advance, to teach, to inspire, and to show what other souls can achieve. Look at the lovely trip you have just taken with Annabelle and Samuel in order to understand them better and in order to work hard to integrate them into the business at a level they can accomplish. Look at how you are remodeling the business you've help build for their future. Our planet Earth is helpful in preparing others for the universe we live in. Earth is a microcosm of what our universe is all about. In obtaining mastery, we are ready for greater tasks here and onwards from this place."

"You have obviously achieved that."

"Yes, in the terms of my creation. We are all different. The divine has created different souls to achieve different tasks. Some of us achieve our destinies more easily, because we have chosen different paths. Others of us choose more-challenging journeys, and that takes more time. Don't forget that any of us can return to Earth if we want to develop other skills that we might become acquainted with here. Earth is one of many planets that are testing grounds to obtain mastery in whatever goals we may desire to achieve, and, of course, in synchronicity with the divine. It's a complex subject that you will come to know after this lifetime. Camilla is with you for a very special reason. You have known each other before, and you both want to make something work that you had not achieved before."

Sabrina continued, "It's as though, in some magical way, we all blend together, each person with that person's other twin to eventually create a greater result—like atoms, molecules, and so on becoming a part of a greater creation. When I see you,

I feel exactly the same way I felt when I saw you for the very first time. It's comforting to know that you are happy and that we will see each other once more. I'm sure you have seen your mother and even Marco."

"My mother, yes, but not Marco."

"What happened will take time, even in this state. We attract only those that we have a connection with now. Who knows? With time, all is possible! We are all loving and forgiving. Other souls who are different or who have not yet reached a certain level of spirituality will not enter our field of energy. It is rare that you can do this. It shows that you, too, James are a truly loving soul and are more than ready to come and join us and be a teacher and a guide to those who are here on Earth, as I do. But have no worries; I'm extremely happy in this state, for now. I have so many souls to reengage with—the list is endless. Always know that my heart and my thoughts are with you every day of your present life, and I am not jealous; it does not exist at this level. I live and breathe for your love and happiness—from now on."

"I understand, and I almost get it in this positive state. The energy I feel is incredible. It's like being a teenager all over again, but with a lot more wisdom."

He came close to Sabrina and reached out his hand to hold her. As they began to embrace, James was dumbfounded.

"Sabrina, this is an experience to behold; I feel every inch of you, yet we are energy. The feeling is so complete, yet my level of attraction and heartfelt feeling is magnified beyond anything I could ever experience in the material form. I can see how beautiful it is to experience love here, and, with this amount of energy, I feel an enormous desire to be creative. If this is what it feels like, as we aspire toward God's light, why do we cling to our earthly existence for so long?"

"It's simple; we choose to master different experiences in order to accomplish our goals in a broader way within the universe. Those that choose to constantly reincarnate in the third dimension have lost and forgotten the heart and love that you feel here. They have become consumed with materialism and the physical form. That's the danger we face when we go back to learn new trades, arts, and knowledge. In the third dimension, our knowledge is accelerated. On Earth, there are two forces: positive and negative. We are tested by learning to balance these energies; that's how we achieve success. It can be accomplished here, but testing one's progress is best served by being in the third dimension. Here, it takes longer to develop a skill, and then it may not stand the test of the opposite! When persons have mastered their particular vocations, they can then implement their knowledge with ten times the energy and greater perfection here. The danger is that we can forget the real reason why we chose our earthly existence when we are there. The physical and opposite force has its own laws of magnetic attraction. That's why we are taught all those principles of how to live correctly—so we can find our way back to our true home."

"It makes complete sense," said James, thinking it all through.

"When we first started our cycle on Atlantis, we had the ability to be either in the third dimension or this one. We could come and go as we needed to. This was many, many thousands of years ago. We were then more spiritual beings. The great masters and adepts retained that ability, as do a few who live in the Himalayas today on Earth. To do this, they have separated themselves from material things in order to preserve this level of spirituality. They exist to teach and guide, and they are sought out by many who want to gain a deeper insight into the spiritual realm. However, with time, we lost that skill. We could transport ourselves with technology, but the age of materialism took over, and some of that inner beauty we all had was lost. As a result, the gravitational pull of the Earth today is much greater. People aren't as tall as they were in the Atlantean era. We slowly adapted to the change in environment, and, in a sense, we moved away from our Garden of Eden, which the Bible refers to."

Sabrina continued, "We are working hard to restore that age and to lighten the burden that Mother Earth has to bear. The people of our planet must see our planet as a living-breathing organism that has deep love and compassion. In order to survive, she has to change her environment when the souls living there do not respect the spiritual laws of the universe. Mother Earth is much more advanced than any human walking its surface. When we all understand the beautiful existence that she provides for all mankind, life will change for the better, and a place of love will start to transpire once more."

"You have truly become wiser; I could listen to all that you say for hours on end. It makes complete sense."

James looked at her, recognizing the very beautiful person she was and what she was slowly transpiring to become.

"Fascinating; so few see this. The physical reality is so demanding that we see that illusion as real, yet it couldn't exist without a higher energy."

"In the third dimension, there is a balance between the positive and the negative. However, in this form, we can truly experience the building blocks of our universe. In complete energy, there is innocence. It takes great courage to go to Earth, and many souls go there for their own progression within the universe. It also takes great strength to overcome the attractions of the physical body: food, self-indulgent pleasures, sex, and so on. All is good, but only in moderation. Sex without love is just a physical gratification that can become an addiction and that has caused great problems in family values. It's an illusion, because our physical body dies and returns to the Earth of its creation. The soul or the spirit within can get lost. It has become the work of many angels to help those find their way back. So much unnecessary pain is experienced, and it's especially hard on the newer souls who delve with excitement and curiosity into this experience. The best way I can describe it is this. It's like experiencing a virtual reality game on your computer, but once you have crossed over into this illusion, you don't know how to get back."

"I fear that danger, as our computers advance with the younger generation. They are already captivated by the idea of being in a false reality, not only like watching a movie but also like becoming a character in the movie. It would be scary if we couldn't find our way back. I completely see. I now realize why Czaur was so tough on me when I was becoming too obsessed with my business."

"James, I so miss you, even though I am very happy here. I look forward to the day when we can become one and move on from here."

"Move on from where you are?"

"Yes, hold my hand, and I will show you the very highest reaches of the fifth dimension I now live in."

As James held onto Sabrina's hand, he found himself moving through a portal of pure light. The portal released them into a place that James saw as blinding light.

"Sabrina, I can barely see you."

"Just wait, as your eyes adjust to this higher frequency of energy."

James could feel the immeasurable force of energy and was

busily trying to find the words to describe the sensation he was now feeling.

"Where are we? All I see is blinding white light!"

"Be patient; we are now at the very edge of God's light and his divine essence. This is the central force of creation of everything. Without this energy, we would live in an empty, nonexistent dark space."

As James's eyes adjusted gradually, he could see beings of light who appeared to have human form but who seemed to flash in and out of sight.

"What is happening here?"

"These beings of light and energy are distributing the very life force our universe needs to the highest masters of our fifth-dimensional reality. Beyond this dimension lies the inner core of our life force, and we are now on the edge of the line between the beginning of innocence and the highest form of knowledge known. Beyond where we are now lies the world of the angelic, which evolves within a structure completely unknown to most of us, except for those adepts, who will transpire to cross over to what we know as complete energy and who will then look like the light, which is similar to looking at the Sun from the Earth."

"So, is this the source from which we are all derived?"

"Exactly; without this, you and I would not be!"

"Wow; it's a lot to take in, yet it all makes complete sense!"

"To us, it looks like blinding light, but, within this existence, lies an unimaginable creation that belies intelligence. This can only be seen by those who are at the highest levels of spiritual understanding and pure knowledge, by those who are without any need to control and impose, by those who just love and who know the natural laws that go within this realm! Many of those evolved souls are aware of our existence, but they have no understanding about us. This existence is guided by those souls that have established themselves through action and wisdom—souls who have taken on the challenge to overcome some of the greatest obstacles in the lowest dimensions of evil and who have succeeded with overpowering love and forgiveness and who have risen to the highest level of spiritual existence. This, then, is the true home of our angels. When we can evolve to this level of thinking, we will be a part of the central force of an absolute power and a beauty that is unimaginable, where love proves its unconquerable essence, of which a part exists to evolve in every one of us. It is in this place where we can become cocreators of our universe, helping the growth of new solar systems and of an endless list of new understandings of how creation works."

"Cocreators; I like that. So we don't sit around all day in what we call heaven? What a long way you have advanced since you left your life with us. To meet you here now shows me the complete purpose and goal of my life. Words cannot do justice to what you have shown me. Your love and faith stand head and shoulders above my goals. In this most valued, wonderful moment, I can now see why God has placed you here: to make way for my journey toward our future. You've already accomplished that. It remains for me to now do my part."

"James, I know you must leave, but I believe this visit has allowed me to show you what all of us who love you want you to be such an important part of. I will watch over you all and will bless the day when we are, once again, one in eternal life together."

James was sad, as he embraced Sabrina again in her new life. For the first time in all his incarnations, he now saw the value of serving God and the divine essence as his primary goal and purpose. Sabrina had achieved breaking through that door for James, who had been locked away toward earthly accomplishment for generations.

"James, when the time is right, teach Samuel and Annabelle. They are highly evolved souls, and, as their mother, I anxiously await the day when I can see them and help them on their journey of life. I love you all so much, and know that when you think of me, I'm there!"

James reluctantly returned to the place where he arrived. He left the little vineyard and veranda she had created in her new life. He watched her waving and blowing kisses, as he returned to mother Earth, with a completely reformed outlook.

James returned to his kitchen to make a cup of coffee; he sat down and thoroughly processed all he had now experienced. He looked at his watch; it was nine o'clock. The crowds would be soon making their way to the Throne room. Fortunately, he remembered to push in the plugs at the rear of the Throne. Seeing Sabrina was more than he could have dreamed of, but to see her so happy and knowing that they still had that unique connection completely healed all his concerns. It was sad that their life on Earth was over, but the hope of a future together was more than anyone could wish for.

How does Camilla fit into all of this? He thought.

He knew he was attracted to her, yet Sabrina didn't mind. That, to him, was something he had to think more about.

He then thought, *Well, if it's all part of a greater plan, what the heck!*

He desperately wanted someone in his life; being a bachelor was too lonely, and now destiny had played her hand in his meeting such a beautiful woman, yet she was so different.

After finishing his coffee, he snapped himself out of his thoughts and decided to go over to see Sarah at the school and to see if she was free. He also noticed that he had an unusual amount of energy; he felt like a schoolboy again. To validate his thinking, he rushed over to the nearest life-size mirror in the front hallway, and, to his amazement, when he looked at his face, he looked noticeably younger; he still had a few grey hairs, but the trip had not only a mind-changing effect on him but a physical one, too.

*****

"Sarah, how are you?"

She was sitting at her desk, going over her notes for the ten o'clock class she was preparing to teach.

"James, what a pleasant surprise! I know what you've been up to. You've taken that trip with your full body, and just look at you; it's knocked a few years off you, by golly!"

"Sarah, you look remarkably younger, too, not that you were not a youthful person before," remarked James diplomatically.

"I know; I just wonder what the long-term effects of this are—whether we get older looking younger more quickly or the reverse. Anyway, if I feel like I do, I'd rather live out the rest of my life feeling like I do now than be old and crotchety," said Sarah, laughing. "So, tell me all about your experience."

"I met with Sabrina, and I can only say the whole saga was mind blowing."

James went into detail, telling her of his experience, while Sarah listened intently.

"I just have to see how Camilla fits into all of this."

"James, there is a reason; don't over analyze; just go with the flow. You are indeed a lucky man to meet what sounds like another beauty, too!"

"Also, she is a psychic and a seer, so you two will have fun getting to know each other."

"James, that's what makes you so unusual; most men would be suspicious of a person with those gifts. When I met Victor, I went very cautiously at first and over a number of years, when he found my advice to be helpful; I did share with him my gift. This lady must have known that, by your aura and your intuition, you would accept her. If you two hit it off, I could definitely use the extra help. All I do is work. That being said, I have met someone else; we are taking it slowly. He runs an estate on the other side of Boston, so not too far. I can't wait to introduce him to you!" Sarah was excited as she spoke.

"When I bring Camilla up, the four of us must go out for a bite at the Armoury in Lincoln; then you'll have a chance to get to know her."

"Well, James, I must be off to class; good to see you again, and you're looking so happy after all that's happened."

CHAPTER 13

CAMILLA'S ARRIVAL

There she was, exiting customs with all her luggage; her face was beaming with happiness after completing the long flight from Buenos Aires. She looked exactly the way James had remembered her: her flowing strides, her magnificent, long, black hair swept behind her shoulders, her petite features glowing with joy after making the journey from across the South Atlantic to the northern climes of England.

"James, at last!" she said as she dropped all her luggage and ran toward him to give him a big hug; then, momentarily, she looked deep into his eyes, before sharing a long-awaited kiss.

"I can't believe you are finally here; it seems like an eternity since we parted in Sydney; you are a tough woman to forget about, a wonderful distraction from my daily routine."

"Just wait; I aim to be your one and only distraction from here on out!" she sexily responded with an engulfing look of abandonment.

It reminded him of the days when he would pick up Sabrina and how excited he was to see her, wondering what new outfit she would put on to tease him.

"I can't believe you're here. I have to pinch myself and say finally our trip across the Pacific wasn't a dream!"

"It's the same for me: all the preparation and wondering whether you would still feel the same."

She hurriedly collected her baggage, as James helped.

"Camilla, you look better every time I see you!"

The happy couple walked to James's Bentley to drive toward London to spend the night before going onto Penbroke the next day.

"My favorite city!" said Camilla. 'He who is bored with London is bored with life,' as Lord Byron once said!"

"I'm impressed with not just a pretty face but with a learned woman, to boot!"

"We've so much to share and teach each other about who we are. I can't wait to discover your world. Will you take me to your offices in London before we go up north?"

"Of course, but I didn't think you would be interested."

"I want to see you in your world before you come and see me in mine."

"Not just a fun lady, but I do believe I'm looking at a business woman, too!"

"It's not every day one gets to see inside another business from the top down. I'm fascinated with all you do and want to help and understand you and your life."

"You are the first woman that has shown that kind of interest in my work. Sabrina always cheered me on and supported me in my business affairs, but she never actually showed the same interest you apparently have. So you are a woman that doesn't mind your man talking shop?"

"Not at all; I love the hustle and bustle of the world of enterprising people. It's what I've been doing for years. It's nice to take a break, for sure, but one must have a passion for what we do so that energy flows to all those around who work with you. I can see you have that twinkle in your eye."

"You've got me down, but I have to say I've been working hard to slow down a bit, as I want to enjoy life a little more, as work has been my obsession for too long."

"Work hard and play hard; nothing wrong with that."

James could see that her whole vibration was very different from that of Sabrina. She was a no-nonsense woman but full of life and energy. He thought her work had been her way of distracting herself from the loss of her husband, which, in a way, had been the case for him.

"Well, here we are," said James as he pushed his card into the gate opener and drove toward his Muse."

"Wow, I know this part of London, having been a frequent shopper at Harrods. To think you have a place behind it is out of this world."

Most men would be worried, but James knew she had more than enough of her own money to splurge on the trendy fineries of the day.

"Now, be truthful: are you tired after your long trip, or are you up for a bite at my favorite restaurant?"

"James, as a businesswoman, I am a frequent flyer. I got some good sleep on the way over because I wanted to look my best for you, and, besides, if I go to bed now, I'll be up during the night, so let's go and have some fun. I've waited for this day for far too long."

James loved her fiery energy and was feeling famished, as he was on tenterhooks, awaiting her arrival. He hadn't eaten a thing all day. They entered the flat, as James helped her take her luggage upstairs.

"James, I love this; so is this where you take your mistresses at night when you are working in London? Quite the hangout."

"I didn't realize you were such a teaser; unfortunately, I'm a one-woman-at-a time man, although I do have my moments when I'm blessed with some eye candy!"

"So, do I fit the bill, your Lordship?"

"More than that, and then some!"

"Now I hope you are not going to be a stiff Englishman and stick me in a room all by myself."

James hesitated; then he spoke, "As my lady desires, your wish is my command."

"I don't want to wake up in the middle of the night and wonder where I am."

At that moment, they both dropped the luggage onto the master suite floor and flung their arms around each other in deep embrace.

"My God, it feels good to hold you again; I still remember the day we spent in bed on the ship, not something one forgets," stated an overjoyed James, feeling that spark of love they felt was still alive in their hearts.

James thought twice about taking her to the Brass Bell because the owners were Italian and might want to ask questions about Sabrina. He would go there in time on his own, or on business. He decided on another restaurant he liked very much, which had recently opened next to Harrods store, called the "In Crowd."

"James, I like this; it's swanky and upbeat with the times, not the typical old-world English surroundings."

"Yes, you will have plenty of that before you leave, my dear, too," quipped James with a smirk.

"I'm sure; don't be offended. I like all that British tradition; it's what signifies the English to the rest of the world. Horses and guards and all that pageantry—it wouldn't be England without that."

James ordered a fine bottle of champagne, as they received the menu, to celebrate her first night on English soil.

"Tomorrow I have something very special I want to show you at our ancestral home in Lincolnshire."

"Indeed; what?"

"Something that's going to, I hope, intrigue you. I'll give you a clue; it goes well with all those telepathic gifts you are blessed with."

"Now, I'm all excited: it's something to do with some past ancestral mystery that defies logic. A revelation that's a best-kept secret; am I getting close?"

"Yes, that's close enough; those antennae of yours are far too sharp for us lesser mortals."

"Oh no; you don't fool me for a minute, Sir James; you love keeping me on tenterhooks."

"You're too sharp; you don't miss much; I'm anxious to see what you think."

"I'm excited already, but I still want to see your business first."

"Yes, but this is only the headquarters; it would take me the best part of six months flying you round the world to get a grasp on that."

"Really? That's quite an operation."

"One of the reasons I took my young adults on the cruise was to see how to plan for the future and what their interests and ambitions are. We are a private organization, and it isn't everyone that can run such a wide-flung multidimensional business as we have, or, indeed, as we want to have."

"You must have good staff, yes?"

"The best, but they need leadership, one who has the vision

and the qualities of understanding finance and business. Charting those new waters for the future cannot be achieved by trained professionals. Entrepreneurs are not a dime a dozen. I have to make decisions to either divest, to take certain parts for a public offering, or to keep the business that we have been closely aligned to private. In this way, in the event of a change in the economic affairs worldwide, it would allow my children to have the financial resources to survive a severe economic downturn.

"Always planning, James. People like us are considered fortunate, but people never know the weight we carry on our shoulders. No one will love us if the business goes bad or we start to lay off employees. This brings me to my own thoughts about my future. If we do become involved together, what kind of life are we going to have with my businesses in South America and yours, being that you live here?"

"We won't solve that tonight; right now, you and I are the two most important people in our lives, and as the week passes, we will solve that dilemma."

"Amen to that!"

They toasted each other, wrapping their arms around each other to give each a drink of champagne. Camilla had a light dinner, and James his usual steak. The couple chatted away, but, by the end of the meal, James could now see that Camilla was beginning to feel relaxed and that sleep was what she now needed.

Camilla awoke, first bringing early-morning coffee to his bedside table.

"Wakey, wakey, sleepyhead!"

"Camilla, you're an angel; early-morning coffee; you don't know how long it's been since I had this privilege, and to awaken to such a beautiful maiden is a delight to behold!"

She jumped into bed beside him and then leaned over to give him a kiss.

"I'm so sorry I fell asleep on you, but if you are ready, I am, too."

It didn't take long for the eager couple to take advantage of an early-morning passionate arousal.

"You're every bit as wonderful as I remember. I'd lie awake at night, wondering when I'd be back in your arms again, and guess what? I fell asleep! Hopefully, that made up for it."

"Oh, Camilla, you're everything you were on the ship and more; how can I be this lucky?"

"You're not alone; I feel the same: to be with a man who I feel I can share anything with, who understands my quirky, psychic ways, who makes beautiful love, and who makes time stand still. I think to be in love has to be one of the most beautiful experiences anyone can feel. It's as though nothing can equal that; we are so fortunate!"

They both dressed casually for the day and for the next leg of the journey. After gathering all her things, James had his driver from the bank pick them up. It was Saturday morning, so it would give Camilla time to see the bank without the employees there.

They arrived around 9.30 a.m. James told the driver to stand by, as he wanted him to take them to Battersea Heliport afterwards.

They both entered the now newly renovated building, with all its paintings and history, as James had desired.

"James, I love the way you have all the businesses that are a part of your operation on display for people to see places they may not know you own around the world."

"It's all marketing, and it gives confidence to those that choose to do business with us. We can offer an international banking service worldwide—for governments, corporations, and individuals that want to do business with a private bank rather than be with a bank where they are one of many. Roger Bell, who manages numerous investments, is able to cater to almost anyone's investment needs with his staff anywhere. You also see my forefathers and how the bank grew from its humble beginnings in 1838."

James operated the lift without aid and took Camilla to the top floor. Lo and behold, as he walked down the corridor to his office, he caught sight of both Claudia and Kimberli putting in some extra catch-up time.

"So, you two workaholics are still at it?"

"It's much easier to do this when everyone is out and there are no interruptions," chimed in an intense Claudia, anxious to accelerate Kimberli's training as quickly as possible.

"James, whom do we have the pleasure of meeting?"

"Claudia, Kim, I'm proud to introduce Camilla, who has come over from Argentina to visit."

Claudia was a little off guard, as she took full notice of Camilla, and Kimberli was certainly eyeing up her dress code.

"It's a pleasure to meet you; James has told me all about you, so now I have the pleasure of seeing you for real. I do hope you take time to visit us in Hampstead Heath during your visit."

"I would love to; James has told me how you are his right-hand when he's on the road; it's always nice to place a face with a name."

Camilla was sizing her up, using all her abilities; Kimberli was also sizing her up. There was nothing like having two women meeting a potential partner to James for the first time!

"I thought the place would be empty, but I'm impressed; you ladies don't let the grass grow under your feet. We will let you get on with your work."

As James left Claudia's office, he looked back to see her raise her eyebrows and wink with a nod of approval.

"I like them both; Claudia is still a beautiful woman, and smart. I felt a little underdressed; if I'd known, I would have put on something else. Kim looks like a hard worker, too; she strikes me as being ambitious."

"You've got them pegged; they understand; you are on holiday; they don't expect you to be dressed to the nines!"

James took her back to his office and was proud to show her photographs of his father and mother and his many memoirs.

"James, I love the opulence and taste you've chosen."

"It's not all me, but we wanted to display an image of success, without overdoing it or appearing flashy. When you deal with other people's money, confidence is everything."

They toured each floor in order to give Camilla a general feeling of what James's world was all about. Camilla was no understudy, either; she was as sharp as a hawk and had the eye of an eagle. She had helped her business partner and husband build a considerable mining empire and was well informed in the affairs of business; in addition, she spoke five languages fluently.

"Very impressive, James; I can see you have not rested on your laurels, as many would have done. I definitely feel and see your signature on this establishment."

James's driver hurried his way to the front door to see that his boss and lady friend were properly attended to for their drive to James's helicopter.

"Now that's what I call going in style!" shouted Camilla, as the noisy propeller blades started up.

"I have to treat my princess in a manner she's used to having."

"James, I have a lot, but a helicopter at my beck and call—that's going in style."

"England is, for the most part, a crowded place, until you get well out into the countryside. Normally, this journey to my estate would take over two hours and, on the weekend, even more; this way, we will be there in thirty minutes."

After they strapped themselves into his jet ranger, James asked the pilot to fly down the river Thames and over Tower Bridge to give Camilla a sightseeing thrill. This gave her the opportunity to look out at a few of the landmarks London had to offer, then afterward, close to, but not over Buckingham Palace, to view Pall Mall and then onto the north. Camilla held James's arm and leaned her head on him in complete exhilaration, as they crossed out over the M25 motorway and A1 toward his home in Lincolnshire. James enjoyed pointing out various landmarks, including the famous Cambridge University in the distance.

James had the pilot fly over the property to show Camilla his estate.

"James is this all yours, even the village?"

"Yes; my family started the building and the acquisition of the land in 1704. Of course, there has been some dramatic change since then."

"That's no country house, and it must require a lot of upkeep to maintain it in the manner you have it today. It's absolutely beautiful and so characteristic of what an English country mansion looks like—what we see in the movies. The wing that juts out from the main house looks interesting. Why are all those people visiting this part of the estate? You must have some interesting artifacts to see."

"Ah ha! After I've shown you around the house, we will take a peek when we close during the lunch hour to give our staff a break."

The helicopter landed on the pad next to the hangar, where James's Lear jet was stored away.

"So, you have your own private jet and runway; now that's impressive. Are you surrounded by a community that's all yours?"

"Yes; my ancestors and I have contributed a lot to bring these properties to the standard it is today. If we were not in the world of international business, all this would not be possible. Many estates today barely survive because of the massive debt burdens they have and the continuous repairs that have to be made."

The couple stepped out of the helicopter and made their way across to the main house.

The butler quickly ran out to meet the couple and to take the luggage into the front hallway.

"James, I like the way you have a separate courtyard; it makes the house very private. Wow! Quite an entrance, and all these life-size paintings of your ancestors! I feel as though I'm walking into a dream or onto a movie setting. So few could ever imagine this kind of life style. No amount of money could re-create what has taken hundreds of years to be the way it is."

After taking the luggage to the master suite, Camilla had to remark, "James, this view of the sea is so captivating. I could sit in this chair and go into deep meditation with the window cracked open to listen to the sounds. Knowing you, I bet you're too busy to do that often."

"You are so right, but the thought of what you are saying does make me think I should do that."

"So healing: the vibration and the pure air."

James took Camilla on a complete house tour, then back to the little alcove that sat next to the kitchen to have a light lunch. His house staff members had been a little concerned about their future since the departure of Sabrina. Some had been dismissed, and, over the year, James had spent little time, if any, at the estate. The arrival of his new lady friend put a smile on all the house staff members' faces, and they were now eager to please the happy couple.

"Let's see; we will eat, and then we can take a sneak preview of the East Wing. Then I want to introduce you to the woman who runs what you were seeing from the air."

James enjoyed keeping it all a surprise, and he couldn't wait to see how she would react to seeing the Throne.

CHAPTER 14

THE THRONE ROOM
AND A SURPRISE

James's heart was beating fast as they made their way down the long corridor and past his father's old study and out through the side door and down the path to the main entrance of the East Wing.

"James, now tell me all about this room; it's enormous. It's beautiful: all these artifacts and, there in the center, a magnificent throne."

"Yes, of course," said James. He then went into detail and told the story of the seventh Earl's travels and collections and how the Throne arrived here in England.

"James, this throne or chair—I know what it is; it's from Atlantis. How on earth did it make it from there to here, and now?"

"Wow! I had purposely not mentioned this, because I thought that if you remembered Atlantis, you would possibly recognize this. I certainly didn't know of its origin, like you, but I felt something, and, after reading the seventh Earl's notes, it all made sense."

"This was your teleportation chair; I remember it clearly. Have you used it?"

"Yes; I have lots to tell you now that I realize you do understand this device."

"I have a lot to tell you, too! I suppose you know that you have to pull out those plugs behind the gemstones in order to make a complete physical voyage. Do you have the base of the chair set? Let's see: to the Pleiades star constellation. This is where our masters and our guides live, and Sabrina is probably there; however, you can visit many other systems if you care to."

"Camilla, you are remarkable; I have wanted to explore other places, but I was scared of not making it back."

"Your intuitions are right; there are many different planets to visit, but not all are fifth-dimensional. The Pleiades constellation is the most advanced and the closest to the angelic realm, as you probably know already. There are others that are more advanced than Earth, and there are those that have some scary-looking creatures that will do everything to keep you there. This a huge subject."

"Look, let's go and meet Sarah who is the administrator of this whole area; she's. like you, a psychic; both of you will have a lot in common."

"James, you're back again, and who is this beautiful young lady you've brought?" remarked a curious Sarah.

"This is Camilla, who is a psychic, like you, and who knows all about this Throne and who was on Atlantis when I was there. She remembers this Throne or teleportation device."

"Really, it's a pleasure to meet you; I can see that, by your aura, you are a highly spiritually developed soul. It's not often

I meet someone of your level of being, if ever."

"Thank you; I can see that you are, too, so if I am correct, you take classes to teach people to align their chakras in order to travel the vortex to get guidance from their masters. Not that you don't have that ability yourself. I can now see why James and I have met; this is the most tremendous moment of my life; I couldn't be more thrilled."

"Sarah, why don't I leave you two together for a while; I'll return in about half an hour, as I know you have a class at 2.00 p.m."

"Thank you, James; I was beginning to wonder if I would be the one and only person to run this place until my dying days; now I think I've met my answer!"

*****

James returned as promised, after sitting outside and observing the teeming masses of people who had all heard about the magical Throne from a different age.

"Well, ladies, what's the prognosis?"

"James, you meet the most interesting and most different people. Camilla here is light years more advanced than I; she and I could talk for hours. James, Camilla is a shaman of the highest degree; there are very few souls walking this planet with her knowledge. I am telling you this, as she is far too modest to tell you. The race of people she derives her heritage from comes from a tribe in Patagonia, like the Swiss Alps, only in Argentina. They come from the Incas, who left Atlantis toward the end of the last ice age. This sect traveled south to find a place where they could keep their sacred knowledge, because they wanted to keep their spiritual powers, which they could see their brotherhood losing with the new challenges of starting over. These gifts have been handed down to her in the present generation, but not all her kind have developed their skills to her level."

"What you're saying is I've found myself a genius, or my little genie!"

"James, I'm serious; she uses almost 40 percent of her brain. We all had these gifts when we came to Earth, but the physical magnetism of this dimension has pulled us away from our heritage. Have you ever asked yourself why we have such a large brain and yet we only use a maximum of 10 percent? We are slowly working our way back to our former selves, but it's taking time, and our brain size is living proof that there was a time when we used so much more and a time when we knew more than we do now."

"That is truly astonishing, Camilla; I thought you were smart, but you've been holding out on me!" laughed James, who was pleasantly surprised.

"I must go to my class, but this, I hope, will be the beginning of a great future friendship; it's been a privilege to meet you," said a very impressed Sarah.

"We must talk further; I want to understand all that you teach and maybe help," said Camilla modestly.

"It would be a pleasure," remarked an upbeat Sarah, full of joy at meeting someone who was more than her equal.

"Camilla, you are full of surprises. I had already thought you were smart, but Sarah is no lightweight herself, and for her to compliment you in that way speaks volumes. So, what do you know that you haven't told me already?"

"James, let's sit outside and watch the people; we can have something to drink, and I will tell you all the things you want to know," she commented in a commanding way and with a smirk, knowing that she had a one up on the curious Lord James for the first time since they had met.

They decided to take a glass of chardonnay, like they had on the boat, with some shortbread biscuits. The house staff members were busily attending to them, glad at finally seeing his Lordship after so many months of absence. They all missed the family, now that they had grown up, and they looked forward to the day when James would find happiness again, after all he had gone through.

"So, my beautiful Latina mystery woman, fill this half-brained nitwit with all your words of wisdom."

"James, I knew you on Atlantis, and I can recall who you were, what you accomplished, and who you were like."

"Have you known that from the very moment we met?"

"Yes; I was astonished after all my incarnations; I've been looking for you, and there you were, at the other end of the captain's table; I thought it was you in the hallway, but, that night, I knew. I didn't know how to introduce myself. I didn't want to seem too forward. I know you, and you don't like bossy women; you like feminine women. I therefore used all my power to send you subliminal messages of attraction."

"Sneaky: using all your high-powered trickery to pull me in?" joked James. "Let me tell you: power or no powers, I'm ecstatic you did. Unfortunately, I didn't remember you from a previous incarnation, but there was something about you besides your very pleasing feminine appeal!"

"James, you were a very powerful man on Atlantis, especially in your final incarnation. You were not evil, but your work and your power were your central axis. There were women you liked and loved, but work came first. You were a good father, and all your children loved you; they wanted for nothing; in fact, after your work, they became second, and your wife became third. The only hobbies you had were intense racing on vehicles, like you see in the movie *Star Wars*, and the throwing of a ball, like you see in cricket, but the games were a cross between cricket and a form of baseball. It was not an age that lived on gasoline and oil; the energy came from the pyramids, which accumulated power from the magnetic fields of the Earth, and from crystals absorbing sunlight into vats. The environment was cleaner, not like this age, which is going to upset this planet. We can get into that later."

"It sounds as though I was selfish for my own desires."

"You could say so, but you were a great and fair leader, and you enjoyed your political power as premier of all the islands; your knowledge of science was in the forefront. People loved your writing skills and philosophy. In todays' world, you are similar, but you show more heart, and you have a real chance to evolve beyond this dimension that you have become so attached to. When the floods came and life started over, you had fewer incarnations; it was hard, and as you played a part in the end of Atlantis, you were subconsciously aware not to repeat the same mistakes."

"You mean I was partly responsible for the fall of Atlantis?"

"Yes; as you became more powerful, you saw less need to develop your spiritual side of life—not that you were intentionally evil. Those that suffered on the other continent of Lemuria were poorer, but more spiritual. Many people of Asia and the Pacific islands are survivors from Lemuria after the great flood. All this could have been thwarted. The people of Atlantis had the power to help the Lemurians, but you and many others saw them as a scourge to humanity and saw their society as a cheap form of labor to increase the wealth and power of Atlantis."

"Not unlike the way the world is headed now?"

"Exactly; you must understand that this planet is a living, breathing entity that gives and gives, but when injustice and

THE JUSTIFICATION FOR INJUSTICE

greed take the forefront and the true values of this universe get lost, it has the power from within and above to cleanse itself. This is not the first age of man. There have been at least four civilizations before this one. We have an atmosphere to protect us from meteorites, and so on. This planet, the Moon, the Sun, and the solar system are the design of extremely advanced spiritual souls with a knowledge of science that far exceeds three-dimensional theory. This Earth is molded by the hands of a power so infinitely superior to humankind, and the Earth itself is far wiser than those of us that live on the surface. When the time comes for her to change and reinvent herself, she will."

She continued, "The minds of present-day man are increasing the density and weight on the surface of this planet; when that happens, the planet has to save itself from implosion. Yes, we can be too much to bear! Our love and spiritual ways and treatment of this Earth are the food this planet needs. This lessens the weight, because, through love, comes positive thinking and solutions; we then become more energized and therefore lighter; multiply this by a few billion times, and you see an enormous difference. You may say this is not right for our Earth to take this action, but the Earth must survive; like we do, she knows we won't be lost; we can live again and learn. Then she can heal and rest herself for the future in the hope that a people will come and raise the spiritual level from this third dimension to one that's much higher; this is the goal of everything in the Universe. Yes, there are those dark planets below our dimension that live in what is known as evil, but as time passes, they can evolve, or they will perish and die with the entities upon it."

"Wow; you and my masters would get on fine; how do you know all this?"

"James, you, too, can master this; why do you think I'm here with you at this moment?"

"To help me evolve to a higher state?"

"Yes, but I happen to love you, and I have been incarnated for that very purpose; I have met my own twin soul already, and now we are one and complete."

"So, you and the man of your life are one?"

"In a way, but it could be a woman; you are part female and part male; we all are, or more correctly, feminine and masculine; when we meet that other half, we become complete. Male, female—it doesn't matter. It's whom we love, and although Sabrina is your twin, that doesn't stop me from loving you and, more important, from teaching you for your future place in the universe."

"So, when I become one with Sabrina, we can love others?"

"Yes, but that first merging is the core and center of your being. I know that you are still tied up in being part animal and that, therefore, you know jealousy and all those feelings of want and desire. Love just is; we don't choose whom we love; it just is. It's the way this universe began and then split up. Anyway, that's enough for now; I will teach you more, as time goes by. Let's go out and have fun!"

"Since my meeting Sabrina in her other dimension and since my meeting you, I have so much to process. All I know is that my master and guides said I would meet you, so all that you're telling me must be gospel."

That night, James took Camilla out in his Aston Martin, after making a reservation at the Armoury Hotel. He knew their food was the best locally, and here they could talk further on the basis of today's surprising outcome.

"James, I love the English countryside. There's something so beautiful about your country. Compared to so many other places, one feels a sense of normalcy and civilization. It's all that history, I suppose what a nation goes through to become truly recognized on the world stage."

"A lot of what you say is true, but we are no longer the world empire we once were. I remember my history teacher showing us a map of the world, where the British Commonwealth had almost half the world under its influence. The British Commonwealth was the master of the high seas; now the United States has become the master of the air!"

"Yes, I see all that, but the legacy England has left the world will live on; like all empires, there's good and bad, but what is the international language of the world? English, of course; that speaks for itself."

The headwaiter quickly ushered them to a quiet table, as James had requested. He had many memories of being there with Sabrina, Sir Nicholas, and others. People knew of his loss, and he wanted to spend a quiet evening with his intended fiancée.

After ordering the wine and the dinner for the evening, James started in, "Camilla, I know you must still feel a little jet-lagged, so I hope you don't mind me asking: what plans do you want for your future?"

"I've been thinking seriously about this since we first met. After meeting Sarah and seeing your Throne room, it's clear to me that my future is here with you—that is, of course, if you want that?"

"My dearest Camilla, nothing would delight me more. However, what about your business, your son, and your life in Buenos Aires?"

"James, I want to sell my business; I don't have a lot of friends. I have enough money to live comfortably, with or without you. Had I not met you, it would be life as usual. But it's meant to be; we met for a reason, and we understand each other. Where can I meet a man like you? Most men think I'm peculiar. Having abilities and being, as you say, smart isn't always great; life can be lonely. I feel people's energy, and they are not ready for a friendship with someone like me. Here, I meet a Sarah, and, instantly, we have so much in common. I can help her so much; she has a beautiful soul; she needs help, and I can teach her all I know. This will be good for your school and so on."

"Camilla, I'm thrilled at the thought, but that's a big decision. Next week, I will introduce you to Roger, who runs all our banking interests worldwide. As you are in the mining industry, his experience may be helpful, as what you do is another form of commodity trading. His advice could be useful. In addition, I would like to take a trip back with you; I'd like to see your world before you make such a big decision."

"James, I adore you; you would do this for me?"

"Of course, this is a big decision. I want to understand, first, what you are giving up, how it will affect your son, and if there are other possibilities that we may not have thought of. There's no immediate rush; you have a business that you have worked hard to build. We must look at all the alternatives."

CHAPTER 15

BUENOS AIRES

After staying the night at Penbroke, Camilla and James went back to the bank via his helicopter, to meet with Roger that afternoon.

On arrival, James looked in on Claudia and asked her to find Roger. "Have him come to the conference room." He also asked Rose to bring some coffee. James and Claudia then walked down to the conference room.

"Ah, Roger, I would like you to meet Camilla, who wants to discuss her business interests with you in South America. She's in the mining industry and would like to pick your brains. She's thinking of selling, but there may be other options."

"Yes, it would be a pleasure."

After the introduction, James wanted to catch up on any business and talk with Claudia, so he left the two to talk alone.

"James, I like your new partner; she has a beautiful Latina aristocratic flair about her."

"Thanks; she's well-educated and runs her own mining business; her husband died several months ago, but as she works in the business, she's looking at various options to divest herself."

"Is this the woman you met on the cruise?"

"Yes; why?"

"If she's thinking of moving here, will this be a big change?"

"Yes and no; she loves England and has been here many times before with her husband of late."

"So, is this the woman you've set your eyes on for the future?"

"Don't be concerned; she's wealthy enough to live extremely well without a penny from me, but, being the curious being I am, I want to go an explore her part of the world before making the next move in both of our best interests. To tell you a little about her, she knew exactly what the Throne was and has already met with Sarah. Camilla is a psychic and a seer, and she is extremely advanced in her knowledge to the point where I can see she could be of tremendous help to Sarah. They were thrilled to meet."

"Well, Sarah is the person who could size her up quickly."

"No worries; believe me, she's for real. We had a great time getting to know each other on the boat, and we get on very well."

"James, I am happy for you; you need someone. That you've put some weight back on tells me you're happy. As your life-long friend and business partner, I'm always protective only for your best interests, as I'm sure you know."

"How are things here? Any pressing engagements?"

"All is moving along smoothly; it's a good time for you to get away after all these years. I'm working to do the same. So, are you two going to spend the night in London? I'd like us to have dinner tonight with Thomas, our son, and, of course, with his new fiancée. Let's meet at our house around seven, and I can make arrangements for dinner."

"Absolutely; it's time we all met up, and I look forward to seeing Alexander, too. On another note, I had some good family time with the young ones, and it appears that, right behind Kim, we have Annabelle who one day wants that job but who would play a part in the business vision. She interestingly takes more after me. Samuel is solid, like my father, and he will make an excellent chairman. He has good people skills, so I think that, in time, they will make a perfect match. I therefore see no reason to take our companies public, provided that the family interest and the continuity are there. I see that, obviously, Samuel will inherit the estate, as is tradition, but Annabelle, if she shows her mettle, could be an equal shareholder with Samuel in the business."

"Excellent, James; I'm so glad for you that we are developing this kind of backup. For now, Kim is going to be great. It will be another three years before Annabelle is ready to start here, and Kim should have matters firmly in hand by then."

James returned to the conference room to see how matters were going.

"James, if you are thinking of going to South America, I'd like to take one other person and do an audit; then we can advise Camilla on her best course of action. As a commodity trader myself, I would like to probe what opportunities we might have there."

"Camilla, how does that work for you?"

"I believe Roger is very talented at what he does, and his opinion would be well worth his time. I would, of course, reimburse you for any expense this may cost you."

"No worries; let's take a good hard look at everything: your business, your staff, your facilities and then arrive at an overall conclusion."

"James, could I have a moment with you?"

"Yes, of course; come down to my office. Camilla, go and pop your head around the corner and have a chat with Claudia while Roger and I attend to business.

"James, this might be a golden opportunity for us to add another string to our commodity trading for the bank. In this way, we could cut out the middleman and go direct to the retail market, leaving more margin for both parties."

"I thought you might see an opportunity there, so if this dovetails with our operation, without increasing overhead, this may be a great shot and an entree into the mining business."

James went on, "We plan to leave toward the end of this week, so check out some travel plans for all of us. She has a ticket already, so I will discuss what she's got in mind. While I am a little apprehensive of doing business in South America, if she has the right team and the staff that has good experience, together with what she knows, we may have a good chance of making a go of this."

*****

That evening, Camilla and James arrived at the Ringstone home in north London.

James introduced Camilla to everyone, with Sir Thomas eyeing Camilla.

After drinks were circulated, Sir Thomas pulled James to one side to catch up on business affairs and how he was doing after the loss of Sabrina.

"James, you're looking well, I'm happy to say; such an ordeal! Claudia and I were very worried about you. So, is this the lady you met on the cruise?"

Sir Thomas, the lawyer for the family's estate and business, wanted to know James's direction. He knew that James was an extremely wealthy man, and he naturally had concerns about this new lady."

"Yes, she has come over to visit; we enjoyed such a happy time during the cruise."

"Good stuff: just the tonic you needed to cheer you up."

"Amazingly, her husband passed away about the same time as Sabrina."

"Really? Well she's very different looking from Sabrina, but she appears to be another beauty."

"Yes, I'm going to South America to see her business, along with Roger and another auditor."

"So is this serious?"

"Yes, you could say, but I'm not in a rush until I'm sure."

"That's wise, James; it takes time to really know what you're in for. After my first wife, I took my time until Claudia entered my life."

"I'm not worried over the financial side; she's an extremely wealthy woman. That being said, I would have feelings for her, anyway. I'm sure that a joint prenup would, of course, be necessary, but we are not at that point yet."

"Watch out in Argentina! South America is still very corrupt, except for, possibly, Chile."

"True; she now owns silver, copper, and mining companies. Quite an operation, she says. She runs it, and she had been a big part of the expansion before her husband died. Roger and I want to do an audit, as she wants to divest herself."

"James, take it easy, my man. You've got enough on your plate, God only knows! When is enough, enough?"

"You are so right, but maybe we can do some kind of asset evaluation and structure a way out for Camilla. She loves England and wants to educate her son here. I will weigh the best options for her. As you say, we do have enough, and the business is still expanding. Roger thinks we should do an IPO on Trans Global and the textile businesses. This will help out my young ones when the day comes, and, of course, it all depends on the relationship with Camilla."

James and Sir Thomas returned to the group, as dinner was being served in the main dining room. Claudia and Camilla were talking away, and James could already see they were enjoying each other's company, jumping into a little Italian now and then. James had a chance to have a long talk with Alex and to learn how he was progressing with his father's business.

"Now, come on, you ladies; you must let an old guy have a few words with this lovely young woman!" said Sir Thomas. He loved the ladies, but he wanted to evaluate her for James.

As they left the house, after a long-overdue evening, Camilla had a few words to relate.

"What a magnificent home! I love the Queen Anne-style entrance and the whole layout of the property. What a fabulous home to own in this part of London!"

"His father bought it when Sir Thomas was a young man, but today it would fetch a pretty penny to be in this location. This is probably one of the choice locations for having a residence within reach of the city, outside a place in Mayfair, where my mother still owns a large townhome."

"I love London, a city with so much character and history. My Argentinian friends always enjoy coming to Cowdray Park each year in the summer to play polo. I love Claudia; she has a small Latina flair, which makes her so warm and welcoming. That woman certainly has your back. What a wonderful person to have with you in the business and on your journey to where and what you've achieved. Definitely a devoted person to you."

*****

The journey to Buenos Aires was long. They flew to Atlanta and then onto their destination. It was the end of Argentina's winter, because the nation lies in the Southern Hemisphere. Roger and George, the other auditor, came with them to Camilla's office and apartment in the city.

Camilla's downtown apartment was on the top two floors of the building she owned in Buenos Aires. Below were her offices on another two floors. The rest was a hotel, which she owned, with full entertainment, restaurants, and boutique shops—not unlike James's business plan for his own buildings. It was palatial indeed! James had often thought about this for his own bank building in London, but the space was too valuable for his accommodation. Camilla's building was larger, and it was the perfect setup in order to run a tight-knit operation. She could work all hours, go upstairs, relax, and then get back into her hard-driving style for literally being on top of all matters!

After having their suitcases dropped off, James and Camilla returned to her office, where they had left Roger and George.

"I would like you all to meet Serge; he is my second in command in running the business."

Serge was a tall, large man, well over six feet, and he looked like a man that would not put up with any nonsense from anyone. He had a suspicious and intimidating presence. James wondered how trusted he was, but, with Camilla's high level of intelligence and intuitive powers, he was sure he couldn't get away with much.

Serge was brief, and he gave James the feeling he resented his presence. After a short introduction, he left.

"So, is this the most trusted man in your arsenal?" remarked

James, with an eye of suspicion.

"Not really, but he's tough, and nobody will get past him; he knows not to take advantage of me; he has too much respect for me. With a weaker person, I would have my doubts."

"Well, that's honest. So, is he a man, if you let go of the reigns, that could take advantage of another?"

"Yes; that's my dilemma."

"But if you let go of him, could perhaps another person get taken advantage of by others?"

"Precisely; I either run the business or sell out completely, and I see he is nervous about the future and about your presence."

"What a fascinating city, and I've only seen a fraction of this place," remarked Roger, as they sat down together in Camilla's large office, with its panoramic view of the city and on out over the River Plate.

"It's like going back in time to a European city that has so much character and history."

"Ah ha, 'Don't Cry for Me, Argentina,' stated a smiling Camilla, "I tell you that if only these very walls could speak to you, they would speak of the passionate and diverse history this country has lived through!"

Roger then replied, "On my first impressions, I notice the Parisian architecture, a staff that reminds me of being in Italy; I could also be in London by entering this lovely building you own, Camilla. A magnificent property you have proudly developed!"

"Remarkable, Roger; you couldn't have captured my home-land more accurately," said Camilla. "I am impressed, James; I can see that Roger is an extremely astute man." She was swing-ing in her large leather chair, with a flirtatious appeal, in her short, black skirt and white blouse, teasingly making James feel that she was being a little too familiar with Roger.

"Now you can see why Roger is on our team," said James. "His abilities excel in the art of making valuable assessments, particularly when it comes to making money!" James was trying to put matters in their proper place, with a slight tinge of jealousy.

Camilla spent a good hour discussing all the mining sights they owned across South America. Her holdings were considerable, and that meant that, after doing the audit at her downtown office, they would be on the road for at least two weeks. Roger and George were then ushered into another office after they had been introduced to the woman that headed the accounting for the conglomerate. The day was moving on, and they were all tired from a long trip.

"I will have her then take them both to our hotel below afterwards, where they can eat, relax, and sleep.

*****

James and Camilla then proceeded to go upstairs from her office to a very spacious and well-decorated suite.

"Magnificent! I love your taste in furniture: comfortable, yet beautifully chosen. A fantastic view and, to boot, on top of all your business! I wish I could have a similar setup in London."

"Yes; it was my late husband's choice; he was a master at choosing this location and a property like this. We spent many hours talking business and enjoying each other's time here."

There were two floors, with three bedrooms on the lower floor, and an internal staircase to the magnificent panoramic view saved for the drawing room, the private study, and the master bedroom suite. The main kitchen and eating area was on the lower floor so that any live-in staff could sleep over, as well as guests for business and all her social friends.

"I like the way you have your complete privacy on this upper floor, with your own small kitchen for personal use when you are alone."

"Yes, it's beautiful, but very functional."

After pouring them both a glass of wine, she sat down on the sofa next to James.

They both embraced, and it wasn't long before the anxious couple were together in bed, in the master suite. It had been a long flight, and the pair were missing each other's warm embrace.

"James, I could never believe that, here and now, after several months of pain for the loss of our partners, we have both found love again, and may I say I've waited a long time to love such a man as you!" said an elated Camilla, smiling.

"Likewise."

The next morning, they arose early, and Camilla said, "James, I've thought matters through; I want to take Roger, George, and myself; Serge can stay here. I want them to see and to understand my business from my perspective. You can come along or take a break. I have a large home around forty minutes south of here. If you would like, I can have my driver prepared to take you there, if you should want to get out of the city into the suburbs."

"Okay; I think I'll take you up on that; a little alone time to explore would be nice. Now be careful with Roger."

"Oh, James, you're jealous," she said and started laughing.

"Well, you are a captivating woman, and I know your penchant for older-looking, distinguished men."

"You must be joking," she said. She could read too easily his thoughts with her intuitive abilities, but she was flattered, in a way, by his feelings for her.

"Oh, I'm just teasing," said James. But, deep down, their relationship was still new, and although she was nothing like Sabrina, it had been a while since he had regained those feelings for another woman, and he was a little sensitive.

He continued, "Another place in the suburbs? Yes, I'd love to visit and to kick off my shoes, so to speak."

James wanted to do his final analysis for his own personal reasons. Camilla knew that about him, and she gave him the full, personal opportunity to explore, and James somehow realized that.

The next day, the group were gone, all well-organized by Camilla and her staff. James decided to wander around the hotel property, but he first went down to meet with Serge.

"My Lord, I am most honored by your intrusion. What brings you to my office?"

"Oh, I'm just learning about how you guys operate on the other side of the planet, a first for me, so if you have time, please show me around, or show me around later, if you are busy."

"No sir; I would be delighted." Serge was surprised; he'd always seen the upper-class Brits as a bit standoffish, and he was intrigued by James's interest.

"You are the man that is Camilla's right-hand, and, as a businessman, I'm always fascinated to learn about other countries and to understand how people conduct business. We are an international operation, so I am very interested to know how you manage a mining operation, and I would like to know how you run things, if that's helpful,"

James knew he had his ways, but he was intrigued to know more, but, more important, he knew Serge was concerned for his own future.

"I worked here for many years, but when Camilla arrived,

she became a dynamic force in our growth. She is greatly respected for her drive and knowledge."

He wasn't about to offer too much about the business; he was going to let James dig it out of him.

"We are quite scattered, controlling mines in Peru, Chile, Ecuador, Brazil, and here. This means a lot of travel within South America."

"That's what interests me: how do you keep a tight control of the various products you mine, with regard to the exact amounts of, say, copper, nickel, gems, and silver?"

"We have selected an experienced management group, who monitor daily what we mine, and that is reported on a daily basis to our office here."

"Would you say that these reports are accurate, or, to the best of your knowledge, are close to what is reported?"

"We do have monitoring: electronic, pass-out gates for each of our employees. In the old days, it was much more difficult, but now, with the introduction of more advanced equipment and fewer people, it has become easier."

"Would you say that a group of employees could work together to carry out small amounts that your equipment would not detect?"

"Our equipment is not the latest, but it's possible that could happen. Employees are able to cheat the system, yes, but the amounts would be small. In addition, if a group is working together, other employees would know, and they can report them, and we have inspectors that are skillful at detecting if that's happening. We have implemented a bonus system for productivity. Most of our mines are in remote places and the only places of employment. So, they are very careful not to get caught, as it would be hard to find another job in the vicinity, and they would be marked men, for much lower pay in another job or mining community. In the mining community, we work together to protect what we produce."

"Is there more advanced equipment?"

"Yes, but the implementation and higher costs outweigh the investment for now," said a slightly concerned Serge. James could tell by his aura that it may not be possible at the mining level, but how many managers could alter the tonnage and documentation? He thought Roger would quickly sense that.

"Interesting; are you mainly here? Or do you travel a lot, too?"

"Not so much, but since Camilla has been away, I look after all her personal and business interests. Don't misunderstand me; Camilla is a very astute person herself; I just ensure that the matters we discuss are taken care of."

"Well, Serge, I'm going to take leave of you, and I appreciate our talk. I can see that you take your responsibilities very seriously.

"Yes sir. May I ask you something without sounding impertinent? What are Camilla's plans for the future of the company?"

"Serge, she is trying to decide on that herself. Roger is my right-hand man for investments and banking, so he and Camilla will arrive at a conclusion. It's too early to say yet, but if Camilla decides to sell, which is a possibility, you can rest assured she will respect all her staff and their future. Mining this far away is an industry I'm not familiar with; however, that will be Camilla's decision."

"Thank you, sir, for your frank position."

James decided that evening to take a meal in the main dining room of the hotel on the ground floor. He would have a drink at the bar and take a snack there. He ordered his usual scotch on the rocks, then took out his favorite cigar, as the barman crossed over to light it for him.

"Thank you."

"Senor, are you the gentleman that's staying with Senora Camilla?" he asked in excellent English.

"Yes."

"Then, welcome to our country; Camilla Ortiz is greatly respected here, and I'm proud to be of service for anything you may need."

"Your name is?"

"Pedro, Senor."

"Pedro, do you have a snack menu?"

"Of course."

At that moment, a lady came to the bar and sat two places down from him.

James turned to look at her, and he quickly recognized this was no ordinary lady. She was tall, with long, black, flowing hair. She had on a dark green-and-black summer dress. Certainly not the kind of dress any woman could afford. The open side of her dress hung away, and he could see that she was a refined lady of means. As their eyes met, he could see that most men would notice this stunning, large, bold-eyed beauty. Her jewelry was expensive, and he liked the gold anklet she wore at the base of her long legs. He turned back to look at Pedro; he was pouring her a vodka tonic, with a splash of lime; as he turned, he raised his eyebrows and rolled his eyes, and that told James he knew exactly who she was.

"Good evening; how is it that such an attractive lady would grace my presence next to me?"

"Ah, Senor, I could say the same."

"You obviously know this place well?"

"Yes, you could say that." Her English was good, too, but it had that Spanish accent that sounded seductive with her deeper tone. She pulled out a cigarette, and James leaned over to light it for her."

"Thank you, Senor."

"So what do I owe the pleasure of having such a fine lady coming to keep me company?"

"I know who you are, do I not?'

"Really?" asked a curious James.

"Camilla asked me to take care of you; do you mind?"

"No, not at all; however, you are a very attractive woman, and although I welcome your presence, I wonder: do you have an ulterior motive?"

"Of course," she said. "She wants my opinion of you. She loves you very much, and she wants to know how vulnerable and weak you could be in the presence of a woman you find appealing." She laughed.

"Wow, she's got great choice," said James. "I doubt I could top you!" James raised his eyebrows and grinned widely.

"So am I here to please you in any way you may want?"

"So does that include favors?"

"Yes, if you desire that."

"Why would she want me to have an intimate time with you?"

"This is Argentina, and men of wealth and position often have a mistress, and we women of means are not jealous, but we do want to be loved by the man we are with."

"So it's perfectly acceptable for us to have a fantastic few days, enjoying one another."

"You have it."

"Let's move on; tell me about yourself; I'm most intrigued. What is your name?"

"Nicolette; well, that's an epistle within itself. I grew up in a poorer part of the city, like the famous Evita, but I made my way academically to university, where I studied political science. I won't go into the way I paid for my tuition; I will leave that to your imagination! A girl has to survive. I'm not proud of my past, but I am proud of where I am today."

She was a straight shooter, and James liked that. He was talking to a woman of the world who told the truth without mincing her words, because, deep down, she knew that Camilla would tell him anyway.

"I like your direct answer; to become the beautiful lady that you are, you probably had to be very creative. However, to become a trusted friend of Camilla speaks volumes. I'm no prude, but I don't think you would be with me here tonight if you were anything less."

*****

"Let's have dinner, and I can tell you my story."

"I would love to hear all about you; thank you, James."

James filled her in, but he knew that Camilla had probably briefed her before. He thought that her free way of offering herself was a test of his moral compass, and he knew that Camilla wanted to get her feedback. As tempting as this temptress was, he was going to hold his personal desires in check, but he would have done so anyway. It was like meeting an Argentinian version of Lisa, but a woman much higher-powered intellectually and physically. It would be hard for most men to resist her advances. He could tell, by her bright aura, that she was attracted already.

"So I'm here, sitting with a British lord, who could possibly sweep any woman off into his arms, yet you are so respectful. It's funny that, in the upper classes, we love the English playing polo. Here, Spain, Cowdray Park in England, and Palm Springs in California, and yet we have had our struggles internationally."

"You mean the Falkland Islands, or 'the Malvinas,' as you call them?"

"Yes, it's strange; all that way for those small islands."

"It's principle. Those islands have been farmed by English families for years; one just doesn't take them."

She held her head back and laughed, "Oh, you Brits just love a fight: 'God and country, master of the seas,'"

She went on, "That's why, in a way, we love your traditions and values."

After a great evening of banter, James asked, "Do you know where Camilla's home is in the suburbs?"

"Of course; will you take me?"

"You'd like to go?"

"With you, anywhere."

They both got up and James felt that incredible urge to pull her into his arms, and she felt it. The two kissed each other on the cheek and then parted.

"Until tomorrow, here is my number; call me, and I will be here to escort you as your friend and confidant."

CHAPTER 16

CAMILLA'S HOME

Nicolette arrived at 10 o'clock sharp at the hotel; she chose to bring her own car, as she did not want the chauffeur gossiping to Camilla's staff about their possible romantic interlude.

"You drive in style, my dear lady."

"You should be impressed; I drive a Bentley. I love everything British, and I hope to make you part of my collection."

"Collection? You speak with such confidence!" said an astonished James, with his eyes raised at her bold statement.

"I meant every word; I thought about you all last night; you are soft spoken and very captivating. Most Englishmen I've known do not have the same approach; I can see why Camilla has fallen for you."

"It's not just that; I find her not only beautiful; she also has a magnificent mind; the two are a rare combination, don't you think?"

James was purposely pushing her buttons. Nicolette did not flinch; she knew how to get what she wanted, or so she thought.

After driving south through the suburbs, from lesser homes to nicer ones, they joined the AutoRoute.

"Don't worry; it's only another twenty minutes to her house; this is the fastest way."

"I thought you might have some devious alternative," remarked James, laughing.

"Well, you may be right; let the hours unfold!"

After taking some small side roads, they arrived at a pair of magnificent, wrought-iron gates, behind which, as they opened the gates to her code input, stretched out a long pond hosting several fountains. There was an oblong dual driveway on each side of the pond.

As they approached the house, James started to realize this was more like a small palace, a miniature Versailles in his midst. He was shocked at all the beautiful shrubbery and at the gardeners busily attending to their duties.

"Quite a place! Wow!"

"So, his Lordship is impressed; I thought you had something equally as magnificent or more," stated a slightly sarcastic Nicolette.

"Yes, but in a completely different way; this house is remarkable in its presentation and architecture; how many acres does she have?" James was obviously taken aback by this very stunning display of outright wealth.

"It's not huge, in terms of property area like an English estate; however, for this region on the edge of the suburbs, it has to be the most magnificent home, supporting around ten acres."

"Certainly large enough to encompass a home of this magnitude comfortably."

"Yes; ten acres in this part of Buenos Aires is enormous."

They arrived at the stair-stepped entrance to the front

doorway. James looked up at the beautifully carved and polished mahogany doors. Staff ran out to greet them and carry their bags to the hallway. James looked back before entering the house to view the fountains aligned toward the front gate.

Majestic, he thought. *Such a home for just Camilla and her son.*

He shook his head in amazement.

"I'm astonished. When is she ever here? And all this for two people?"

"Oh, she holds the most spectacular parties and functions for charities. She invites all the elite from here and many others in South America. They give generously to her foundation. She is devoted to the underprivileged, and she is highly respected in this country. Her husband built this home twenty years ago. She would never lavish this kind of money on a home like this, and she has talked many times about selling the property. She can well afford the upkeep, but there are few people who could, or would, afford such a spectacular home."

"I can believe that this economy would not have many such homes. Who would want a home of this size, even if they could afford it?"

"There were better times in Argentina, but not in the present-day economy. She has a unique position with her business interests. She's thought about turning the home into a resort because she spends so little time here."

"That's probably the best idea, as I'm sure she would not realize the true value that has been spent here."

They walked through the main entrance onto marble floors and under a double entrance staircase to the upper floor. James looked out under the staircase to floor-length windows that had patio doors to the rear garden. On the patio outside, he witnessed the huge swimming pool and the tiered garden that fell away to a spectacular view of the river Plate. A dream house, for sure, but, like so many fabulous homes, the staff enjoyed the facilities more than the owners.

"Well, I'm going upstairs to change into my swimsuit, so you should do the same and catch a few rays!" Nicolette invitingly exclaimed.

"Well, it's time I took some playtime, so I'll do the same!"

The staff escorted them up to their rooms, excited to have someone to care for and to take interest in a place that was so often empty.

James arrived downstairs, and, after ordering a glass of champagne, he lay out on the lounge chair in front of the pool. Not long afterward, Nicolette arrived in a jaw-dropping swimsuit that left almost nothing to the imagination.

"That's quite an outfit, my dear lady; most men would be eye-riveted to see a woman in a swimsuit like that."

"Now I have your attention, obviously. Did I do a poor job last night?"

"Not at all; you looked fabulous then, but this ups the ante."

She laughed at the attention James was giving her, while ordering her special cocktail.

"Tell me: how is it that a beautiful woman like you has not settled down with that significant other?"

"I know; I ask myself the same question."

"I can't think of a man that would not want to be with a woman like you. Confident, ambitious, fun, great conversationalist, apart from all your other attributes."

"I'm looking for an older man, eventually."

"Why?"

"Younger men would be with me, but they are too possessive, and, with my past career, they would be insecure if I didn't play by the norm for a married woman. In other words, because I'm an independent person, they would not have the same trust level."

"I don't understand."

"A woman like me has, and would end up in, arguments if I was out late at various functions with other men who know me only too well. I would be faithful, but, with my background and reputation, it's hard, and men can be very jealous, as women can be, too. An older man who is well-to-do and who has lived life would be freer and more understanding."

"How old?"

"Sixties to seventies."

"You'd throw away your life for a man of that age?" remarked a shocked James.

"Yes; I want a man that loves me and trusts me. I've been with enough men to know. I want the full package: children and a life where I'm in a position to do charity work and to be among the socialite community that I've been in for a long time."

"So, looks don't matter; you just want to be loved, and yet free to live your life without judgment?"

"Exactly."

Nicolette went on, "I've been independent too long, and I don't want my life shoved in my face every time I'm not home when I'm expected to be. That being said, I would be a devoted mother."

"Interesting; so looks are not a priority; it's the person and being loved and trusted for who you are?"

"Yes; I like what I do; the physical aspect becomes less important; I would make love, of course, to the man I love, but if I'm allowed the freedom to be me, that means everything."

"I know that would be hard on a younger man, but a man who has lived life and who is more mature could overcome that in order to have a younger woman. I can see that. I think you would have to start over, though?"

"That's not a problem; I meet people from all over the world, and I would settle down with right person and then create a new life. Leaving here would not be difficult; it's past that, I don't regret it, as it has elevated me to where I am."

"What if this man doesn't live very long?"

"I'm prepared for that; I will devote my attention to my children and to my new life, and I will take whatever comes."

"What a fascinating person you are; you are so real about life and practical, yet you are capable of a love that's deeper than the physical, truly wonderful. I suppose that living the life you have had makes people judgmental, instead of realizing that you are a beautiful woman inside and that, through your journey, you have found an insight so much deeper. People think that just because a woman has had multiple affairs, she doesn't have a heart and soul inside. You are woman like any other, with feelings, emotions, and love. You deserve all those things."

"James, the life I've lived so far doesn't mean I loved every moment of it.

"There are times I've had to do things with men that make me sick, but once you have a label, it sticks, and you are seen as something else, when inside you are still that little girl who grew up with so little and just chose the best journey you thought was available to have something. In this Roman Catholic society, which is highly hypocritical, men can do what they like, but as for women? No; there's a different standard."

"I do believe I've had an education from a woman of the world; for me it makes you all the more interesting. I can see why Camilla trusts you. I would take her advice over anyone else's. If she follows you and loves you, so will I."

With that, James ran off and jumped into the pool; Nicolette immediately followed. The couple swam up to each other and took a hard and long look before embracing. She slipped her legs between his, and he could feel the fullness of her whole being against his body. They kissed and held each other again, and then James, realizing the uncontrollable passion he was feeling, pulled himself away.

"Why did you do that?" shouted a scorned Nicolette.

"Not because of you, but I don't trust the desire I'm feeling to have you."

"I've told you Camilla won't mind; I promise."

"She may not, but I would mind; I love Camilla, and I cannot progress further; I want to be your friend and to love you in that way, to embrace you, to kiss you, but not more. We must show our loyalty to Camilla."

"James, you are the first man to reject me after I've made an advance; don't be this way; I will never come between you and Camilla."

"Nicolette, it's not you; it is me whom I don't trust. I already have feelings for you. Please know that I push away because I don't ever want to lose your friendship."

The couple swam quietly; then they played Ping-Pong; then they went to the pool table in the enormous house, giggling and laughing like school kids. There was a powerful attraction, which they both knew was there.

That evening, the staff had laid out a table by the swimming pool. James and Nicolette would enjoy the fantastic beef that Argentina was known for, along with a fine bottle of Malbec wine from the cellars below. The couple enjoyed more light conversation after enjoying a sumptuous meal. Then Nicolette started in.

"James, so Camilla is the one you want to marry?

"Yes; she's an unbelievable woman that has my admiration in more ways than I could explain."

"Do you know she's a psychic?" Nicolette thought her question might sway his opinion.

"Yes, and that's what I love about her. A mind that is so advanced and aware is her most captivating quality."

"You don't find that a little scary; how come?"

"When you come to England, you will understand the very reason why she is perfect for what I have in mind," replied James forcefully.

"You strike me as a down-to-earth type. I would never think you would be into that sort of thing. I'm intrigued!"

"Would you be surprised if I told you I have some of those abilities, but not to the degree Camilla has? She's taught me a lot, but when you come to England, you will understand why. It's a lot to explain right now, but it will all make sense; you will see."

"I can't wait; as Camilla's best friend, I will always be there for her, but, having met you, that goes for you, too.

Nicolette got up from her chair and walked over to James. She took him by the hand and motioned for them to take a walk. The couple walked hand in hand around the beautiful grounds. Below the swimming pool was a swinging sofa that looked out over the river. The two sat down together, and there they embraced and indulged each other with a long, passionate kiss. They did everything but make love. Nicolette skillfully worked her hands all over his body, and James knew he couldn't resist her advances any longer. She was too beautiful and alluring; he wouldn't make love, but the very touch of her perfumed body brought him to a climactic reaction that he felt powerless to control. He felt ashamed, at first, but then he realized that Camilla somehow wanted to share her with him. He would enjoy the moment, but there had to be a stopping point before he lost himself to a bedroom with her for the night, which he was absolutely not going to do.

"Nicolette, you are indeed irresistible; I've never met a woman like you. Wow!"

"James, thank you; I needed to feel you, and that meant a lot. I know you are Camilla's, and you have respectfully drawn the line. I am a woman; I just wanted to know that I meant something; it was personal and from my heart. I do not wish to hurt your relationship with Camilla; she trusts me, and I now know you are a man of principle. And you can be trusted also. Very few men would resist my advances; what we shared was loving and affectionate, and that's the place it should stay. I just always want to hug you and love you, even if sometimes from a distance. You are a lovely man; I hope I can meet someone like you one day."

That night, James tossed and turned; he was troubled by the thought of Camilla's close relationship with Nicolette; he thought of all kinds of erotic encounters between the three of them, and then discarded the idea as preposterous. Maybe this was going to be a different experience. He just couldn't get to sleep. Finally, he fell into a half-sleep and started to feel a soft, soothing feeling. It was Sabrina comforting all his conflicting thoughts about things that he had never encountered but that he never could see himself acting out.

"James," she whispered. "Rest; let it all go; stop trying to solve everything and do let things be; all will work out; you will see."

He finally fell into a deep slumber and didn't wake up until he received a nudge from Nicolette the next morning.

"James, come on, sleepyhead; here's a cup of tea to bring you around."

"Oh, Nicolette, how thoughtful of you; you had me thinking a lot last night!"

"Really? It's about time someone shook you out of your routine life and stop overanalyzing; nothing bad happened."

James knew Camilla would be back on Thursday, so he was going to make the best of his time with Nicolette, to enjoy the good weather, to drive around the local area, to let life play its hand, and to let go.

CHAPTER 17

A DREAM COME TRUE

Nicolette dropped James off early on Thursday morning in anticipation of Camilla's return.

Later that afternoon, as James was catching up on his business in London with Claudia, Camilla came running through the door to give him a hug.

"Oh, James, we have some exciting news to share; Roger is downstairs in my office, so let's go down and let him tell you his thoughts."

"A whirlwind tour, I bet? Good to see you guys back in one piece."

"You can say that again; Camilla has quite an operation!"

"So, what's the plan?" asked an eagerly awaiting James.

"Roger wants to buy the operation from me."

"Really?" asked a surprised James.

"James, if this meets with your approval, I would like to make an offer to Camilla for her business."

"Absolutely, but what about your work at Bannerman's?

Will that be over?"

"James, I can do both; I want to move here, and I can run the same commodity markets that I've been doing for you from here; I will get help, as they can all coordinate through here; nothing has to change."

"That's a big change. What about Kate and your kids?"

"Peter can manage, and I'll help him buy out Kate's share; then she can help me here. It can all work, James. I've worked hard for you, and you gave me the chance of a lifetime, but I have delivered, as you know. This allows Camilla to be with you. It can all work."

"Camilla, what do you think?"

"James, it's what I want, and Roger would be great at this and still oversee your financial investments at the bank," said Camilla. "Our life together means everything to me; I hope that means the same for you." Camilla was concerned about his reaction.

"Well, in fairness, you have worked hard for me, Roger, and I know you have the money; you deserve this opportunity. What the hell? Let's go and have dinner and celebrate."

James knew he had more than he could ever want, and to give Roger his head was only fair, and, not only that, it would secure Camilla's life with him.

"Camilla, that's quite a house you have in the suburbs; do you intend to sell that?"

"Yes; I can't see any use for it. I'm never there, and I'm always here, since the day Alberto died."

"Do you have another place, Camilla?" asked a surprised Roger.

"Yes; you are welcome to see it, but it's very large and about thirty to forty minutes from this office here."

"I'd like to see it." Roger was thinking of big ideas.

"Roger, it's huge," said James. "I've no idea what it's worth. Camilla what do you want for it?" James was curious about what it may have cost and what it's worth would be today.

"I know that when Alberto had it built twenty years ago, it cost him a good seven to eight million in US$, but now I doubt it would fetch that."

"It must be quite a house," remarked Roger.

"Believe me," said James. "It is a miniature Versailles, with fountains and pools on about ten acres. It's a fabulous place, but quite a staff is needed to keep it up. Nevertheless, I'm sure servants are not expensive to hire here."

"That's true, James, and they've been there for years," said Camilla. "They are all very devoted to the place."

"I'm interested," said Roger. "I want Kate and the family to be happy; if the price is right, maybe this is a worthwhile proposition."

After dinner, they retired to their quarters, and James couldn't wait to talk with Camilla about Nicolette.

*****

"I know what's on your mind, James; it's about Nicolette."

"Yes; my God, why did you set me up with such a seductive temptress? It took everything in my arsenal to resist her advances, and, on occasion, I have to say, I was very weak, but I never lowered myself to my physical desires, although I was tempted."

Camilla threw her head back, laughing, "Men! I knew she'd push your buttons, so why did you hold back?"

"You ask me that? Why, you of course? Camilla, that was very sneaky of you. I also heard that you two have been intimate before knowing me."

"It's all true; are you jealous?"

"A little; I have to be honest."

"James, you have nothing to be concerned about."

"Why test me that way, knowing she's a professional? Although I do believe she wants to settle down."

"She's my friend; I trust her. Even if you had sex with her, I still know you love me."

"Thanks for telling me that now. Camilla, this could get ugly; no man wants to be played for a fool. I'm sorry, but I'm getting angry; that was inappropriate. If that's how little you think of me, maybe we need to rethink things."

"I was available to have a romantic interlude with Roger. He's a handsome man. How do you know what really happened, other than that I'm here to change my life? So is he for the better? So, get over your misunderstood feelings and see what's in front."

"That's the point; if we start off like this, what is there in front?"

James was angry; he got up, stormed out of their suite, and descended to the bar on the main floor.

Who should come crawling up but Nicolette?

"James, what's wrong?"

"Everything. I feel set up by you and Camilla, and it's hurting our relationship. If we had sex, it wouldn't matter, and if we didn't, it doesn't make a difference. Here I am, trying to be the best version of myself, and nobody gives a damn. I feel completely taken advantage of. What should have been honest and aboveboard has turned into a sneaky prank. Camilla should have introduced you properly, and we should have all met with the best intent in mind."

"James, we had a great time; she's going to be with you! Her mind is made up, so what's your problem?"

He took a moment to think, then answered.

"I guess you are right; I'm making too much of it all. My feelings have got involved, and that's never good."

"On the contrary, it's very good. James, you take everything too seriously; we are a lighthearted people. Maybe we are a little freer in our ways, but my purpose is true, and you are a very good man; Camilla is lucky to have you. Camilla would be very mad if she knew you felt this way and very angry with me. I came to pick up my coat, which I left the other day, so return and make peace. All will be good, I assure you."

"Thanks, Nicolette; I will recompose myself. I don't give my heart easily, and you, too, are a woman that will leave a lasting impression on me. I don't play around, but I must swallow my feelings and look ahead; this has definitely been a maturing encounter, one I won't forget easily; you've helped me a lot."

"You care; I can see that. And I care, and my feelings for you are true, but that cannot cloud the love you have for Camilla."

The pair kissed and hugged, and James felt some relief; he had taken it all too seriously, and he had to let logic rise to the surface and see his interlude with Nicolette as fleeting, but a great diversion.

He arrived back at the penthouse.

"Camilla came running up and said, "James, never do that; I love you too much. There are no games here, Nicolette enjoyed your company, and I know you were both true to me. She's already called me on my way back from the airport. So don't have feelings of guilt and confusion. We are going to be together; I have dreamed of this for months."

*****

Roger got up early and went to see the house with Camilla. He was gobsmacked at the enormity of the house and its beauty. Ideas were flowing through his head like a torrent. He knew he wanted the house; it was just a question of price; he must have it evaluated in light of the current market; he asked about the schools, as he would want his children to have private education and quickly learn Spanish. It would be a huge change in his life, but one that he would welcome and one that he could now afford.

James was now getting anxious; many thoughts were also crossing his mind. He wanted the best for Roger. He knew that if he kept up his loyalty with Bannerman's, he had to let him go free. Roger had left too great a legend already and thoroughly deserved this opportunity. James would miss his advice and friendship on a near-daily basis, but it would always be there. From time to time, he and Camilla would return to her hotel, which she would keep, and this would maintain the valuable relationship they had enjoyed thus far.

"James, that place is out of sight!" exclaimed an excited Roger.

"So, you want that palace?" asked James.

"Absolutely; if the price is right."

Camilla politely left her office to let the two men talk.

"James, I realize that's an extravagant home. However, with good staff at modest costs, it could be a gem."

"Not a noose round your neck?"

"No; I would set up the house as a business, run part of it for Bannerman's and the other for the mining business."

"Brilliant; now that makes sense; then you could write off a lot of the costs, lease from the business, and write it off and depreciate the asset, if you can swing that with the government here. I'm sure they will be only too delighted to have us both represented here. Don't worry; Camilla can swing that deal."

"I'll pay her $5 million for the house, and it will cost over

$100 million for her business. That way, I'll include the house in the deal."

"What's her business worth, do you think?"

"She's cash flowing over $20 million a year right now, and, over the years with what she has received from her husband and savings, she is a very wealthy woman, not that you need her for that."

"Then if her business is that successful, will she ask for more?"

"I know, but that's where I'm going to start. She's rich enough already, and this would take a huge weight off her back."

"What if she can get more?"

"I will pay it; I want that business. I can increase the mining capacity with further investment and also with state-of-the art detection equipment. What she's got isn't bad for the sales she's doing, but, with increased production, it will easily pay for the improvements."

"I wish I could join you, another tremendous opportunity, but, this time, this one's for you; you deserve it," said a proud James, remembering their early trip to China, when Kate and Roger both met. How her fortunes have changed! And how her mother, Sarah, and her father, Victor, would be so proud!

"Okay, let's get Camilla back."

She was down the hallway, talking in Serge's office.

Camilla hastily returned to hear the news.

"All right, Roger, let her know your thoughts!"

Roger got out of his seat to politely receive her presence, and then returned to the small conference table she had in front of her desk.

"After reviewing all the figures, I am prepared to offer you $100 million, if you throw your house into the deal," he said coolly and cleverly, as he was now in his element. His genius for the deal would now go to work. He knew it was worth a lot more, but he had to start somewhere.

"Mr. Roger, I may look stupid, but my business is worth a lot more than that. I know you think I want to be with James, but I didn't help build this business up without knowing, down to the penny, what this company is worth. I have other offers that would blow yours away."

She brilliantly looked him firmly in the eye, as James started to see another side to his intended life partner.

"Well, then, pray tell me, what do you think it's worth?"

"If I stayed in here, I could easily raise this business up to at least $200 million; however, I'm not a greedy woman, and I have sufficient savings of my own already. I'm prepared to work with you, but if you want this business, you'd better be prepared to offer a lot more than that."

"All right; $125 million."

"$175 million, and not a penny less," she said sharply.

"$150 million, and that's it; not a penny more!" said an agitated Roger, thinking that this woman was far too sharp and that he had clearly underestimated her. He had tried to soften her up on their trip, and she had given the impression she just wanted out.

"I will split the difference; $162,500,000, and that's it."

Roger was prepared to go to $150 million, but this was more than he was prepared to pay. As always, he had another plan up his sleeve.

"If the house is in the deal, then yes," replied Roger. "Also, I would like you to finance $62.5 million at 4 percent, if it cash flows what your saying on the books in the first year. Otherwise, I will have a loan with you payable over five years, and I will pay 5 percent only if the cash flow is above $20 million on the unpaid balance of the loan." Roger always had to, somehow, get the better of the deal.

"James, can I trust this man?"

"With your life."

"Then, I will remember your words, and if he falls short, can you make up the difference?"

"Steady on; I'm not in this deal. My dear Camilla, Roger will see you right; I promise."

Roger and Camilla got up, shook hands, and then laughed their heads off. They both liked the challenge, and she wasn't worried for a moment, because she knew he would have to personally guarantee the loan, and she also knew he was worth a lot more money than that. He just wanted to buy money cheaply and to use his money where he could make better returns, as the opportunity arose—the same skills Roger had so brilliantly achieved with James. It was more than Roger wanted to pay, but he knew he could make the money back and pay her off earlier. It was just a way of getting something, when she had firmly gotten her way.

"Let's go downstairs and celebrate, and I want to come and see you when you're living in that fantastic home," said an excited James.

CHAPTER 18

CHANGES FOR GOOD AND SAD

The year was now 1995. James had celebrated his fiftieth birthday. James and Camilla were now married and spent their honeymoon in Bora Bora, Tahiti. They had invited close relatives and the immediate family to the wedding. Camilla's son now attended an English boarding school. James's mother and Antonio were also present at the wedding in Lincoln Cathedral. The bishop was proud to wed the couple. Everyone adored James's new bride and saw her as totally befitting his status in life. His mother and Antonio were still active for their age. Obviously, the good Tuscan air had kept them healthy. Many had become senior citizens. Sir Thomas was still active, part-time, in his law firm with his son, Alexander, but Claudia had been under the weather with a bout of flu. Kimberli was firmly in place as the group managing director. Annabelle was a step away from being behind her. Samuel was now returning from the bank in Hong Kong to join his father, having cut his teeth on the nuts and bolts of the banking and shipping businesses, or so James believed. Sir Nicholas was going through major trauma with the loss of his beloved wife, Davina. Only in her mid-fifties, she died in a sudden car accident on some icy road near Tarporley on her way home. Fortunately, she had been alone, but the injuries to her head had been too severe.

After catching up with all the news, James called Sir Nicholas, in shock.

"Nicholas, how are you doing? I just heard the news."

"Not too good, old boy. I don't get over something like this too easily; I can only imagine what you went through with Sabrina. We enjoyed a longer period of time together than you and Sabrina. It takes a moment. The kids are devastated, but it's life: one minute, you are here, and, in the next minute, you are gone."

"Camilla and I are back from Argentina. Come over to Penbroke this weekend, and let's have some good banter together."

"Sounds like a good tonic, old boy; I'll see you this Friday night. At least the business and the family keep my mind off this horrible event, and you, James—we've had a long journey together; I've always been your admirer: so much damn talent. You inspire me."

"Come on; you still know how to crack a joke; you are the best at that. Let's get the old prankster back in you."

James was shaken; he adored Davina; it was a shock. He thought about the Throne room for Nicolas, but maybe things were too fresh for that yet. So much was changing now, with Roger planning his life in Buenos Aires. He thought about Peter and the possibility of Annabelle taking over from Kimberli. Let her be free to work with Peter, and work to buy out her share with Peter, in the business to replace Kate.

At that moment, Kimberli came into James's office.

"Am I intruding, James?" she asked politely.

"No, not at all; it's time we had a little chat. So much is going on in all our lives, and a lot of change."

"Yes. Indeed, Anna is doing so well; for such a young woman, she's brilliant; you definitely have a rising star, sir!"

"How are things going between you and Peter?"

"Well, I never thought so in the beginning, but he's really talented and such a thoughtful, kind man; we have seriously been thinking about tying the knot!"

"Excellent; I have an idea: what would you think of going to work with him?"

"That's news, indeed. Roger has decided to move to Buenos Aires to take over Camilla's business, and, of course, Kate and their children will want to be with him. So maybe this is an opportunity for you?"

"Wow! We had talked about being together more. I could certainly help him out. I would miss my job here, but Anna is more than capable, and it's a great future for her."

"We are not getting any younger. I have decided to take Trans Global and the textile manufacturing business public; this will make the bank, the newspaper, and the property business less difficult to run for the next generation."

"You've built such an enormous, worldwide business now; I believe it's a good time to do that."

"Roger believes that this constant expansion won't continue forever; he sees the accumulation of world debt by the consumer getting out of hand. I think he's right. It's time to shore up and bank our money to protect our assets and minimize our risk position."

"When do you see yourself doing this?"

"By the end of this year and through to March of 1996."

"Well, Roger has certainly made a big change in his life."

"Not really; he will still run the investment side of our banking business, in conjunction with Camilla's business. We have a good staff in place; we may have to promote a few, but Roger will be the guiding light and the decision maker—with me, of course."

*****

After some time apart, it was exciting to see Sir Nicholas and James meet up once again. He had lost a lot of weight. James could see the pain he must have lived through.

"It's like good medicine, old boy, seeing you again," said Sir Nicholas. "None of us are getting any younger; we've got to prepare matters for the next generation." A happier Nicholas smiled at seeing James. Now in his late sixties, Sir Nicholas wanted to take life easier.

Camilla was excited to see Sir Nicholas after hearing so much about him from James. She was busy weighing him up, while the two shared old memories.

"Well I'm taking the shipping business and the textiles business public so there'll be less burden on Samuel and Annabelle," said James. "It's time to shore up and reduce debt; Roger believes we are in for some change." James knew that although he, too, was still able to continue on, he now wanted to spend more time with Camilla in a way he hadn't done with Sabrina.

"James, that Roger is smart," said Sir Nicholas. "As big a risk taker as he is, I would take his advice. We've all done well; I'm going to do the same with my businesses but keep my outlets private for my daughter; she has the flair, like I have, for design. My son can focus on the manufacturing side."

"Nicolas, are you wanting to get some answers from

Davina? We can go to the Throne room, if you'd like to."

"James, I will, but I'm not ready yet; it's like you felt that if I saw her again, I would feel lonely and miss her. I have to focus on my work and then slowly get myself over what happened. Like you, I'm angry, and time will only rationalize my emotions. You know I like Lisa so much; she has become such an asset to my business, and I know she's had a tough time with her boyfriend. I'm thinking seriously about her. She's a good woman, and I know she thinks the world of you, but she's loyal, and I trust her. She's down to earth and will be a great asset in working with my daughter."

"Great idea; I couldn't think of a better person to keep your spirits up and to get you back on the right road. She did it for me and look at the wreck I was."

"She's still a very pretty woman in her fifties; she keeps herself in shape and has such a great sense of humor."

"That's a good choice; get yourself out of the rut I fell into!"

The two talked away over a bottle of champagne, as Camilla went to prepare herself for dinner.

"Well, you've got yourself a hot number there?"

"You think so?" smirked a happy James.

"James, she's fabulous; she could have any man, but, of course, none so desirable as Lord James."

"You're still good for another round, Mr. Nicolas!"

"Yes, but it takes time; eye candy is great, but finding another Davina—now that's a tall order."

"Yes, I agree, but look at Camilla, completely different from Sabrina. I never thought I could find anyone like her. She has a friend called Nicolette, who likes older men, and I would hazard a guess that she would be the perfect tonic for you."

"Tell me about her."

"When Camilla went off to show Roger her other mines

in South America, Camilla had this outstanding young lady show me around. I've never been so tempted in my whole life."

"Really? You devil, tell me more."

"She's quite the operator, and a definite ten in looks and personality."

Sir Nicolas started to perk up at the thought and asked, "You think she would be interested in an old buzzard like me?"

"I will let Camilla answer that one, over dinner."

The three of them drove over to the Armoury in Lincoln. Sir Nicholas started to chat his head off with Camilla. After cocktails at the bar, the three of them were ushered to James's favorite table.

"Nicolas, I have the perfect woman for you. Not only is she my best friend; she would also be a woman you would like."

"It's a bit soon, Camilla, but if she's anything like you, who knows? Ah, I can see James has been talking to you."

"No, he hasn't, but I'm pretty good at weighing up people, especially men."

"I can see that," said a curious Sir Nicholas.

"I like you already; you are humorous and handsome, and I feel you have an eye for the ladies. You would find it hard to top my best friend."

"If she's anything like you, bring it on!" laughed Sir Nicholas, thinking maybe James could be right.

"Nothing ventured, nothing gained," said James, thinking it would not only help Camilla feel more at home in England but also that it would make Nicolette have the same kind of spark about her as Davina had.

"Do you have a picture of her?" asked an intrigued Nicolas.

"As a matter of fact, I do," said Camilla.

Camilla had the idea, and, after reading James's thoughts, she had appropriately brought a photograph over with her.

She dived into her handbag.

"There, what do you think of her?" asked a smiling Camilla, hoping to bring some happiness to Sir Nicholas.

"Wow, it doesn't get hotter than that. James, are you sure, you weren't a naughty boy?"

"I was damn tempted, but Camilla is one of a kind for me."

"Well-said, Lord James; most wouldn't," laughed Camilla.

"This woman would shake anyone's rivets; at the very least she would make a great model for my new line of clothes! How in God's name is this woman still on the market?"

"She's fussy, but she prefers older, more mature men. I believe she's just the ticket for you, but take your time; she won't be in any hurry, but it would be hard not to like you, Nicholas!"

"You're kidding! It would be hard not to like this beautiful gem. If she has the personality as well, hard not take a shot at it?"

"The four of us would have so much fun," sparked Camilla, excited at the thought.

CHAPTER 19

REVEALING NEWS

Camilla couldn't wait to call Nicolette. After she left several phone calls, Nicolette finally called back.

"How's my naughty girlfriend doing after stealing the man of my dreams?" announced an always-provocative Nicolette.

"How dare you! I found him first," claimed Camilla, laughing.

"I miss you, girlfriend; it's not the same here without you."

"As much as I am enjoying my time with James, I miss you too!"

"So, when are you coming back again? Or have I lost you for good?"

"On the contrary; would you like to come over to England and visit?"

"Like a shot!! Can I believe that you need little old me to keep you company?"

"Yes, of course; James and I want you to come over and stay a while."

"Really? to be with the woman that has everything?" Nicolette was like Sir Nicholas in a way, always teasing and joking.

"Nicki," as she always called her, "you never know what life has in store. You might like to meet some of these stuffy old Brits."

"Not if they're like James; you hit the jackpot with him." Nicolette knew that Camilla was always premeditating, unlike her own flair for the moment.

"Come on Nicki; where's your spirit of adventure?"

"I do have a number of matters I must attend to first, but the thought of seeing you two again is intriguing. Can you give me a couple of weeks? And then I will be up, up and away."

Camilla was excited at the thought of showing her long-time friend a little of how the British upper class lived.

James arrived home from London, after a quick trip to check on matters, his daughter, and his returning son from Hong Kong.

"James, I have good news. Nicki returned my calls, finally; she will be here in two weeks!"

"That's great."

"She will bring us up to date; if I know her, she's already met up with Roger."

"Roger would better watch out; Kate needs to get over there."

"Don't worry; Nicki won't do anything to jeopardize my trust; that I know."

"I'm sure I trust your intuition on that one."

"On another subject, I would like to make use of your Throne. I have so much I want to evaluate, not only for me but also for you and me," said an insisting Camilla.

"Let's not waist another moment; we will go to the Throne

room during the lunch hour and do just that!"

Camilla followed James to the Throne room, and she was slightly apprehensive, as she couldn't remember all her experiences on Atlantis.

"Gently sit on the Throne, while I pull the plugs."

It took no time at all; then she was completely gone. James waited with bated breath. As the time passed, he knew she was into deep conversation, as it normally took less than a minute.

All of a sudden, she reappeared. She was surrounded with an aura of brilliant, white light. He knew her experience had been special.

"James, I feel renewed; I have so much to tell you! Let's sit outside on the balcony of our bedroom; I want peaceful surroundings; there I can explain everything without distraction."

They made their way back to the house, where James told the staff that they needed a private moment and that they didn't want to be disturbed.

"James, that has to be the most incredible experience I've ever had; that beats all. What an incredible teleportation device that Throne is!"

"You look like a teenager again; I know how I felt," claimed James, anxious to hear of her experience.

"I arrived to see my guide; he was a tall man that I had met in another life, not in a romantic way, but which had evolved after the demise of Atlantis. He told me the following.

That this was definitely my last life before coming home and that it was amazing that I had chosen to go back to Earth. He knew my intense love for you and recognized that I was the one to stop your hard-driving will to want to continue with your earthly existence. He sees the changes you've made, and he could already see the effect I was having on you.

"Good; so, did you see your late husband?"

"Amazingly, no; I so wanted to, but apparently he's chosen life on Earth again and is already reincarnated. I didn't see anyone from my family. He did tell me that you would pass over in time, but not now. I did meet Sabrina. James, she is so beautiful; we immediately connected; what a beautiful soul she is, and she's so glad I met you."

Camilla went on, "She understands everything, and, after meeting me, she can now connect to us both."

"Was she okay with that?" asked James.

"She is so happy that I'm with you to assure your reconnection with her."

James eyes started to shed tears at the beauty and selflessness that Sabrina had always displayed.

"Sabrina is worried about Samuel; he's not working as hard as he should, and he's been with women that are not good; he's taken drugs and drink, and he's done things you would not be proud of. She wants you to come down hard on him. Otherwise, he will lure women over to England that could be bad for his future reputation. He's weaker than you, James, so she suggests that you hire a private eye to spy on him. He's been given too much freedom; your staff members know about it in Hong Kong, but they would be afraid to tell you."

"Really? I guess he's got to sow his wild oats, but the last thing I want is a reputation that could carry over into the business here. He's innocent and gullible, with too much at his disposal. It's time I had a serious word with him."

"They see me carrying on after Sarah at the Throne room, and I'm so glad that I've sold my business. You must exercise more and watch your diet. You are still young, but because you have such a passionate heart in all that you do, it could become strained, as you've put yourself through a lot already. I will live on after you. There are a lot of people to help. This

Throne room and Sarah are very necessary to accomplish that. Not that I'm here for the money, but this Throne room is going to grow beyond imagination. I can help with the business aspect of this, too. James, this is like a dream come true for my last life. I could not imagine God and you granting me such a magnificent opportunity."

"That's a lot, and a lot for me to think about. What about your son?"

"James, I know he's my son, but I was told he could be a far greater entrepreneur than his father. You don't have to worry. I have all the money to get him started in life, so that will not be on your shoulders. I see him working well with your daughter, Anna, in time, in something to do with the biotech industry. Becky could also be a huge influence, because she's already in the medical field."

"It's amazing how life evolves, isn't it? Samuel has all a young man could ever dream to have, but, as of yet, he is lacking in the personal disciplines to be great."

"Sam can be a good figurehead, but it's your daughter that has the talent you have. If she's anything like you, she won't put up with any nonsense."

"I thought that, in letting him have the freedom I didn't allow myself, he could be better. It just goes to show that it's either inside you or not. It's disappointing for a father to hear that."

"Let him prove himself; do your homework on his time in Hong Kong, and if it's what I suspect, put him in the armed forces, and let him learn the school of hard knocks; however, with his personality skills, he's going to be hard to marshal after so much privilege. God has his way of teaching us all, doesn't he?"

"It's funny how we can control so much, but not people. A

son that could have everything, yet he has so much to learn."

"Some of us must go down before we can go up."

"By God, he's the heir to the Earldom."

"Yes, but we are moving into a different era; after nearly 300 years, how many great families have come and gone? It doesn't have to be that way, James."

"I know; it's hard to plan what we want for our children."

"There's more; my fear is that if you leave him this estate, he must not have control over the finances; your daughter must control Bannerman's and keep him on a strict leash. Even though he is the heir, have your daughter own 50 percent of the estate and have control over the business; in time, if he doesn't change, he will need money, and your daughter will have to deal with that. I don't think she will want it, but, at least, she has the power to block him and to retain your heritage. He can show his best colors if he changes, but all these matters must be carefully written in your will."

"You can see all that?"

"More than that; your own guides will confirm it. I'm just preparing you, as I don't want to be seen as a designing woman that wants personal power over what you have achieved. I can have everything materially with what I have; however, I'm concerned for the Throne room, if I'm supposed to do the job well without interference."

"This a huge revelation; my only son, and this could be the outcome? Wow. I don't know whether to thank you or to have a stiff drink or to do both. You can rest assured I will not let this go without complete research into his activities. It's a shock! Material things are not the purpose, but our heritage is, and that must be maintained at all costs."

"James, this is one of the reasons that I'm with you. I don't need money and power: I have that. But what your forefathers have achieved must be preserved—and all that you've done, too."

"So, my sweet Annabelle is the one? I felt it deep down, but what father wants to denounce his own son?"

"You have plenty of time; at present, it's food for thought. I want to enjoy my time with you as long as it's allowed, because you are my greatest joy; without you, how could I have such an amazing future? After my sad time at the loss of Alberto and after your sad time at the loss of Sabrina, the sad times are somehow all there again. Your hard work and efforts will be known for centuries to come, and I will be your greatest ambassador, among others."

"That's what I must do; the pain of life is great, but no one will ever downgrade what my ancestors achieved."

*****

James was deeply disturbed about what Camilla had said about Samuel. He couldn't wait to get to the bank, and as it was Monday, he knew Claudia would stop by.

As James passed by Annabelle's office, he asked Claudia to come and sit with him.

"Claudia, tell me about Samuel. He was noticeably absent after spending the weekend at his London home."

"What do you want to know?"

"I've just got wind of some disturbing news about Samuel; what have you heard?"

"I was wondering how long it would take for the news to reach your ears. It's not good; Harold finally warned me; he was reluctant to say anything before now, as he thought it would have a reflection on him."

"I realize that it can't be easy talking about Samuel without appearing to be a sneak, but now that he's gone, I guess he feels a responsibility to inform us."

"Exactly; apparently, he showed little or no effort to learn about the bank or the textile business, and he spent many of his days going out with women from strip clubs and escort agencies, professing that he had fallen in love. Also, he was going to make the best of his time learning about the acting profession and fulfilling his desire to follow his acclaims for acting on stage at Oxford and his prior school days. This is what he wanted to do, and Harold was under strict orders not to tell anyone. Harold had wrongly thought that he would come to his senses after many long discussions. Samuel was adamant that he had no desire to follow in his father's footsteps, and, I might add, he was extremely disrespectful to the staff and to you, personally."

"By God, after dealing with my sister and now my own son and heir, what must he be thinking? That boy has had everything, nothing but the best."

"Quite a different story from your amazing daughter, Annabelle?"

"Samuel has similar qualities to those of the Seventh Earl, who did nothing but travelling around the world, collecting artifacts, and writing, but, at least, he found the Throne in the East wing! Samuel is a romantic, with dreams of personal fame in Hollywood. It's best I know now; at least I can see him tonight, if he doesn't show up here."

"I doubt he will; he complained he was tired from jet lag, and he said he wanted to catch up with some of his old school friends that went to Oxford. There's more: he apparently has developed a serious drinking habit, and Harold believes drugs are involved, too. He was seriously concerned. He hopes he won't be blamed for his behavior."

"I wish he had told you before now, but I understand his

concern. Does Anna know?"

"Yes, and she's deeply upset with him."

"Okay, Claudia, many thanks for the update; can you ask Anna to come and visit?"

"Yes, right away; it's good that you talk to her."

"My darling daughter, how are you?"

James got up to give her a hug and a kiss.

"I'm sure Claudia has filled you in on the latest," said an anxious Anna. When a family member has sad news to relate, it weighs on everyone.

"Completely!"

"What are you going to do, Daddy?"

"I must talk with him first, and then I will make my decisions from there. Anna, have you seen this pattern of behavior in him before now?"

"Yes, I thought it was just his youthful zest for life, but, left to his own devices, he lacks self-discipline and is overconfident in what he can do. In all reality, we have been apart a lot; it was only during the school holidays at home when he and I would have our moments. But even though I was so different from Sam, for the most part, we got on well. He has so much personality and humor. It's sad what's become of him. I noticed a change in him after Mother died; I believe this must have affected him more than I realized. Sam is very proud; he holds a lot inside. That's the only explanation I can give. I guess a mother's love is important for boys."

"Good thoughts Anna; well evaluated. I thought that I had given him more time as he grew older, but obviously not enough."

James caught up on the affairs of the day, and then returned to his London home in order to see Sam.

James waited and waited; hours passed by slowly, but still

no Sam. Then, all of a sudden, the door burst open, and who should arrive but Sam. He was stumbling across the living room to the kitchen.

"By God, you are drunk, so no more drink for you, young man!" shouted an angry James. "It's nearly midnight; I hoped you would have had more respect for your father, instead of arriving like this."

"Father, I don't need a long speech out of you," said Sam, slurring his words. "I just met up with my old school buddies, and we had one over the top; it's been a while."

"Go to bed! We can talk tomorrow."

Sam barely got up the staircase to his room, as James watched in silent disgust.

*****

James was up early and patiently waited for Sam to appear. He thought deeply about all that had been said over his morning tea and toast. It was nearly nine before Sam came down in his pajamas.

"I've fixed you your tea; it's cold, so heat it up in the microwave."

"Thank you, Dad; take some aspirin and then come and sit with me."

James wanted to start gently, and, with all that he was feeling, he wanted to control his anger.

"Well, the cat's out of the bag now, isn't it?" moaned a hungover Sam.

"Yes, indeed. Why, in God's name, did you hang out in Hong Kong, feeling the way you do?"

"I had to experience things first, Dad; then I realized this is not for me—stuck in an office doing numbers. Money has no interest for me, or business, for that matter."

"So, give up, just like that?"

"I gave it a few months, but then I started to dread going to work. Harold tried, but, with all his efforts, he never gave up, always giving me the latitude to reconsider. I'm more interested in the arts, in acting, in teaching the classics, in music, and in sport. You know I'm an okay student, but my heart is not in what you do."

"One day, you will be the Eleventh Earl; how are you going to run an estate if you feel like this?"

"I know, Dad, but, by then, I will have matured. The force in me to want to be an actor is too great. I'm sure this is a great disappointment to you, isn't it?"

"So, are you happy for your sister to own and control matters?"

"If it's better for the future of the family, I'm okay with it. Who can live up to your achievements?"

"That's not necessary; it's a question of maintaining what we have. You have leadership and authority; you proved that in school. Why walk this crooked path and lose your inheritance?"

"I've got to find my own way; things have come easily to me. I know I'm spoilt and need challenge, but this way of life, your world, is not for me."

"You didn't need to waste two years to find that out. I understand you led an existence with women, booze, and God knows what else. Have you no consideration for the reputation of your family?"

"I was lost, not knowing how to face you, being the disappointment I am now. I felt lonely, and a fish out of water. I did everything to escape the day today."

"Do you realize that, without all the support you've had, it would have been impossible to live the playboy lifestyle you've managed to acquire?"

"I felt free for a while, and then I realized how self-indulgent I've been."

"So, what's it going to be?"

"If you agree, I would like to go to an acting school like RADA, the Royal Academy of Dramatic Art, to gain my accreditation, and to go from there."

"Was Oxford a waste of time?"

"Yes, Dad."

"Check it out; stay here for now. I will seriously cut your allowance, and if there's any more report of your immoral behavior, you will be on your own until you develop some personal self-control."

James went on, "I must be off; I've people to meet. Go into action right away; there's no more time to mess around. Work hard at this, and you will gain my respect, but, more important, your own."

When James arrived at the bank, he talked with Claudia and Thomas about hiring a personal detective in order to keep a watchful eye on his son. He also made arrangements with Anna to cut Sam's allowance and to have his bank statement sent to their bank. He was determined to monitor his progress. As much as he wanted to share his disgust with all that he had been trusted, he felt it was useless at this stage. He would be careful so that he could keep the door open for further discussion. James thought this was not the end, but the beginning, of truly trying to understand his son. He was young and immature, and mistakes had been made, but he would give him the opportunity to come to his senses.

A tired and dejected James arrived back at Penbroke and into the loving arms of Camilla, who was anxious to hear the news.

"James, how was it with Sam?"

"Not good; I saw no sense in getting angry and belligerent; I accepted his request to attend acting school. He will soon learn that whatever you do in life takes every ounce of effort to become successful. So, let's see how he does, and how he can show me that he can be competent at something."

"Very wise; he's got a lot to learn, James, and he's still young enough to redeem himself. It takes a lot to build an empire, and even more to run it. He's probably overwhelmed at the thought. If he can do well, he can still play a part in the business and still carry out the role of being an earl in time. I've yet to meet your children, but when I do, I will tell you more."

"Let's go out, my love, and have an evening with some laughter and fun; enough of all this heavy stuff; life will determine the future, won't it?"

CHAPTER 20

NICOLETTE

James and Camilla anxiously awaited the arrival of Nicki at London's Heathrow Airport. After passing customs, she finally appeared in all her finery. She naturally attracted the view of all the onlookers, as she made her grand entrance.

"Nicki, you made it!" shouted an excited Camilla.

Nicki, as always, looked incredible. After hugging Camilla, she came to James, and as she hugged him, she whispered, "How's my sexy man?"

James automatically blushed. Then he remarked, "How can you travel eighteen hours and look this good?"

"Inspiration, darling; I couldn't wait to see you both."

She winked, with her normal, teasing ways.

James whisked them both off in his Bentley to his London home. Nicki could then get some much-needed rest after her long flight. Nicki sat in the front seat next to James. He noticed that she was wearing a very high-cut dress, with a mink jacket. It was now fall, and although it was a beautiful day, the English weather could be changeable. He thought that Sir Nicholas would definitely take a second look at this magnetic woman.

"I'm truly looking forward to seeing your world, my Lord, and I want to ride one of those fine horses you have,"

She was already up to her high jinks!

Camilla was laughing her head off, but she knew how much she trusted James. She found it fascinating to see how British men were politely awkward around a beautiful woman—very different from men of her own culture.

They all chatted away, until they passed by Harrods department store on their way to his home.

"Now, James, that's a store I want to visit; that's on my wish list. We used to have one in Buenos Aires, but nothing like the one in London!"

Camilla laughed, as James thought, *Here we go!!!*

"Your wish is my command!"

"So, can he spoil me, Camilla?"

"Of course," she remarked, just to see how James would respond.

"I must have something to remember for my trip, your Lordship."

"I can see that." He wondered what else she would want before she left.

Nicki loved the townhome. As James carried her luggage to the bedroom, she followed him to her quarters; then, as he was about to leave, she came up to hug him and to give him a kiss. James was a little shocked at her forwardness, but he played along.

"Well, you know where I am; if you get lonely, I shall always welcome a visit."

Yeah, right, he thought, as he gently closed the door of her bedroom behind him.

Camilla was downstairs, fixing a snack for them.

"Is she always like that?"

"Oh, that's Nicki; take no notice; she's just having fun teasing you."

"You could have fooled me."

"You find her attractive, don't you?"

"Yes; who wouldn't?" said an aroused James.

"I love to see the way she plays you."

"You are not jealous, are you?"

"Not in the least. I know you love me, James."

"Thank God for that!"

James and Camilla decided to let Nicki rest. It was midafternoon, so they would let her take her time, and if she was up, they would take her out for the evening.

James thought about the Fantasy Bar, now called the The Trend Setter, under new management. It had been remodeled after twenty-five years, but it was still a favorite hangout for the elite. Then they would go to Harrods the next day and spoil Nicki. James booked a table, knowing Nicki was the type to go out at night.

*****

Sure enough, after James had dozed off, while Camilla went to do some grocery shopping, Nicki showed up.

"So, what's the plan, young man? Are we going to hit the town?" She was up and alert in her chiffon nightdress, and she wanted to make a cup of coffee.

"I've booked a table at a chic place, where we can dance and eat, around 8.00 p.m. Are you ready to deck yourself out?"

"Absolutely; where's Camilla?"

"She's out shopping; she'll be back shortly."

"So, we are alone—even better. I've thought a lot about you,

James: the time we were together. There's not many men like you in the world. Do you know someone that could put up with a woman like me? I know I can be intimidating, but it's just my way; don't take me too seriously. However, when it comes to you, I do have a weak spot. Lucky Camilla, but she's a lovely woman; I'm so happy for her."

"How about you? Have you found your one-and-only?"

"I'm a hard woman to please, so if you know a fine English gentleman, I'm all yours. I miss Camilla terribly, so who knows? I can adapt."

"I do know a fine English gentleman; he lost his wife some months ago, and he needs cheering up; I think you could be the person. I'll let Camilla fill you in; she will have a woman's opinion."

At that moment, Camilla walked in with her shopping and said, "So I see you guys are busy chatting away."

"I've booked a table at a great place for eight o'clock. Nicki is up for it, so, hopefully, you are, too, my dear."

"That's sounds like fun, of course."

The three of them took a taxi to the restaurant on the King's Road.

As they entered, heads started to turn. The new owner knew who James was, although they had never met. He sat them at a table close to the dance floor. The renovations were incredible. James always thought that the dance floor was too big and that the tables were too small. It was now more in keeping with the times, and the acoustics were greatly improved. Much to his surprise, in the far corner, he could see Sir Nicholas, who had taken the evening to spend the night out with Lisa.

He walked over to invite him to his table.

"Good to see you out! Nicholas, this is what you need."

"Fancy seeing you here," said Sir Nicholas.

Then he got up to whisper, "How in God's name do you meet these women?"

"I don't know. They seem to find me!"

Lisa was excited to see James and meet his new wife.

"James, I'm so glad to see you looking well."

They both chatted, as they walked over to meet James's two anxiously awaiting women.

"Well, this calls for a celebration," said James, as he ordered his favorite Crystal champagne.

He purposely sat Sir Nicholas next to Nicolette, but he made sure he didn't offend Lisa, as she sat on the other side. James sat in between Nicolette and Camilla.

After a few drinks, Sir Nicholas got up to dance with Lisa. Camilla now had her chance to tell Nicki all about Sir Nicholas.

"He's older, but, on first appearance, he looks like fun, and he is still a handsome man."

"And a very wealthy one at that," James chimed in. "Now that's your dream man, if you like women's fashion."

Camilla got her up to speed. Although she hadn't been to Sir Nicholas's home, she knew about his business affairs.

"What about the lady he's with?" asked Nicki. "They look good together."

"She's his number-one person in his retail fashion shops. Lisa knows what he's been through with the loss of his wife, and they would be having a night out to talk business and have a good time, as Lisa is a valuable asset and a hard worker in his business."

When they returned, James and Camilla got up to dance.

"What do you think, Camilla?" asked James. "Are they suited?"

"It's early days, but I think he's a little overwhelmed, first at the shock of this encounter and also not wanting to hurt Lisa's feelings."

"I know Nicholas, and as much as I respect Lisa, I know she's a good person, but Nicholas's background is different, and Nicki, I think, would be a better bet. That being said, I don't know Nicki like you."

"I think you're right, but Nicki can be hard to read when it comes to choices," said Camilla, thinking deeply about the subject.

They all sat down to dinner, and it would be interesting to see if Sir Nicholas would ask Nicki to dance.

"James, I feel so privileged to have an opportunity to see you again after your difficult time when Sabrina passed away," said Lisa. "You are back to your old self, and I can only think that Camilla has played a big role in that." Lisa spoke in a polite way, eyeing up Camilla.

"Thank you, Lisa," remarked James. "Camilla has lived through a similar situation, so our meeting on our cruise to Australia with my kids changed my life, in a way. You also played a role in coming out to see me at my worst." James wanted to give her full credit for her kindness and her loyalty.

They all started conversations in order to know Camilla better and her best friend, Nicki. James saw how enamored Sir Nicholas was with Nicki, as he was busy trying to understand how she knew Camilla.

After the dinner, Sir Nicholas asked Nicki for a dance. James waited his turn to ask Lisa. It was slightly awkward with five people, as James didn't want to leave anyone alone at the table without a dance partner.

James then got up, as Nicholas returned, and he saw how well they were getting on.

"Camilla, do you mind if I ask Lisa for a dance?" asked James politely.

"Not at all; you guys have some catching up to do. I'm so enjoying the evening."

"James, you certainly know how to pick 'em," she said, in her sexy cockney accent. "Where do you find two women that are so elegant, and smart, too?"

"Thank you; I'm so glad that we're all together. Isn't it time we met up, Lisa? I owe you. You were a godsend at a very critical time in my life, and I will never forget that."

"This Nicki, she's a ball of fire. I hope Nicholas likes her; he needs someone after all he's been through."

"Do you really think she would be a good bet for him?" asked James, carefully treading the waters of where her affections might lie.

"James, thanks to you, I have experienced a fantastic career with Nicholas. I have someone else in my life I care about. I've been seeing Nicholas when he's in town, but I'm just there to cheer him up; as much as I care and respect him, he's also great company. I wouldn't want to hurt my job. Maybe this young lady could be good for him, as she's a good friend of Camilla. I really like Camilla's disposition; apart from her beauty, she seems so calm and intelligent. Good choice, James."

"Thank you, Lisa; you are very good at sizing up people. I welcome your thoughts. I guess it's all about chemistry. Davina was great, and I know Nicholas likes an extravert woman, so who knows? Nicki might be the right person."

"Nicki's not only beautiful; she's also a bundle of energy. I think you could be right."

They returned to the table, while Sir Nicholas and Camilla went to dance.

As the evening went on, they all took turns to dance, and

they enjoyed the opportunity to know James in his new life.

It was a chance encounter, thought James.

He would get with Nicholas later and see what he thought of Nicki.

*****

The next morning, James couldn't wait until he phoned Sir Nicholas to pop the question, "So Nicholas, what do think of Nicki?"

"A real smasher; she'd light up any man's fire. Is she on the market, or am I fantasizing?"

Camilla took the phone and then answered, "Nicki does want to settle down. She's a socialite, but she would like to settle down and get married. Because she's such a dynamic force in the political and social world in South America, she's had many opportunities. She's no fool when it comes to men, and she doesn't trust easily. To answer your question, she wants a more personal life, with the hope of having a child, and as we are like sisters, she would like to be closer to us."

"I like a challenge, and she could be helpful in promoting my clothing line. She's a natural for modeling, and I can see that women would like her look, especially in the Asian and European world. Definitely food for thought."

James then took the phone back and said, "If you'd like, come over to Penbroke; we will be there tomorrow."

"I have a thought. Why don't you come over to Tarporley? It might give Nicki and Camilla, especially, a change."

"Great idea; we will be there Saturday, late afternoon," said James.

"Splendid," remarked Sir Nicholas.

James felt that Sir Nicholas was starting to be excited and that he looked forward to the occasion.

"I do believe that Nicholas is interested. What do you think, Camilla?"

"He's still a fun person to be with and never at a loss for words. He's older, but he has so much youth in him, so who knows? She could have any man, but he's successful and accomplished, and life is all about timing. I believe it could work. She'll get a kick out of his fashion world. She would be in her element, and she could be helpful to him in design and in what women like. She has a sharp eye."

"There's no doubt that she has had a hard life and that she got to the top, educated and elegant and that she would certainly be, I believe, of great value to him in business and socially."

The next day, as promised, James took Nicki shopping, then left them. They were in the right part of London for that; in addition to Harrods, there were countless other stores that would catch her eye.

It was time for Nicki to be with Camilla; James gave his credit card to the couple so that they could share some girl time and catch up on their lives to date. He said he would join them for a late lunch after attending to business. From there, they would take the helicopter to Penbroke to spend the evening after a hectic week.

Naturally, Nicki was having the time of her life, as the helicopter made its way across the sights of London to his home in the north.

*****

They all went to bed early, after a busy day. James got up to have breakfast, and then to take Nicki riding.

Camilla lent her riding attire to Nicki; she was of similar size, and it would make the experience more enjoyable.

There's nothing worse than riding a horse with the wrong clothes. She was used to the English style of riding, but it took her a moment to get comfortable. The couple wandered down to the beach.

"James, it's all so beautiful; what an amazing life you have!" shouted Nicki to James, as the wind gusts were stronger than usual.

"It's been a while since I went out riding; I'm so glad you're here; it's not Camilla's favorite pastime, but you have more of the tomboy in you."

Then he shouted, "Are you ready for a good gallop?"

"Bring it on, Lord James; I'll give you a run for your money," said Nicki, laughing with joy. James felt that, somehow, as great as her life had been in Buenos Aires, she had become tired of it. She needed challenge and a new outlook on life.

Now he was going to see how much measure there was to this woman. He was riding his favorite horse, Bullet, who was now older in his years, and Nicki was riding a young, English, thoroughbred mare, which was being trained to race. She was on a horse that she had no clue about.

Let the games begin, thought James.

He gradually let Bullet out into a canter and then a gallop; he shot off and kept a careful eye on Nicki. The mare, called Black Fighter, got the message, and, to his amazement, she started to catch up . . .

"James, this horse is crazy; I've never ridden this fast!"

"Catch me if you can," he said, laughing.

They ran a good mile, and she stayed with him.

"By God, woman, you can ride!"

James slowly brought Bullet down to a gallop and then to a walk. Black Fighter was not going to have it and shot out in front. James wasn't sure whether she had control or not, but she was still up there, as she slowly brought the mare to a walk.

"James, that's a thrill; what magnificent horses you have," she said, laughing. But James could see that this woman knew how to ride. Not many could take out a blood horse and contain her mount in the way she had done.

They turned their horses around, and James started to talk.

"Not your first rodeo, my dear; does that tell me a lot about you?"

"I do have horses of my own, but not as close to a beach like this. What a lovely ride this is, so fluent and powerful. I can feel she loves every moment; it's so exhilarating to breathe this salt air and to oxygenate our bodies."

"Come alongside, now that we have the wind at our backs; it's easier to talk. Can you tell me more about yourself and your intentions for the future?" asked James, weighing up a different Nicki, who was obviously competitive and who seemed fearless at the opportunity to ride a horse like Blacky.

"James, I doubt there's many men available like yourself, but my clear intent is to find a man that I can settle down with, as I'm in my late thirties. It's time for me to change direction, as I do so want a child of my own. I've done well for a woman from the school of hard knocks, and I can comfortably live alone; however, as much as I've enjoyed the social agenda, I want to live a more purposeful life. I've done my part with charities and will always enjoy my time in helping others. It's hard for us independent-minded women to find the right person."

"Explain that, will you?"

"I can't say all, but Latin men are very controlling and are programmed to more submissive women. It's okay for the man to fool around, but we have to maintain a different standard. Nicholas seems like fun. I've had my time with wild romance, and I am looking for a relationship that's lasting and where I'm not suffocated. I've put up with too much jealousy from wanting to be possessed; I don't see those qualities in you, and although Nicholas is a lot older and probably not at his best after the loss of his wife, I see a spark there. It would be so great for all of us to be friends, as I know you and Nicholas seem to have a lasting friendship over many years."

"True, but in my early days, Nicholas was quite a sparring adversary. With time, a mutual admiration has grown between us; his advice has been invaluable to me; he's like an older brother."

James continued, "Are you ready to go and see him tomorrow? I think going today is too much; it's a long drive; we could, of course, take the helicopter, but there's a lot here to absorb first, and as you can see, this is quite a different way of life from London and city living."

James looked into her eyes and could see the brightness of her aura. He couldn't deny the attraction he felt.

"James, do you feel like I do?"

"If it's what I sense coming from you, the answer is yes."

"I don't know how to get you out of my mind; it's so powerful and real, and yet, in the same breath, it could be something that could hurt all of us. I love Camilla, as I know you do. Seeing you again is even more intense than the feelings I believe we both had at Camilla's home."

"The strange part, which I don't understand, is that Camilla is not jealous in the least. Camilla has an insight and perspective that I've never known in another woman. You two are very different, and as much as I hate to admit this, it's as though the three of us are connected with a force I have yet to understand."

"I know. But talking with you and the two of us understanding that reality are so amazing."

James could see her eyes watering up; it was clear her feelings of love were true, yet who could ever understand such a crazy notion?

"James, my fear, and you know I'm outspoken, is how this can work for the future, knowing how we both feel about each other."

"That's a tough one; knowing what I feel for you, I could take you off that horse right now, and take you!"

"If only we could! Let's dismount and hold hands, and if I can kiss you, it would make my heart flutter with joy," begged an inviting Nicki.

"My thoughts are that if we did make love, would that decrease our feelings or intensify them?" James was quivering at the thought, as the energy passing between them was so powerful it took all his restraint to hold back.

They slowly trotted over to a patch of grass, where the horses could graze, while they held the reigns and dismounted.

Taking off their hats on the empty side of the beach, the two held each other with passion, flinging their arms around one another. They kissed intensely for a moment that was intoxicating.

Then James pulled away, as Nicki started to open his britches.

"Not now Nicki; we have to figure out our feelings. I'm not ready to do this!"

"I understand James," she said. She was so ready to make unabandoned love, but this was not the time or the place.

"Nicki, I do care, but I have to work this out."

"I know you do, James; forgive my feelings; what I wanted to express just got the better of me!"

They kissed again, and then remounted their horses and returned to the stables. James now knew that he was at a crossroads of an attraction he'd never experienced with such intensity before in his life.

*****

They arrived back to the house, where Camilla was busy fixing a midday snack for the three of them.

"So, you naughty couple, how was the ride?" asked Camilla, knowing, by the color of their auras, what had happened between Nicki and James. She could see the glassy eyes of Nicki and James trying to regain his composure and feeling a sense of guilt he couldn't hide.

"It was exhilarating, to say the least!" exclaimed Nicki.

"Old hat for you James, as you've been on the beach so many times before."

Camilla showed a smirk, which was making the couple uncomfortable.

"Come on; a little horseplay never hurt anyone." said Camilla, laughing, relieving the tension. She wasn't fooled for a moment, but she knew that this would be a challenge that James had to grow from.

"Camilla, do you think that Nicki would be ready to sit on the Throne?" asked James, thinking that, therein, may lie the answer to his thoughts.

"Yes, I do; she's a very free and a very advanced soul, and it was a suggestion I was going to recommend."

"What do you think, Nicki?" asked Camilla.

"I know you've told me a little about this Throne; perhaps it would do me a lot of good and answer questions for my life's direction," she answered apprehensively. But, being a woman of courage, she was always up for the challenge.

The three made their way over to Sarah's office. James knew the Throne room would be shut down until 2:00 p.m. for lunch, so the timing was perfect.

"Sarah, please meet a great friend of Camilla, Nicolette; she wishes to take to the Throne. So, we are here for your blessing."

"A pleasure to meet you, Nicolette, and such a beautiful lady, too. Can you please come over here and be seated, while I check out your chakras?"

"I would be delighted to," said Nicki anxiously.

"You are nervous, and that's natural; calm yourself by taking deep breaths, holding them, and slowly letting them out."

As Nicki started to calm herself, James could see how bright her aura was becoming, and Sarah was studying her energy field intensely.

"My dear, you are a beautiful soul; you are aligned, but you have yet to understand the spiritual world. This will be an experience for you. I can see you've been too busy in our world of the day-to-day. You are more than ready for what you will learn, and I'm here to advise you afterwards, although Camilla can also help you as well."

Sarah and Camilla could see that her chakras were aligned but that her colors were deeper, so they knew this would brighten her outlook from the material world that she had worked so hard to rise up from in life to make something of herself.

As Nicki sat on the Throne, she worked hard to keep calm; this was a completely new experience for her. It took a moment for her to release herself. Then, all of a sudden, to everyone's joy, she was gone.

James then joked, "Well, we don't have to worry about

sending her back to Argentina, do we?"

They all laughed, as Camilla said, "I can't wait to hear her news."

She took over a minute to return, and as Camilla knew Nicki, she would have questions beyond questions, as talkative as she was.

All of a sudden, she gently reappeared, as the enormous energy surrounding her dissipated. She sat there for a moment, and, unlike her normal self, she was quiet, processing all that she had experienced.

"I have so much to tell you all; I don't know where to begin. Who could ever believe that this would be possible? I could get on that horse of yours, James, and gallop for miles, I have so much energy!"

"Nicki, if I may call you that, this Throne has helped so many people to see life differently," responded a polite Sarah. "Please share your thoughts. I realize you probably have private information to share with Camilla and James, but your experience overall is always helpful to learn and understand."

"Yes, of course; what amazed me was seeing obviously my guide, who is a woman, and seeing my parents. Brought up with modest means, I was so excited to see how much I was loved. In life, we had so little that my parents were very strict; I didn't have some of the things others did, and I was embarrassed. This made me feel inferior, not understanding and appreciating all the good things they did do. As a result, I became a staunched feminist and, in later years, very mistrusting of men. I recognized I was attractive, and men were very anxious to meet me. I sensed their reasons, and I became very manipulative in order to get a good education and find a determined way to climb the social ladder. I had not seen myself as I truly am. As I'm older, I'm starting to feel this more, and, of course, by meeting Camilla socially over the years, we grew closer, and that has changed my outlook enormously. It's such a profound experience that I cried; the love and the beauty of what is above us is breathtaking."

Nicki started to cry, which was a rare emotion for her to share publicly. She had so much to release, and this was the first time in her life.

"Nicki, I've always felt that and saw that in you, and I realized that your provocative and teasing style was a coverup," said Camilla. "But, in truth, I enjoy that side of you; it's how you cope with life." Camilla was feeling a lot of emotion at seeing Nicki so overjoyed.

"Well, I'm so glad you experienced the beautiful person you are, not only physically but also inside too!" declared Sarah. "There's no way you could have travelled the vortex if that was not truly within you." She was always fascinated to listen to the many experiences she had learned over the years.

"I believe you have much to share with Camilla, so I will let you all go, and it was such a pleasure to meet you, Nicki. Please come and see me anytime you wish to have an outside opinion."

The three of them left and returned to the main house. Camilla and Nicki went to the drawing room to have girl talk. James wanted to call Sir Nicholas and to make the afternoon tea.

"Nicholas, is it okay if we come tomorrow?"

"Everything all right old boy? I guess it must be hard when surrounded by two beautiful women. Yes, of course, I planned to take Monday off, so you can all stay over."

"Great; see you around midday, and I'll bring the champers!"

"Excellent idea! Can't wait to see you over here; it's been too long."

James brought in the tea and the afternoon snacks to the busy women, who were talking in their native Spanish.

"Can't understand a damn word!" said James. "Time, I learned; just know enough to be dangerous, Nicki." James woke them up from their in-depth discussion.

"Carry on; don't mind me."

They continued talking, as James poured the tea and placed the available cakes and biscuits in front of them. Camilla finished her tea, then got up to leave.

"I'll let you two naughty kids talk, as I know Nicki has a lot to share with you, too. I want to change out of these clothes and to take a nice, long bath, as I'm sure we will eat out."

"Yes, and I called Nicholas, so he's expecting us tomorrow, as it's a lot to do in one day."

"Sounds great."

James couldn't wait to hear what Nicki wanted to tell him.

"Another cup, my dear?"

"Yes, please." Nicki eyed him with a spirited look.

"James, I cannot thank you enough for that experience; it was an eye-opener. No one would believe that you have such an incredible device in order to understand that there is truly something beyond our lives here."

"Every time I return, I learn more; it takes some getting used to."

"I met your incredible first wife; she's so beautiful. She didn't stay long. She told me how happy she was that you and Camilla are together. She knew me in a previous life, but we were not close. It was in the time of the French revolution; I was a courtesan. I guess that explains my life now, a little. I was advised to take marriage and to have a child, as it would change my outlook tremendously, and it's something I've wanted for so long! I'm sure you know we are all from Atlantean times; it's why we all feel such a connection."

"I felt that, but as you were not knowledgeable of those matters, I didn't express that."

"You and I have been together, but in more modest circumstances, so that's why we have the feelings we do. Camilla knows that, as she's very intuitive about all those things, as you know."

"It's as though we are all meeting up to move onto a higher purpose."

"Exactly; I've never delved into the more-spiritual side of life; only knowing Camilla and her brilliance has started to open up my understanding. Otherwise, I could never experience such a magnificent opportunity. We've all grown a lot since those times."

"So, have we been intimate before?"

"Yes; very much so, and we were, and are, extremely compatible, but Camilla is the one to take you to the place you've never been. I only hope that, by knowing a Camilla and you, I, too, can reach that level of understanding."

James was very moved by her modesty. It was a part of Nicki he hadn't felt before.

Nicky continued, "On a physical level, we are extremely attracted, and Camilla knows that, and I honestly doubt that I could be as objective as she is. Mentally, she is more than your equal, and it's that which is your direction. She has a tremendous future for your Throne room, and when she really gets going, which Sarah welcomes, your place here will grow phenomenally. She has so much knowledge to impart. She's here for you, and for so many others."

"It all makes complete sense; meeting you really threw a wrench into my feelings, because I would never believe, even with Camilla and now with you, that I could feel this way again."

"The irony is that we would probably be a better couple, but it's bigger than that, and I can see why I've found it so difficult to meet the right person; our love was, and is, very special," said Nicki, with great emotion.

"But that's the way it must be. That being said, it would be hard not to love you; just know that that's the way it will always be."

Nicki started to tear up and stretched out her hand. James pulled her up to give her a hug. He thought that the feelings of their hearts were true and that as much as he wanted to believe it was an infatuation, he now knew that he was wrong.

They all went to Horncastle, James's favorite restaurant, for an evening meal; then they turned in early for another busy day at Sir Nicholas's home.

CHAPTER 21

TARPORLEY

After they had breakfast, they packed some overnight luggage. They all piled into the helicopter. It was a pretty ride over the English countryside toward Tarporley. James had told his pilot to look out for a castle this side of the village. The helicopter ride wasn't long—about twenty-five minutes. James sat in the front, while Camilla and Nicki could view another part of England. He told the pilot, from his GPS, that it was several miles east of Tarporley off a lane known as Barrington and that he would easily see the Barrington Estate from the air, as it was a castle.

"Oh, look over there, Camilla; there's a castle in the distance. Can we fly over it, James?"

"Indeed, we will fly lower to take a closer look."

As they got closer, the women looked at the old building.

"James, do you know who lives there?" asked Camilla.

"Yes, I do; as a matter of fact, you are about to meet its owner."

The surrounding countryside was more open, with fewer trees than there were in Penbroke. It had a unique beauty of its own. The estate looked immaculate, as only Sir Nicholas would have it. His eye for perfection was well known, all the way down to the stitching on the hem of a dress.

"Oh, we are going to land; is this appropriate?" asked Nicki. "It looks very private and well cared for."

Once the pilot had found the landing pad, he set the helicopter down.

"James, do you know this person?" asked Nicki again.

Nicholas had heard the sound of the helicopter and had sent over his new chauffeur to pick up the landing party. The blades started to slow, and it was now safe for everyone to disembark. The women were holding onto their hair, as the blades slowly turned. They could also see a Rolls arriving, to collect them.

"James, you never told me Nicholas owned a castle; I knew he probably had a beautiful home, but this is beyond magnificent," remarked Camilla.

"So my lady of vision is surprised; at least I can do some things without you, knowing them before you see them." He laughed at their shock and excitement.

The chauffeur ushered them to the awaiting car and then collected all their baggage. James had told the pilot to meet them around 4:00 p.m. on Monday for their return.

"James, what a place to come and visit; you are a devil keeping us all in suspense," said a laughing Camilla.

They drove round the perimeter of the castle and then entered across the drawbridge and into the front courtyard. James could only remember the last time he was there with Sabrina. He could feel her presence, and that brought many memories flooding back into his mind.

This time, Sir Nicholas stood at the front doorway, dressed in his tweed suit, proud to see them all at a home that he had manicured and loved.

"Well, ladies, welcome to my humble abode." After all the hugs, which Sir Nicholas loved doing to the ladies, he walked them into the front lobby.

"No place like home," said Nicholas, proud of all his years of work and renovation to make his old castle the spectacular place it had become.

"Nicholas what a place, and how beautifully you have made the décor within the house in keeping with the castle," said a stupefied Camilla at such a magnificent and palatial place for anyone to live in.

"James knows me well; since he was last here, I have meticulously collected artifacts from many places to enhance the period and the history of the time when this castle was originally built," announced Sir Nicholas proudly. "It's been a hobby of immense pleasure."

"What period of English history would this castle have been built?" asked a curious Nicki, with eyes looking upon this place of antiquity with astonishment that people still lived in homes like this in the modern day.

"Around the turn of the of the fifteenth century, after Henry VII won at the Battle of Bosworth in 1485 and united the Lancastrians and the House of York by marrying Elizabeth of York. He was anxious to maintain law and order, especially in the northern part of England, where the loyalty to the Roman Catholic Church was still very strong. I won't continue, as I'm sure you are possibly not up on English history. It was a period of time when the nation was sick of the war between the two houses of York and Lancaster, known as the Wars of the Roses. His marriage combined both houses, known today as the House of Tudor. The red rose of Lancaster and the white rose of York became their emblem. I treasure this castle, my refuge, in a time where peace was hard fought for."

"How brilliantly you have captured this period in your history, yet I'm sure you have combined it with all the comforts of modern-day living," answered an intelligent and observant Nicki.

"Yes, we Brits love our history and work hard to maintain it; as with all nations, we've had our ups and downs; nevertheless, we have survived so far!"

Sir Nicholas took them all on a family tour, and, much to his amazement, he was gratified by all the questions he was asked by Camilla and Nicki.

It was now later in the day, so Sir Nicholas had arranged a magnificent dinner to be served in the Great Hall; he had brought in staff to give the atmosphere of those bygone times. Having a great meal was in keeping with the surroundings.

After all the guests were shown to their respective rooms, they all gathered at the long refectory table, with its gleaming candelabras.

"I do believe a toast is in order, so, to my dear and best friend, Lord James, his new wife, Camilla, and not without mention, the beautiful Nicolette, welcome to Barrington Castle! May your time here be as joyful as the many years that I've spent in this great home—to God and Country!"

"Here, here," they all shouted, and then clapped. Nicholas had seated them in a way that he and Nicki were opposite to James and Camilla. He could take time to be closer to Nicki, whom he was eyeing with great admiration.

After the meal, Nicholas stood up and asked Nicki to walk out onto his veranda so that they could take time to talk and get to know each other more intimately. James and Camilla went for a short walk outside, to catch the evening air before departing to bed.

"Do I see that Nicholas is taken with Nicki?"

"Yes, indeed," she said, with a twinkle in her eye. "I do hope they get on. It would be so great to have her here, and I know you would want that, too, James."

"There's nothing I can say that you don't know already, but you have your feelings, too."

"Yes, I do; we know each other too well."

They laughed and kissed.

*****

The sun rose on the rear lawn, and as James remembered, the castle looked west toward the village. He and Camilla rose early to have tea and then to take a long walk together. They had no idea how Nicki and Sir Nicholas were getting on, but they knew they would hear all about it later.

"James, you know I don't mind you being with Nicki; she adores you, so don't feel guilt and embarrassment," said Camilla, finding the appropriate time to open the discussion.

"I know, and it's that which amazes me; I feel guilty in what I feel towards her, yet you don't seem to mind in the least."

"James, you have something to learn; we don't choose whom we have feelings for. It just is."

"I know, but we are married, and I feel that it's wrong to be around someone I want to have in a way that violates our vows."

"I agree, but that's the indoctrination of this world; we don't control whom we love or care for; I know you wouldn't have sexual relations with anyone unless it was a feeling and a want inside you. It's not you; you guard and protect yourself way too much from indiscriminate affairs."

"So what's your point?"

"If you want her, have her; you will learn something—I promise you."

"I don't understand. But if it's to be, we are certainly not doing that at Penbroke. One mistake, and the gossip would fly everywhere. If it's to be, it will be at our London home, not here."

"I respect that; people here will not understand—that's true. Now, stop feeling guilty and let it go; what will be, will be."

"Camilla, how God invented you is beyond understanding; you are brilliant, so balanced in thought, yet so unconditionally loving." James, in a way he couldn't explain, loved her more and more, as he learned so much from her. He thought, *It's funny that when we feel restricted from something we would secretly want to experience, the more we want it.*

He took her in his arms, gave her a long kiss, and said, "Camilla, outside Sabrina, I don't know a woman I could love more, but then it's in a completely different way."

"Now, you're beginning to expand your thoughts from tradition and to open your mind and heart to a reality you have yet to experience," responded a woman that very few would be capable of understanding without taking the time to do so.

They slowly walked back to the castle in peaceful harmony, enjoying their alone time together, in surroundings where neither of them felt the burden of everyday responsibilities and were free from the hustle and bustle of the day.

They arrived back at the castle and saw Sir Nicholas and Nicki talking up a storm in the small breakfast room off the side of the kitchen.

"Where have you two love birds been?" asked Nicki.

"Oh, just enjoying a walk in the beautiful grounds of your estate, Nicholas."

"Come and join us; I've just made some pancakes, the very finest, as only I can make."

"A chef, to boot?" joked James. "More qualities I've yet to learn about Sir Nicholas."

The four sat down, and Camilla could feel a glowing happiness from Nicki, and Sir Nicholas was humming, as he served the new guests.

"James, I'm starting to wake up again; I haven't felt like this in months. I've been on my own a lot, not a bad thing to experience, a lot of matters to think out. All of you coming over is such a joy, and it makes me realize I've got to get back on my horse and move on with life."

"Nicholas, I know you miss Davina, but you are very resilient, and when you are ready, you must come over and take a Trip to the Stars. It will answer a lot of questions."

"Yes; Nicki was telling me all about her story. What a wonderful device you have! And to think that, at one time, I thought it was all hogwash. We've come a long way from those days, haven't we, James?"

"It's natural for anyone to think the way you did; believe me, I was as nervous as all get out the first time I tried it, but it changed my whole perception of the world forever."

Camilla was watching Nicki, and she could see that she and Sir Nicholas were very comfortable with each other.

"Nicki, have you got a moment? I would like to show you something." Camilla said, diplomatically. She wanted to get the latest so that they could have some girl time together.

"Tell me: what do you think?" Camilla asked, as the two women went upstairs to her bedroom.

"Camilla, he's great. I don't feel that same attraction as I have done in the past, but I feel so comfortable with Nicholas, and he's also funny and easy to be around. I love fashion, as you know, and we have so many interests in common. In a way, I find that, for me, it's probably better not to have the sexual attractions positive and negative that I've had before. It makes for an easier life of compatibility."

"You don't find him attractive in a sexual way?"

"No; please don't misunderstand me; I would not hesitate to make love to him, but it would be out of love for who he is and the great man I admire. Of course, I'm talking ahead of myself, because it depends on him, too, but I truly believe it would be a relationship without drama, and something that I've not experienced before that would be so healing. I know he's enamored with me, but I am also enamored with him, but in a different way."

"So, you believe you two could be a great match?"

"Yes, I do, and I would be a very fortunate woman, indeed, especially if we could have a child together. I would feel so blessed."

"Nicki, you are changing, and it's for the best; I believe this man can give you the stability you desire without suffocating you or overposessing you, as I know you have experienced. Englishmen are less domineering in my experience than the men in our own culture, and the funny thing is that we give back in return."

"Nicholas has something special planned for tonight, so James may want to delay the helicopter for tomorrow, if that's all right; then I may stay on for a while in order to learn more and to understand Nicholas."

"Of course, my dear; let him show you his world, if you truly believe this is the man for you. After all, you didn't come all this way for nothing. Nicki, I'm so excited; I know the four of us can have some great times together."

In the meantime, James and Sir Nicholas were having some

alone time, too, in order to discuss matters.

"How's your family doing, James?"

"It's my son; I let him spend a couple of years out in Hong Kong to make a return on our shipping line, and, to my shock an amazement, he can't stand banking or anything I do, and he wants to attend acting school. He believes he was so good at Eton and Oxford."

"My God, that had to be a shock. Can't you knock some sense into him?"

"I've tried all that. Maybe I'm wrong, but I've lowered his allowance, put a PI on him, and told him to get on with it. Sometimes we have to experience life. Who knows? He might be successful and eventually join the bank later, but I will certainly alter my will. The problem is a lot of people who get into the artistic world go down a path of drugs, alcohol, parties, and women. Could this way of life be an excuse for that? I know that's already happened, fortunately in Hong Kong, but it won't happen here; otherwise I will cut him off. It's up to him, and if he can make it, fine. I've done all I can do as a father. The choice is now his."

"I can't disagree with that, can I? What a disappointment! So much opportunity! Unbelievable!"

"What about your two?" asked James.

"My son, Robert, is working at the mills in Lancashire and doing a good job. He's not the best student, but, like my father, he's good with his hands and the employees. Melissa works under Lisa at the fashion shops, and, between them, they control the products here, in Hong Kong, and internationally. I obviously have a general manager over the new facilities that we moved out to China. I refurbished the old building downtown into modern, low-income flats, and it's turning a good income."

"Sounds like you've done a better job integrating your family into the business than I've done. However, Annabelle is my gem; she's a chip off the old block, and she's dedicated and runs the finances with a rod of iron. Also, I mustn't forget Becky, my sister. She's become invaluable in helping with the growth of Trans World, in the medical field, as well as in human resources. Felicity, my younger sister, is also doing well, after being an anchorwoman at BTV; she is now running our newspaper business. I guess that, all in all, I must say it's worked out well, as family is not always easy."

"You can say that again; fortunately, I was an only child, but, like all of us, we all wish for something we didn't have."

After their long chat, Camilla and Nicki appeared.

*****

"Ladies, go and get yourselves fixed up. We can drive into Chester and see the sights; then I have a lovely restaurant for all of us to enjoy."

Experiencing Chester with its old-world charm and Nicholas knowing the Duke of Westminster allowed them to visit the fabulous estate of ten thousand acres at Eaton Hall. Nicki was delirious at all the small shops and at the way of upper-crust English life.

To imagine a Norman ancestor arriving in London during the eleventh century and buying up, at that time, around sixty acres of what is now larger, and part of the West End of London was unfathomable, and to think a family could have an heir over nine centuries later. *Welcome to England,* she thought.

On the way home, Nicholas stopped at a well-known pub, The Alvenly Arms, for a sumptuous dinner and evening. British pubs were well known for their food, but this was exceptional, so both Camilla and Nicki got another look at England's social life. Country life was different from city life, but it always provided a unique charm. Although much maligned by tourists, it could serve great food at the right places. The pub's roast beef was renowned. Tarporley was a-larger-than-the-average village and could supply much of the necessities for the surrounding community. Of course, Chester was not much further and could be easily reached for a great day's outing.

A wonderful day was experienced by them all, especially in allowing Nicki and Camilla the opportunity to know England from its rural countryside.

The tired group snatched a cocktail and sat outside on the drawing room veranda.

"Nicki, now that you've seen a very different part of England, what are your thoughts?"

"I know you have less-privileged people, as we do in Buenos Aires, but it amazes me how many upscale places you have in the countryside that can provide superb cuisine in more-modest surroundings."

"The British countryside can be so beautiful, especially as we sat outside and enjoyed the night air. It's what a lot of people enjoy in order to get away from city life and to get back to nature."

"James and Camilla, do you mind if I stay over with Nicholas for a few days? He's asked me to go with him to London, and there I can get a taste of his fashion shop."

"Ah ha, what a treat; you will love it, Nicki; Nicholas is the master of women's fashion," proclaimed James, knowing how much Sabrina loved her time working with him.

They all agreed. James had called on the helicopter for early Tuesday morning, as he had business to attend to. They would all meet up in London, and Camilla had promised to bring all Nicki's clothing with her, as she was due to return to Buenos Aires that weekend.

CHAPTER 22

SAMUEL, ANNABELLE, and JEREMY

James and Camilla made their way home to Penbroke Court, after leaving Nicki and Nicholas together. Camilla was excited that the weekend had gone well, and she enjoyed knowing Nicholas on his home ground.

"An incredible place!" said Camilla. "What Nicholas has reclaimed out of that old castle is remarkable. I was looking at the castle in a practical way, and, actually, from the way it's laid out, it's probably easier to maintain than Penbroke." So Camilla shared her thoughts with James.

"Yes, he's done a fine job of refurbishing the exterior, too. It was jaw-dropping when Sabrina and I stayed there for their wedding, but today it's certainly brilliant what he's done—so tastefully in keeping with the historical era."

"I would like to be a fly on the wall to know how those two got on. I have such a good feeling about them. Nicki deserves a lot; she's done so much work in charities for the underprivileged.

She's also been clever in working her way through the political scene in South America, and she is extremely well-respected. Men, of course, she attracts like flies, but it's funny that, deep down, coming from modest beginnings, all she truly desires is to be loved for herself instead of being desired as a sex object by men."

"Nicholas is the right man for her, an older man that has a big heart. I'm sure, knowing Nicholas, he will worship the ground she walks on. The way he was with Davina, he loves extrovert women, and, with her fashion sense, I believe she could be of value."

"Home, sweet home," shouted Camilla. "I can't wait to go for a walk and throw open our bedroom windows to hear the sound of the sea."

The pair crossed the driveway from the helipad by the hanger and into the front courtyard, holding hands. After a light lunch, James kissed Camilla and then went to his office to call Kimberli about the latest news.

"Kim, how are things going?"

"Sir Jeremy would like to meet with you on Thursday for lunch if that's possible."

"Yes; book a table at the Connaught around midday; I will be at the bank early Thursday morning. Anything else?"

"Yes; Anna wants to talk to you. She's going to your office to pick up the phone."

"Okay; thanks."

"Dad, I heard about Sam, and I am thoroughly disgusted with him. I have had a long chat with him, so you might want to talk with him again. If not, know I'm your girl. He's obsessed with this half-Asian girl, and he's got her coming to live here; he's really mixed up. He can't even take care of himself, let alone a girlfriend. In addition, he's not staying at your place;

he told me he's moved out. He's staying with an old school friend in Chelsea."

"Okay, I will be in London on Thursday for business; Camilla is coming on Friday morning, as Nicki, whom you briefly saw, flies home this Saturday; okay?"

"If he doesn't come to his senses, I would cut him off. I don't know whether he's on something, and maybe this girl has led him astray. Isn't it time he grew up? God only knows, you given him enough time away, which he's thrown down the toilet." Annabelle was not one to get angry, but this was a side of her, as James was learning.

That evening, after supper, James and Camilla sat outside to enjoy the season; the summer months were coming to an end.

"Camilla, I've been thinking a lot about Sam."

"You know, he's your father reincarnated, who was the Seventh Earl, too. He likes to do his own thing; that's why he chose to spend more time out at this estate instead of building onto the business, as his father had done. He's got talent. He could well be a great actor—that's the remarkable thing—and he could live here as the Eleventh Earl. He's responsible for bringing that Throne here—from the Himalayas!"

"Wow! That's why he had so much interest in the notes of the Seventh Earl."

"He was a party animal when he was younger; do I surmise that your mother hasn't told you that?"

"No, she didn't! He was the best father a man could have. I just wished he could have lived longer."

"Does that give you a different understanding? Not every-one is the powerhouse you've become. He's had to live up to that in his past lives, but, in this life, he wants to contribute in his own way. So, this time, talk with him, as Annabelle says, and let him express what he has to give; he may become a better earl than you might expect. We all have something to give; his gift is being given in a different way, and he wants this now more than ever, doesn't he?"

"That definitely puts another spin on his life before; I can see why Mother had to be the pragmatic one, and when she met Antonio, it changed her life for the better. It's funny how our parents don't always express themselves; they are so set on keeping up appearances."

"James, it just goes to show we are all different, and now you see his artistic temperament coming to the fore."

"I couldn't dream this up; I do remember Czaur telling me a long while ago, at Samuel's birth, who he was, and, for some reason, I'd put it out of my mind. That being said, my father was nothing like that when he died. Yet, thinking more deeply, perhaps I've got something to learn. If he doesn't go down the wrong path and end up a party animal and lose his way, who am I to judge?"

"Some of us are late developers. He's had a good education; he's got personality and leadership skills, and he's popular; just keep a tight reign on him. Look how your father turned out. Was he not loved by many?"

"Yes; I can't say he wasn't; you're right; who knows?"

*****

James left on Wednesday afternoon for London to get ready for his upcoming business luncheon with Sir Jeremy. When he arrived at the London home, he checked out the room where Sam had slept, and, sure enough, all his clothes and suitcase had gone.

That boy of mine! he thought, *What is he up to now?* He quickly called Anna and asked for his mobile phone number;

then he called it immediately.

Sam answered.

"You moved out. Why?" scowled James.

"Dad, it's best; I know you don't agree with my decision and think I'm headed off in the wrong direction. I'm staying with a friend until I can find digs that will be close to the acting school I shall attend."

"Look, I would like to talk further on the matter. Can we meet at the Brass Bell for dinner at, say, 7:00 tonight?"

"I did have other plans, but, certainly, Dad, I'll be there. Is there anything I should know?"

"No; as you can imagine, our last discussion was a bit of a shock, so I want us to have a civil conversation, and I want to understand your plans."

"That's good; I have had enough browbeating from Anna, and I know it's all been a shock, but I really would like to explain myself in a better way."

"Okay; see you later."

That evening, Sam arrived at the restaurant before James.

"Good to see you here first; let's find a table and have a chat."

The maître d' of many years found James's favorite table, and James ordered a bottle of his favorite wine. After ordering from the menu, James started in.

"Sam, with great difficulty, I have become resigned to what you want to do. I was very assured of my direction as a young man, so I can't criticize you for that. Unfortunately, or maybe fortunately, my father wasn't around to advise; therefore, I chose not to go to university, much to your grandmother's dismay, but I got with a good accounting firm and got my degree in two years instead of four."

"Dad, I applaud all that you've accomplished; no one can

doubt that you are a truly amazing. Look at Bannerman's today—all over the world. I'm sure there will books written about you, if not a movie, one day."

"Sam, who am I to judge your choices is what I'm trying to say. My concern is that the artistic life still takes determination, dedication, and hard work to become the best. If you have talent, which I believe you have, then it can all happen. It's the lifestyle that bothers me."

"I know I've abused my status in Hong Kong, and I'm embarrassed for my disrespectful behavior. I didn't know how to face up to you. Even with all my confidence and extrovert behavior, I felt speechless to tell you how I wasn't cut out for this type of life you lead. There's you, and you are one of a kind. If I evaluate myself, it's my ego that seeks self-definition in order to be a success at what I can do. So I escaped, like a lost child, into a world of women and drink and, to be honest, into a few things I would rather not talk about."

"Sam, the whole point of this conversation is not to downgrade you for your choices but to understand that this life of debauchery you've had in Hong Kong is over, is it not?"

"Dad, I am happy to be home; I was a fish out of water. I got lost."

"Now tell me about this Asian girl you are supposed to be in love with."

"Funnily enough, she called me today. Her father won't let her come until she's finished her studies. She's in her early twenties, and he will only allow her to see me if I'm there. Her family is very strict. She was in tears, but he won't give her the money to come."

"How do you feel about that?" asked James, happy at the outcome.

"It's probably for the best. She could attend medical college here, and I had looked around for her. I will miss her; she was a great strength to me in my weak times and behavior. I'm realizing that I was becoming too dependent on her, so as much as it pains me, time will tell. In all reality, I need to get my life in order first, not hers."

"Now you're making sense. With your knowledge and interest in the arts, have you not thought about the East Wing and the Throne room?"

"Mother had steered me away from that, because she didn't want me to fail in my school studies and because she wanted me to focus on university. I am more than interested, but, with Sarah in control, I never thought you would approve of me getting involved in that."

"Not at all; now would be a tremendous time. Camilla, whom you need to know more about, and Sarah would be delighted for you to take an interest."

"Really? So, could I spend time at the estate on weekends and learn more?"

"Of course; you might find some answers for your own life, if you took the time."

"Dad, I'm overjoyed at your offer. I had wrongly assumed that Bannerman's was all that mattered and that the other was just a side issue." Samuel's eyes lit up, and James could see his aura starting to glow.

"I had no idea; Anna has never shown much interest, but maybe in time. One day, that estate will be yours to run. The Throne room is an important financial contributor to our financial well-being at Penbroke. Running the large property, we have is not easy in today's world. Lots of old English estates have been sold off or knocked down, as few aristocrats can afford the upkeep of a place like we have."

"That makes sense; I've always loved being at Penbroke; I

have my finest memories being there with you and Mom. I love riding, hunting, and all that goes into making the farm successful as an agricultural entity."

"Good Lord; I have underestimated you with regard to the estate. You are a country boy at heart, even if a country gentleman."

"Dad, that's always been my dream; I just thought my way to claiming that heritage was through your business empire."

"No way; we have definitely lost touch; I blame myself for not having this conversation before now, but it's never too late."

James went on, "Come up to Penbroke the next weekend after this, and you and I will personally take a trip in the helicopter and spend the weekend exploring, like we did when you were younger."

"Dad, I can't wait! In the meantime, I'm looking for my acting school, and I want to find digs in Kensington, because it's a little cheaper than your part of London."

"Sam, always know I'm your father and want the best for you. How can a father not love his only son?" James and Samuel laughed, after finishing a sumptuous desert of crêpe Suzette. The pair parted, after James gave his son a big hug.

James was now overjoyed and had felt Sabrina's presence, as he reconnected with Samuel, much to both James's and Sam's surprise.

James thought about everything they had discussed on his walk back to his residence. *How could I have been so blind, again always thinking of their future being like mine. Have I so much to learn, Sabrina?*

James slept in the next morning, and he arrived at the bank at 10:00 a.m., to see Kimberli and Anna eagerly awaiting his arrival.

"Dad, shall I get your coffee? I want to know everything,"

"Yes, yes, my dear."

"So how did it go?"

"Better than I could have imagined. He's more interested in the farm and Penbroke than the business here. I was shocked, but I know he was always wandering around as a boy. He prefers country life to the city. He will pursue his acting for now, and he wants to find digs in Kensington."

"I'll help him, Dad; he doesn't have a clue. Flats are all expensive now. He doesn't need much. He may have to go further out, and he can take the tube, for now."

"On another subject: how long before Kim joins Peter at his home?"

"Give me another six months, and I'll have it under control. I can always call Claudia or Kim, but I see a lot of ways to improve things. I know you are going to say, gently and slowly, so trust me on that."

"Is Kim helping Peter now?"

"Oh, yes; she's here on half weeks, as she's such a hard worker; she doesn't seem stressed. Deep down, I think she's going to miss being with us, but I'm looking forward to taking the reins. My assistants are great. Claudia certainly built a well-oiled machine. She's one in a million, Dad!"

"Do I know it! I'm going to miss her after all these years, since I became a teenager—nearly forty years. However, I couldn't be prouder of you, Annabelle. Look at you, my beautiful daughter, running through the back garden with those pigtails. If only your mom could see you now . . . .. Oops, she probably can." James laughed.

"Since you told Sam about the Throne room, it's time I piqued my curiosity; as a nonbeliever, I'm beginning to feel outnumbered!"

"It's time that you, too, got involved. You might be surprised at what you can learn."

"Mom wanted us to keep focused on our schoolwork, and she said we should learn about all that later, when we got into our careers. I am interested, Papa, even though I'm not much into history and past lives. I will keep an open mind, though."

"You might be surprised; you never know."

"Well, Dad, that you fought so hard to revive the Throne room and that you built this an enormous business must count for something."

"You are a smart one, my Anna!"

Sir Jeremy had already arrived and was waiting on James to go for lunch.

*****

"Jeremy, it's a pleasure to see you again," said James.

They chatted away during the taxi ride to the Connaught Hotel before lunch.

"Indeed: lots to discuss. Since your last attendance at our meetings, I have not bothered you, as I know you have had much to attend to after rearranging your life and your marriage to Camilla. You've been a great component in our meetings up and until this time. I now want to share with you the latest news. First, I am retiring from being in charge of the Inner Sanctum, and I want to hand over the position to you. I see now that you are starting to delegate a lot of your duties; this, I think, will be the appropriate time for you to take charge. We have a number of new attendees, which I will introduce you to; the board wholeheartedly approves of your leadership, as you know I do."

"I'm honored, Jeremy; will you still play a part?"

"Yes, of course; it's been my dedicated effort to steer our

nation in the right direction over the last twenty-five years. I'm now seventy, and it needs younger blood to continue the good work in these changing times."

"We are nearing the millennium, and it's clear that the world is starting to take on a new direction. Could you give me your thoughts as to the present and the future challenges as you see them?"

"It appears the world economy is running at a reckless pace. Alan Greenspan's financial acumen has brought about what appears to be a miracle economy—low inflation, low interest rates, and all under the Clinton administration. The States are reducing debt and balancing their finances for the first time in decades."

"I've been watching that; it appears he has the cure for modern business growth through global financing and investment."

"There is, however, a growing suspicion that this could be a bubble, and, with a potential change of government after Clinton's eight years in office, the world picture could change."

"How so?" asked a curious James, remembering what Roger had also predicted.

"The Middle East has become a source of tension. The rise of Saddam Hussein in Iraq is becoming one of extreme tension. His eight-year war against Iran, in his attempts to take oil from that nation and to unite the Shiite and the Sunni Muslims into a nation of Islam has not succeeded. Right now, he's on the prowl for other opportunities. Having been backed by the United States in the past, there is a growing discord between the two countries. It is clear that he's becoming a dictator that intends to part from the support he's had and that he wants complete autonomy."

After taking a moment to regain his breath, he continued,

"Obviously, he wants to increase his oil reserves in that region. The proof of that is Desert Storm for his slant drilling of oil into Kuwait on his southern border in 1991. The success of the Americans and allied forces in pushing him back to Bagdad has made him feel diminished. Two failures are helping him to lose power in his own country. Being a Sunni Muslim in a majority Shiite Country is proving to have difficulties. As a result, Saddam Hussein is becoming a vicious dictator by using lethal weapons against not only his own people but also the Kurds in the north."

"Yes, I can see that could result in a bigger problem. Why George H. W. Bush didn't take him out when he had the opportunity is hard to understand."

"It's deeper than that. George Bush, Sr, was wise. Even though Saddam is a problem for the West, the truth is that if you take him out, you leave a void in the administration in that part of the world. The Americans are not like the British; look at the chaos of the Vietnam War. The Americans have the power to win battles, but that's only part. Who's going to run the country the day after? We, like the Romans, were colonizers, and when we took places around the world, we left a clearly defined administration to run the country and to integrate them back to a place of law and order. Not always possible, I agree, but isn't that better than leaving a vacuum?"

"Interesting; Napoleon said the same thing after his exile in Elba, when he returned to take over France again in March of 1814. When he called all the heads of government to his palace, his first words were, 'When France wakes up tomorrow morning, the country will need a government.'"

"Precisely; anyway, not to get off the subject, but the growing tensions in the Middle East are of significant concern. In addition to this, Alan Greenspan's philosophy is working for now, but his lack of regulation of the hedge funds, or the entities that we call 'shadow banking,' is disturbing."

"I think that John Major, our prime minister, has done a fair job under the circumstances—after the collapse of the USSR, after the Chechen wars, after the Bosnian War between 1992 and 1995, and the end of Yugoslavia between 1991 and 1992. It seems that we are surrounded by change everywhere. The end of the IRA, the Irish Republican Army, is promising, but it remains to be seen how well Tony Blair will do; he definitely has the gift of the gab; maybe he can help with Israel."

"After John Major's seven years in office, people now want change, so there's a swing back to the left. And don't forget the genocide in Rwanda and the upheaval in the Congo. Africa is still a nation in development. It seems like a new world order is on the horizon."

James and Jeremy continued with their world discussion and with their thoughts of what the future would hold. Then Jeremy turned to a more spiritual discussion.

"James, you've done a magnificent job with the Throne room. Your new wife, Camilla, is a fantastic choice; I met her only when I had a brief encounter with Sarah and your new wife. I never went into detail as to who I am; she just checked me out for alignment classes at one of her sessions. I prefer incognito, especially in the profession I'm in."

"Don't thank me; Sarah, as you know, is a jewel, but Camilla is a highly intelligent psychic, beyond anything I've ever experienced."

"I could see that, by her aura, she's from South America. After the breakup of Atlantis, many went to the southern regions of Patagonia in order to retain their spiritual knowledge. Apart from her beauty, she has a serenity I've rarely encountered. You couldn't have chosen better. She will make your place a landmark—that I can assure you."

"Jeremy, will you retire from the House of Lords?"

"No, but I will take a lesser role. As you know it's been a life-time's passion, apart from my law firm. To continue, your role will be significant; none of us can totally predict the future; having the gift as Camilla has and as you have, to some extent, I can see the following challenges. War is imminent again, and the Middle East region of the world will bring much chaos and turbulence. There will be a financial bubble burst after this massive world growth in the financial arena. We will all sur-vive. The difficult part about these cycles is that those who are financially strong and with little debt will become more pow-erful, as assets will become cheaper to buy out. The problem with this is that people with money will have an even stron-ger control on a nation's policies. The unfortunate outcome is there will be a greater division of wealth between the poor and the rich. This will bring about social strife and civil action. It will be a time of great change, and policies that would be seen as too socialistic will meet with confrontation. However, it's the only way to keep balance between the electorate."

"That's why I'm divesting from my two biggest earners, Trans World Shipping and my textile industries, which I'm in the process of taking public now."

"For you, James, it won't be a problem. It will be a period where modesty must be shown. Having wealth is not a crime; however, smart behavior is a priority. Like myself, James, we are on our last lives before moving on to a higher state of purpose. We are all here to usher in a new age, which will be fully underway by 2030. You can probably see this through the technological advances we are all making. It takes confusion, unfortunately, in order to bring about change, so those of us who can adapt will be living in a different world than what we've experienced."

"Fascinating! I can feel the change, but since we were born, and even yourself, the pace of new developments has been groundbreaking."

"Yes; I chose to be born around the time of the Great Depression, so I was brought up in a more frugal world. It was a time where I saw Hitler's advance to his place over Germany in the 1930s, because of Germany's catastrophic financial losses in World War I, thanks to Keiser Wilhelm's arrogance and jealousy over his cousins in Britain, as well as Britain's world power. Hitler brought hope and then chaos; like all men of his kind, they don't know when to stop; how people obsessed with power can treat life as dispensable, especially his hatred for the brilliance of Jewish people. Creating a so-called superior Aryan race is unthinkable. Power makes people like him believe they are gods. Oh, how history teaches us!"

Jeremy continued, "The day of the baby boomers has played its part and brought about immense wealth and prosperity. This new age will take on a different form and has every opportunity for the betterment of mankind. Throughout history, there have been great changes; this one will be one of the greatest we've yet to witness. A lot of us who have brought this about will not be here. You, James, will see it's beginning. Now you see your true purpose and the reason I'm here today."

Jeremy went on, "There's something else that I wanted to discuss with you, today."

"Yes sir?"

"The Law of Grace."

"Yes, indeed, please explain," said James, who was anxious to learn.

'The Law of Grace is the most profound essence in all that

we learn. It's the greatest power of all, which is humility, and, in fact, true love and compassion; nothing has more power than that. You have shown that quality by honoring your tradition and your forefathers and by creating work and opportunity for tens of thousands of people. You could have sat back and done very little, as many have done in your position, and that's why so many beautiful homes are either hotels, apartments, or knocked down. No one can afford the upkeep. Yes, the competitive nature in you has made you want more, and that's where we must know when to stop. It's not about being rich and wealthy; there's no sin in that. It's about our priorities: the way we manage our lives and help those of us who are less fortunate, leaving an example to inspire others and, above all, understanding before being understood. These are the essence of living a good spiritual life, in spite of all our earthly weaknesses. We try to have a conscience in all that we do. These are the principles of the Inner Sanctum, by acting in good conscience for the betterment of mankind. Unto whom much is given, much is expected, and that doesn't translate always into money! Now I will get back off my soap box."

"Beautifully explained, and they are the very foundation of the principles we stand for."

"All of which you have shown, James; I'm so proud of you."

"A compliment, indeed, coming from you, Jeremy, as you are the very best example of all that you've said," said James, reflecting on his words, which he had understood, but thought, *Should be said more often.*

James continued, "When you come to Penbroke, please let me know. I would love to take you around the estate; it's the least I can do for all the valuable advice you've given me through the years."

"James, the next time, I will. I would be fascinated to talk to that brilliant wife of yours; I've never seen an aura of such magnificence. I'm sure she could teach me a few things."

Jeremy burst out laughing, in one of his rare moments when he wasn't caught up in serious, discerning thought.

James got up after having enjoyed the roast beef and the enlightening conversation he always had with Jeremy. The two parted and would meet up again soon.

James arrived back at the bank, full of thoughts about the future, thinking,

So much to learn and so much to come!

After making some business calls to various department heads, he sat back in his chair after Kimberli had brought him up to date, sipping on his late-afternoon coffee.

The new receptionist, Angela, who had taken over after the retirement of Rose, said he had a personal call.

"Well, who is it?" exclaimed an anxious James, already missing the efficient way in which Rose had always filtered his calls.

"I'm sorry, your Lordship, but they wouldn't say."

James pondered for a moment and then said, "Oh, okay, put them through."

"James, this is Nicki; I was nervous to call you at work, so forgive me for not revealing my name."

"Nicki, you can call me anytime you want, my dear."

"Nicholas had to go up north to take care of some business at the plant in Manchester and will be back tomorrow, so I'm stuck here alone and wondered if I could have dinner with you tonight. That's if you are not too busy, of course."

"It would be a pleasure; let's meet at The In Crowd at seven. Okay?"

"I will be there, your Lordship," she said teasingly, excited to be alone in his company.

Nicki had a style similar to Lisa's, but in a more Latin way; her voice was a little deeper, and the minute he started to think about her, his heart started beating faster. *Oh, here goes nothing*, he thought.

*****

After his long, busy day, he took a long, hot bath and thought deeply about his revealing day, which apparently wasn't over. He laughed out loud and said, "Never a dull moment."

He decided to put on a nice suit, not wanting to appear too casual; it was a business day, after all, and he didn't want to appear too flamboyant. The restaurant was within walking distance from the house, so he took his time and walked down to sit at the open bar and wait on Nicki.

Sure enough, as he was taking a sip of his scotch, in popped Nicki, looking all around; he got up and motioned her to come over.

"I've booked a table, so let's have a drink first; then we can go eat."

"Yes, my Prince Charming; I love your suit; nice to see you dressed up in your refined city clothes!" she remarked flirtatiously.

"Needless to say, you look fantastic, as usual."

She wore a tight, low-cut, gold, satin blouse, with a very short, dark green skirt. Around her neck, she wore a broad gold necklace band, with small diamonds equidistant around the circumference, with a large diamond at the front. Her black, patent high heels were plain and took nothing away from the wide, black belt with gold buckles that supported her waist. Her jewelry was a variety of gemstones, with a beautiful emerald, again surrounded by diamonds, on her left hand. Her hair was pulled back into a golden clasp to reveal her most perfect ears, which could only add to those beautiful, dark brown eyes, graced with the lips that only Latin women were so blessed to have.

"You blow me away every time I see you. You look more beautiful each time." James couldn't resist the opportunity to compliment such an eye-stunning woman.

"If my Lord is happy with my couture, then I'm over-joyed," she remarked, as she leaned forward to give him a kiss. Needless to say, there were no persons in the room that didn't turn their heads.

"I don't know if you are an asset or a liability, when you walk into a room dressed so magnificently," said James, teasing her as he ordered her a vodka and lime.

"Do you still find me attractive, James?"

"No, but the rest of the restaurant does."

"I'm not good enough for his Lordship?" she asked, as she swiveled her stool so that her legs touched his.

"Nicki, you are a riot; you know how good you look. You don't need my approval."

"I've missed you, James; did you miss me a little bit?"

"Nicki, do you remember the first time we met, in Buenos Aires?"

"I'll never forget it!" she said and threw her head back, laughing.

"Deja vous, encore?"

"Okay, let's go eat.

The couple found a table in the corner of the restaurant, and James ordered his champagne while they perused the menu.

"I know we mean a lot to each other, but I do adore Nicholas, and I know he's the right choice for me."

"It's difficult for me, too. Camilla is fantastic, and the funny part is that you two could almost be twins. The same height, almost the same looks; she's just a little more introverted and serious, but it's actually amazing."

"People get us mixed up all the time. I guess that because we are both from that part of the world as opposed to being here in London, people don't see the difference. I have a reason for seeing you. As you know, I'm headed home on Saturday afternoon, so it's great we have this time together again."

"Nicki, I know things will work out with you and Nicholas; he's perfect for you, so don't miss this opportunity, and, in this way, you and Camilla will see a lot of each other—something I know Camilla wants."

"James, I've thought about that often. But what if I do stay in Buenos Aires? When you come over to see Roger, maybe we could spend time together."

"I can't do that; it wouldn't be fair to Camilla; I love her deeply, and you wouldn't want that. Anyway, you are nobody's second; you need a man you love in your own right."

"I know Camilla would be happy if we all lived at Penbroke. But you're right; it's complicated."

"I can't live a double life; it's not because of you or Camilla I would feel wrong."

"We've been together in our lives before, and it's worked, so I know we are fully compatible."

"Look; go home; take time to think things through, and if you think it can work with Nicholas, I believe that's your best option, or move here as a single woman and take a place here in London. I'm sure there are many eligible men here that would love to know you. Only time can unravel this, and what is meant to be, will be."

"I like that thought; would you help me find a place here, if I chose that option?"

"Let time pass, if you don't want to hurt Nicholas's feelings.

Then let's see."

They finished up, and as they started to get up after paying, the owner came over to tell James something he needed to know.

"My Lord, I believe there are some camera men, paparazzi, outside; I have a back entrance; if you don't want publicity, please follow me."

"They are all after seeing who my new wife is, so let's take his advice."

They followed him down a narrow corridor that went down into a basement and to a door that opened into a side street. James knew where he was, and the couple walked another block to circle the restaurant and cross over the Brampton road onto the other side before Hyde Park corner. Then the couple walked among the crowds, passed Harrods department store, slipped back over the road again, and after James took Nicki's hand, they took the side streets to his place.

"You devil, you know your way around."

It was getting darker, so they could pass by unnoticed.

"The last thing I want is that lot following me to my place, as they will never leave me alone."

"You don't like the limelight, do you?"

"No, because once they're onto you, it's impossible to get rid of them."

They arrived at his mews safe and unseen. After opening the door, Nicki flung her arms around him and said, "James, I adore you. You know all the tricks, my mystery man."

"Stay here for a bit; then I'll get you a taxi."

"Let's have a nightcap."

James brought her a stiff glass of brandy as the two sneaked a cigarette and relaxed.

"Never a dull moment with you, but my feet are killing me

in these high heels," Nicki said, as she flung them on the floor.

"I don't want all that attention, and someone at that restaurant who knew who I was let the word out for a kickback. I'm sure the owner will fire whoever it was."

James continued, "Nicki, we both know what we want and, more important, what we should do. So, let's enjoy the moment before I call for a taxi."

"I understand, James; you and Camilla have treated me like royalty, and how fortunate I am to meet such a wonderful man as Nicholas. So, my mind is made up; I will take some time to think it all through, but I know you are right. How lucky I am to have such a loyal friend in you, and a man like Nicholas is one in a million!"

The two parted after a hug and a kiss, and a relieved James now knew how happy his good friend, Sir Nicholas, would be.

"See you with Camilla tomorrow night," she shouted, as the cab driver closed her door.

******

That afternoon, Camilla arrived at the bank to see James.

She talked with Annabelle, while James was busy on the telephone.

"It's great to talk with you, after your father does nothing but sing your praises!"

"Really? I know so little about you, except for the time we shared on the cruise, but I can see you are a very beautiful woman, and I know we will come to know each other better with time."

"I see you are definitely your father's daughter, but you certainly have the looks of your very beautiful mother."

"Thank you; you will see that I and my brother are very different."

"So James tells me."

"I'm sure you've already heard the news about Samuel."

"Yes, indeed, but I sense your brother will find his way, even though he's very different from you and your father."

"I enjoyed our trip to Australia, but we didn't really get a chance to talk, and I must confess our heads were full of onboard romances. However, it was obvious to see how much my father loved you."

"Time has passed, and I haven't wanted to interfere, but please come up to Penbroke and spend some time with us."

"I will; as you and my father are so happy together, I know you and I will enjoy each other's company."

"I look forward to knowing you and Sam better."

James popped his head into Anna's office and said, "I see you two are having a chance to chat."

"Your daughter looks just like her mother and appears to be on top of matters." said Camilla, smiling at Anna.

Camilla followed James over to his office.

"You've been quiet these last two days, so I'm sure you have had a busy, if not fun, time."

"Yes; lots to catch up on." James was not going to discuss the episode with Nicolette, but he would after her departure.

"Are we going to have a farewell dinner with Nicholas and Nicki tonight?"

"Yes; I will call Nicholas now."

"Nicholas, how are you? Heard you had to put out a fire in Manchester."

"Yes. It's Nicki's last night here, so let's meet up at a restaurant I know, called Charlie's. They have a live band, and it's cheerful. Say, around 7:30 p.m.?"

"We will be there!"

CHAPTER 23

JAMES AND CAMILLA

After a great, final evening, it was a sad departure. Nicki reluctantly waved, as she boarded the plane on her long trip to Buenos Aires.

Camilla was sad to see her best friend leave, and she was silent on the way back home to Penbroke Court.

Then James started to talk, "Why are you being silent?"

"Yes; I will miss her."

Camilla continued, "I love you more than ever, James; you are not easily seduced. You've proved that already. In this three-dimensional world, there are rules, which I hate."

"In a sense, it's logical, because, in raising a family of values, it's necessary to have those rules."

"Yes, but if you were born into a world that accepted a different lifestyle, it would be the norm."

"It's been tried in communes, with courtesans, and so on. Our religious teaching states that it's all wrong."

When they arrived back at Penbroke, Camilla grabbed

hold of James, knowing how he felt about Nikki and took him straight to their bedroom. It was late afternoon, and, in this reunification, the two of them felt a beautiful oneness that hadn't separated them but peculiarly brought them even closer together.

"Camilla, you are such an unusual person; I believe I've met a woman that I could never dream to be with. The incredible part is I do realize that the more we are together, the more I love you. As much as I feel a compatibility with Nicki as you do, it's that extra something in your knowledge and wisdom that would make me choose you over and over again."

"That's true love, which is above the physical and which is hard to find in another. The sex is like a pill; it can wear off. It's that deeper force that is so powerful. In a sexual adventure, we keep looking for a more exciting experience, but when there's love, it's not necessary, because we feel the heart and soul of the experience; the sex is just the gravy."

James had learned an important lesson that there was a duality in all of us, After losing Sabrina, he realized that his love for her was far more important than his business, which, in another sense, was his wife, too. He pondered deeply on all that Camilla had said. As much as he found Nicki attractive, it couldn't equal the love he was feeling for Camilla at this moment.

"James, what you have been able to show me with the Throne room goes beyond anything I ever dreamed about," said Camilla. "When Alberto died, I knew I had a purpose, but meeting you on the cruise brought everything in my life together. With all the knowledge I have, this opportunity allows me to share my skills for the rest of my life. Teaching people to understand that life is real beyond our lives here is the greatest gift I could imagine." Camilla wanted James to realize the impact he had given to her life already.

James felt redeemed by her words of appreciation.

The next day, Nicki called Camilla when she arrived home. They spoke for a good while. James was relaxing before a busy week ahead.

"Well, she's expressed herself to me, and she believes Sir Nicholas is the man for her."

*****

The millennium was closing in, and James had taken both Trans Global and the textile business public, thanks again to the brilliant timing of Roger Bell. The shares were going through the roof. The incredible profitability of the textile business lay in being able to ship to all the distribution centers they had set up globally. This action allowed all the properties he owned around the world to be debt free. It also gave an increased cash balance to elevate their Swiss bank account. The reduction of debt placed Bannerman's in an impregnable position. Roger was well on his own way by now to becoming a billionaire himself.

James was spending more time devoting his attention to the Inner Sanctum, focusing on the changing political scene to come. Samuel was making strides in his acting career, much to James's surprise. As for the Throne room, they were increasing the size of the buildings and of the classrooms and were hiring more staff. Camilla was now firmly in control. Her name was starting to be known far and wide, and she had taken to writing books about her experiences, which were now being translated into many languages.

Ironically, by James's focusing on his personal life and devoting his time to the affairs of the nation, Bannerman's wealth was increasing at an unbelievable pace. James was spending more time at his estate and spending three days a week—Tuesdays, Wednesdays, and Thursdays—at his headquarters in London.

Dreams had become reality. James, Camilla, and his daughter were an unbeatable team. With new blood and a younger generation of hard-driving, ambitious leaders, they had now replaced the wonderful men and women who had reached retirement age and who had greatly contributed to their success.

James was now approaching his sixties, and after the housing bubble and the Iraq War, it was plain to see that the writing was on the wall. By the time James was in his mid-sixties, in 2008, he was buying up properties and businesses at bargain basement prices. He was doubling the size of his estate and increasing his ownership in land; his timing was spot on.

His devotion to Camilla was paramount. She had lifted him out of an abyss at an incredible time in his life, and that could never be forgotten.

CHAPTER 24

THE END AND
THE BEGINNING

The year was now 2030. James would be eighty-six in December. His life with Camilla, now in her seventies, had lasted longer than his time with Sabrina. He rarely went to London now. He handled everything from his office in Penbroke. Anna was in charge, and, through her success, she had bought a beautiful estate north of London. She had taken over James's London home to run the business. She had married a famous playwright, whom she had met through Sam, and was the mother of two daughters.

Sam had, indeed, realized his dream of becoming a great Shakespearean actor. He preferred the stage and live acting to movies. Plays were becoming very popular again. They had now become fashionable to enjoy in this new age, where technology was reaching new heights. He had also become chairman of the board at the bank and had taken up residence in Hampstead Heath. He was now married to a beautiful actress and lived close to the place where Alexander Ringstone lived, after the passing of Claudia and Sir Thomas. So much had changed. It was a new world order, and Sam enjoyed running affairs within the Inner Sanctum, where he had taken over from his father's duties. James started to see in him the qualities his own father had, and he was proud of his progress.

Soon after the sad passing of Sir Nicholas, Nicki was now a fixture in working with Camilla in the Throne room. She had settled for a life with Sir Nichola, and after 20 years, their son, Rex, was attending university. After the sad passing of Sarah, she spent more time with Camilla; they had now trained new staff, as they, too, could enjoy more time to travel and do other things with James.

Roger Bell had also passed away. Anna also possessed the same acumen as Roger, and she learned a lot from his investments and timing. Roger's wife Kate was busy trying to sell his business in order to return home to England. Peter Lloyd and Kimberli had married, and Kimberli still kept an eye on his business, as Peter was enjoying his retirement. So many had passed on: Lisa and his parents. Becky and Flick were still alive but retired.

James spent time looking back over the years at all he had accomplished, but he longed to be with his one and only Sabrina.

That evening, in the late summer, James started to feel chest pains. He was not a moaner and retired to his bedroom to rest, thinking he probably had too much spicy food. During the night, as he slept, he felt different. He thought he was dreaming. As he looked down at himself, he thought that it was an out-of-body experience, but he soon started to realize that it wasn't that at all. He had died, and he found it hard to believe, because he wasn't in a hurry to leave.

He was able to move about in a way he had never experienced before, and he went downstairs to see Camilla and Nicki talking away. He thought that they would see him, but they didn't; then the reality of what had taken place started to hit home.

"I've gone!" he shouted out. "Camilla, can you hear me?"

Instantly, at that moment, she felt him.

"Nicki, I'm going to see if James is okay."

"Why, when I saw him downstairs in his office, he looked fine to me."

"I felt something; I can't describe it."

Camilla hurried down to his office to look.

He's not here, she thought. *I wonder where he is.*

She started to go to the bedroom to see if he had gone to take a bath before bed.

She had a funny feeling inside, as she opened the bedroom door. She saw him lying on his bed, appearing to be fast asleep. She went over to where he was lying and reached out to touch his hand. It was cold!

Oh, my God. he's gone, she thought.

She thought about calling an ambulance right away, in case he could be saved, but, deep down, she knew.

"Nicki, come quickly; I think James has passed away!" exclaimed a frantic Camilla.

Nicki confirmed her thoughts, and they immediately called for an ambulance.

"I can't believe this, and so suddenly," said Camilla.

The pair were sobbing their eyes out, wishing they could have one last word with him, but he was gone, and that was that.

James witnessed the whole situation, so he wished to be able to talk to them both.

Just one more moment, he thought.

He just wanted to ease their unhappiness.

*****

News travelled fast, and Flick worked on having a beautiful presentation for his life to be written up in the newspaper. People from all over the world were calling. No one could believe that the invincible James Bannerman had passed away.

Samuel gave the eulogy for his father at Lincoln Cathedral. People arrived from all parts of the globe. Although James had been a very private man, his businesses around the world were known far and wide.

"Ladies and Gentlemen, it is an honor to speak of my father's life on this saddest of occasions."

He took a deep breath, as he was filled with emotion.

"My father, what a man, who walked like a giant among us, proving no dream was big enough and no task was beyond his reach. Instead of resting on his laurels and running his estate, he chose to fight for the preservation of the Throne room, which has been his greatest gift to all humanity. He took a renowned business and built it into a worldwide empire. He didn't even go to university, but he worked to get his chartered accountant articles with an accounting firm. At the age of twenty-one, he was ready to go into action. From that day forth, with many others that have passed away, he took his dreams to the world, creating tens of thousands of jobs. His hard-working ethic was an example to us all. The two things that he valued above earthly pleasures were to honor his forefathers and to improve on all their labors that he had so proudly inherited. Well, Ladies and Gentlemen, he's a tough act to follow!" The congregation could feel the admiration Samuel had for his father, and his words were very moving, as

305

emotion and tears started to become apparent.

"I well remember the time when I was starting out in life after my school and university days, when I told him that I wanted to try my hand at acting. Obviously, he wasn't very pleased. To show you the kind of man he was, he didn't become angry and belligerent. He thought it over, and, somehow, he saw a silver lining in what I wanted to express. Not once did he desert me for my choices. In fact, he did the very opposite: he saw a creative component to my personal dreams. It was in that one moment that I realized that whatever duties my father would expect of me, I would never shy away from them. I am proud that I work with my sister and that I have had the magnificent opportunity to work with Camilla, Nicki, and, once, Sarah, who are, and have been, such beautiful, spiritual people, apart from pursuing my own dreams and aspirations.

"To reveal all his amazing accomplishments would take too long. I know most of you here are proudly aware of his achievements, as I have been. I will sadly miss his brilliant advice and love as a father. As a dutiful son, I only wish to uphold his values, in the hope that our family will continue on into this new world to add in our lives our way of continuing the Bannerman dream."

Samuel had said enough. He had expressed what he had felt in his heart. He then quietly stepped down from the pulpit and bowed before his father's casket.

Camilla, with her exceptional abilities, could feel James, and she knew he had not passed on and away from earthly existence, yet. She felt his love, and she knew that she would see him in his new life with Sabrina by taking the Throne, but not yet; he wasn't ready to leave.

James had always wanted to leave life in a spectacular way, so, in his will, he had written that he wanted to be cremated, but not in the usual way. He wanted a Viking death, where he would be floated out to sea on a raft. He wanted archers on the shoreline to fire flaming arrows. He wasn't going to leave until he saw that happen.

Sure enough, Camilla and Samuel had arranged for this event. Only family and close friends were invited, and he wanted no press. It was his way of passing on with music, leaving a moment of sorrow, but also of joy. He wanted it to be an event where food and drinks were served, where fireworks were set off, and where, for all the people he valued would enjoy the moment and the memory, too. He wanted it to be an event where the torch of his earldom would be passed to his son Samuel, who would now become the Eleventh Earl of Penbroke. He wanted it to be a ceremony where Alexander would announce his title and inheritance, much in the same way Sir Thomas, his father, had done for him.

It was on a Saturday after the funeral. The raft had already been made. His body was laid down on a carefully constructed bed for all to see. They then doused the raft with fuel.

The crew gently pushed the raft out above the lapping waves from their boat. This area was in an inlet, and the rougher waves of the North Sea would not interfere with the raft's gentle journey outward. Once the crew had released the raft, they rowed back to the shore. The archers took up their positions; after lighting their arrows and to the glorious sounds of Beethoven's Ninth Symphony, they all fired simultaneously. The raft quickly caught fire, and the audience, in absolute silence, enjoyed this sad, but stupendously spectacular, event.

As the raft continued to burn, Alexander passed the flaming torch to Samuel, and, on his microphone, he declared him as the now-reigning Eleventh Earl of Penbroke—to which the gathering lifted their glasses to cheer in a moment of joy.

At that moment, after James had been all over the world to observe how his companies were operating, in his astral body, a portal of light shone down over the raft.

He could partially see and hear voices calling out to him, beckoning him to leave and to join them.

*****

James now wanted to leave. He had seen all there was to see; it was time to go.

He was eager to walk into the inviting light, and, within seconds, he was staring into the beautiful eyes of Sabrina.

All his guides and those that had passed over were there to greet him. He was overjoyed at his reception. The feeling of love was breathtaking, as his eyes quickly became adjusted to this higher vibration.

"James you made it," laughed Czaur. "You had us all guessing, but, finally, after hundreds of thousands of years, you are coming back to the real place of your birth."

"Real place of birth?"

"Yes; you will be here for a short time, and then the portal that will take you to the next dimension will open. Sabrina and we, your guides, will be going with you."

"Let Sabrina take time with you to adjust, and then we can all get together to celebrate this great event."

Sabrina whisked James away to her little place by the sea, overjoyed to be with him.

"James, I can't believe you are finally here."

"Sabrina, you look so beautiful; I went through so much after you left, but having the Throne room helped me a lot."

"Samuel wanting to be an actor—knowing you, I know that was a left fielder."

"It was, but he's on the right track now; I'd forgotten he was my father again, and I do believe that he will make it over here again, to stay this time."

"Another person you will be pleased to see is Claudia."

"That makes sense; she was one in a million. I really missed her, but Annabelle has really turned out to be a brilliant businesswoman."

"Yes, she's got a lot of you in her; it's funny how they turn out after school days. Also, Sir Jeremy is here, and Sarah; they will stay here, and they will not be coming with us yet."

"Yes, of course, they are obvious souls to be in this dimension; I guess it's their turn to meet their other half."

"Yes; Sir Jeremy had especially waited for this moment to see you come to this dimension after Atlantis, and Sarah, too, was anxious. I've had many great conversations with them both."

"Tell me more about life here."

"It's so different. As we are at a higher vibration, our bodies are lighter, we naturally feel happier, there's a feeling of love here, and it's abundant. You and I will go through a merging to become one. Then, like Camilla, you will feel complete. She went back for you, and as she's such an advanced soul, it took a lot of love for you for her to do that. There's a risk when we go back to third dimension that we can lose our way back here. She is complete, as she's already merged with her soul mate. When you have that, there can be, but not always, a bisexuality within that person. It's not bad, but, obviously, it's frowned upon on Earth. Sexual behavior is very different here from life on Earth. However, your soul mate is your oneness; when you have that feeling of being complete, you don't have the jealousies that others feel in a lower dimension."

"Yes; I noticed that, with Camilla, she didn't mind me being with Nicolette, something that I found very different."

"You will see a difference, when we are one."

"So, there's only one of us?"

"We can merge and split as often as we like; you'll get the hang of it. That's why I've wanted you to be here so badly. Right now, I feel so complete just having you here. Also, we can astral travel; I can think of any place in my mind and be there. We can't change an event, but we can witness it. Through dreams and thoughts, we can connect and help people with their thoughts, as you and I have often done over the years we've been apart."

"All so interesting!"

"We will all ascend to the next dimension once you have become more accustomed to where we are now. This dimension is a transitory dimension, where we get prepared for our true purpose, or where, in our case, we are waiting for our twin soul or flame, as it's known. All of us, through many lifetimes, try to reconnect with our true mates. It can take time. Now that you are here, we can move forward with our guides to become what they call cocreators in the universe. That's a whole new purpose and experience. It's the place we started out from. After all our travels, we are now returning with a greater understanding of this universe to work in the development of solar systems and planets—the list is endless. You will find this knowledge will come to you very quickly."

"Sabrina, can we lie down together? I'm feeling tired. This whole experience, even though you have greater energy, is quite a transformation from being on Earth."

"This is what I've dreamed of doing with you; you don't know how many times I've lain next to you without your knowing," giggled Sabrina.

"Really! No wonder I slept so well when I was alone. Except for the time I was missing you on that island after your sad departure."

"I was there, even then. You were so angry at life, and I, too, was sad to leave; to see your pain and love for me was hard."

James drifted off into a deep sleep and into a calmness he had never experienced before.

*****

As he awoke, he was confused, and, for a moment, he wondered where he was. He felt so energized, and he realized that his older body was gone. He was youthful and vibrant, as he had been in his early thirties.

"Sabrina, I'm young again, like you; it's like reliving all over again. I feel I could run for miles, I have so much energy."

"That's how it is; we are, in a sense, reborn. You can imagine how I felt after experiencing that ghastly cancer. I missed you, but to feel as I do now is miraculous."

They continued to talk. James asked more questions in order to learn what she had already experienced.

Then, out of the blue, appeared Claudia.

"What a wonderful surprise to see you as I remember you as a teenager."

"Yes: it's fascinating we are all the same age, but I understand we can appear as we choose. Some prefer to keep their older age in order to teach; we are all different."

"Tell me, Claudia: after meeting Camilla, I know you and Thomas took time to travel, I hope?"

"Yes, and we went to many different places, but, being older, he was less adventurous. After he died, I so missed him. We work all our lives to be free and to explore the world. Then, in a funny way, we miss our days at work. Anyway, I did; working with you, James, was a wonderful experience."

"We had a great chemistry. Kim was good, but it was somehow not the same. I guess that, after knowing each other for so long, we could chat about more personal matters and not feel uncomfortable."

"It's true. Alex has now taken up the reins and is doing a fine job."

"I'm not surprised you are here; you are a deeply spiritual person."

"Yes; I was not one for religion, although I always believed in a higher power, and here we all are. It's sad that we don't all come to experience this incredible dimension. Thomas had good values, but he was more pragmatic, and I suppose that he was not ready to leave an earthly incarnation."

"It took losing Sabrina, and Camilla, to teach me what love is. How we don't appreciate it as much as we should!"

At that moment, Czaur, Serena, and Rachel appeared. James expected Morphus, his technology guide, and then he realized that the Seventh Earl, who brought the Throne back to England, was not there. Why? Because he was also Colin Bannerman, and then his son, Samuel. It all went into place. It was only at that moment that he realized that Samuel had been the right person all along to be a part of the Throne room. When James was younger, he didn't realize that he was talking to his father, Colin Bannerman, as he had chosen to appear as the Seventh Earl. They were all the same person. James chuckled to himself.

"Why did the Seventh Earl risk coming back twice?" James asked Czaur.

"Well, now that you see him as a young man, you can understand why. You were hell-bent on him being the leader in your business. It wasn't until Camilla made you aware that you changed course. It was then you understood that he played a big role in bringing that Throne back to England. You were the one that gave the Throne to Jeremy Soames, who was

Orga on Atlantis, and you brought the Throne room into use after reading the Seventh Earl's notes."

"How I underestimated Sam! Thank goodness I had the presence of mind to realize the importance of his life now. I'm still amazed he's come back, first as my father, and then as my son. No wonder he feels like a fish out of water in my world of business; his heart has been in the Throne room all this time, hasn't it?"

"Exactly; it's not only Camilla's passion now; it's his, too. No doubt Camilla is going to realize that and tell him. He will understand everything, too."

"It's funny how we don't always connect our purpose on Earth. I know it must be frustrating from up here, when you can't get through to us, when we get so absorbed in other, less-important matters."

"James," said Czaur, "now you know how I felt when I thought you might be going off course with your obsession for the business."

"Do I ever."

"Anyway, we are all here for a very auspicious occasion; we will, over the next period, depending on you James, be ready to return to the dimension above this one. Yes, we are going back to the place of our origin. What people on Earth call Heaven. This is a stupendous moment in all our lives. After all our travels in the earthly plain, we have aspired to proceed and to be trained to be cocreators with the creative force known as the 'divine essence,' or, more simply, God."

"What does that entail?" asked James, excited at the thought.

"It's as though we are all at the real beginning of our true purpose. The beginning of being taught how to work with experienced souls. We will now meet angelic souls that have advanced to the point where stars and solar systems are being created. That will entail even greater tasks than that, as we grow in our understanding and knowledge. This is the place where we find our true purpose of being what the creator had in mind for us to do. So, enjoy your time here first, and rest, and as we teach you, James, you will be ready. We shall then all go with you to do the work each of us was designed to do."

"I can't wait to get started."

*****

After a period of adjustment, James and all of them were now ready. Czaur took them to a place where the portal entry was created from the upper dimension. It was a pad next to the educational building where James had learned about the various planets as a young man from Morphus. He wasn't made aware of this place of entry before. He now learned that angels from the upper levels would arrive at various times to teach and to prepare souls in order to go to their level sometimes to visit and, at other times to help teach.

They all hugged one another in anticipation of the joy they were now about to receive.

The portal then opened. The light was so blinding that they all covered their eyes, as they were sucked up into its swirling energy.

They emerged on a site in the center of a marble floor, which was elevated and ringed off inside a giant crystal building. It was as though they were the centerpiece of a crowd of onlooking angels, all singing with joy and exultation at their arrival.

They could hear a voice calling out to them with abundant love and excitement at their return to the inner core of the God Light. They looked around at this crystal building that seemed to elevate to eternity, with countless floors that one could only conceive were places of knowledge, teaching, and understanding.

So this is Heaven? thought James.

It was so different from what he could have ever imagined, far from the belief that this was a place of eternal rest. This was a place, or source, of abundant creativity, a place where all creation began. Where stars, planets, and even universes came from. The beginning of eternal knowledge, surrounded with an abundant force of love and everlasting energy!

They all now knew that this was the real beginning of their true purpose, having experienced many lives to reach this most prestigious becoming. They could only imagine that the Transfiguration of Jesus had to be similar.

James looked around, as his eyes started to see them all clearly. The audience and his beloved Sabrina had all made the journey. Not to mention Serena, Rachel, and Czaur.

James noticed he was being downloaded with information at a furious rate. It was as though they were all connected to this divine computer that knew each one of their purposes for creation. The many floors were for their different abilities that each one of them had, and for so many others. This would be the place where they would now be prepared for their work in the universe and beyond.

James was overcome with joy by all he was experiencing. The greatness of minds he had yet to comprehend. For him to finally know the essence of the true author, he could hear only these words in his mind: *"The Power and the Glory for ever and ever. Amen, Amen, and Amen."*

EPILOGUE

It has been an exciting task to write and express the many facets of human nature and how each one of us copes with life in the new world of enterprise today.

These books also display a spiritual narrative and attempt to understand the world beyond and the constructive purpose for its creation. The values of positive thinking and energy that are the essence of higher purpose, for which we all desire to attain.

We all have a passionate desire to know that which is out and beyond present knowledge; these books attempt to present a direction based on the many components of thought in our world today.

As much as we are all tempted by this world of materialism, it doesn't always fulfil many of our questions. Without higher awareness or the aspiration to advance to a greater understanding, we can often be left empty.

We now live in a time where we are all questioning traditional knowledge, this work attempts to combine traditional beliefs with a New Age perspective. In other words, we don't last in this life forever, so it's natural to invest some time in evaluating what indeed lies in front of us.

Hopefully, my work opens some of those doors not only to what exists in the here and now, with this new age of discovery, but also to what alludes to what may exist in all our futures.

This last book contains the remainder of James's journey, from 1980 to 2032. It reveals the distinct changes that take place at the turn of the millennium. The transition of thought and values to be enhanced in this new age of unbridled information. We shall now learn from technology, medical science, artificial intelligence, and so much more to come, which will be in keeping with the up-and-coming students born into this new world today.

It has been a joy writing these three books and to receive so many positive comments and questions. So please don't hesitate to go to my website at davidfcook.com, as your thoughts and comments are always welcome.